Praise for Alexa Mar[...]

'A hilariously fun rollercoaster o[...]
Nathaniel have explosive chemis[...] [...] suburban warfare to
outrageously fun heights! *Next-Door Nemesis* is hate to love at its finest'
Sarah Adams, *New York Times* bestselling author

'Smart and sexy, Martin's *Next-Door Nemesis* is a fun romantic
romp about second chances, embracing the unexpected, and the
beautiful things that can come from failure. A glorious read!'
Ashley Herring Blake, *USA Today* bestselling author

'I've never had so much fun with a homeowner's association. Collins
and Nate set those white picket fences on fire with their electric
chemistry. Smoking hot and delightfully sharp, this book is
one to add to your shelves'
B.K. Borison

'Alexa Martin's books are the ultimate reading escape, filled
with fabulous characters; witty, dazzling prose; and
swoon-worthy romances'
Chanel Cleeton, *New York Times* bestselling author

'Alexa Martin is so good at this; I'm so impressed by how nuanced and
thoughtful this book is, while still being hilarious and sexy!'
Jasmine Guillory, *New York Times* bestselling author

'Alexa Martin is an auto-buy author for me. *Mom Jeans and Other
Mistakes* is a celebration of the strength, joy, and complications
of female friendships that span our lifetimes. I will read
anything Alexa Martin writes!'
Lyssa Kay Adams

'Fast, fun, and absolutely engaging!'
Kristan Higgins, *New York Times* bestselling author

Alexa Martin is a writer and stay home mom. A Nashville transplant, she's intent on instilling a deep love and respect for the great Dolly Parton in her four children and husband. The Playbook series was inspired by the eight years she spent as an NFL wife and her love of all things pop culture, sparkles, leggings, and wine. When she's not repeating herself to her kids, you can find her catching up on whatever Real Housewives franchise is currently airing or filling up her Etsy cart with items she doesn't need.

To discover more, find her online at **AlexaMartin.com**, on Facebook **/AlexaMartinBooks**, and on Instagram **@AlexaMBooks**.

By Alexa Martin

Mom Jeans and Other Mistakes
Better Than Fiction
Next-Door Nemesis

The Playbook Series

Intercepted
Fumbled
Blitzed
Snapped

NEXT-DOOR NEMESIS

ALEXA MARTIN

HEADLINE
ETERNAL

Published by arrangement with Berkley
An imprint of Penguin Random House LLC.
First published in the United States in 2023

First published in Great Britain in 2023
by HEADLINE ETERNAL
An imprint of HEADLINE PUBLISHING GROUP

1

Cataloguing in Publication Data is available from the British Library

ISBN 978 1 0354 1270 9

Book design by Elke Sigal

Offset in 10.65/16pt Minion Pro by Jouve (UK), Milton Keynes

Printed and bound in Great Britain by Clays Ltd, Elcograf S.p.A.

HEADLINE PUBLISHING GROUP
An Hachette UK Company
Carmelite House
50 Victoria Embankment
London EC4Y 0DZ

www.headlineeternal.com
www.headline.co.uk
www.hachette.co.uk

For the readers:
may you always find a home
in the pages of this book

NEXT-DOOR NEMESIS

Chapter 1

*I*f I hear *live, laugh, love* one more time, I'm going to die, scream, rage.

I know my mom means well, but my phone's almost out of storage thanks to the abundance of uplifting memes and Bible verses she won't stop sending me. Maybe I'd appreciate her unrelenting positivity if I was still in LA, enjoying my oat milk latte from the adorable café I wrote in almost every day. But for some reason, the never-ending text stream hits a little different when I'm fifteen feet away, sitting in my childhood room, and notifications keep interrupting the shame spiral I've been living in for the last two months.

I swipe away her latest text message and nestle deeper into the frilly comforter of my childhood past. I make sure the volume is all the way down—after all, who needs sound when every single word is ingrained in my brain?—and hit play on the video that has quite literally ruined my life.

To say the camerawork is shoddy would be a massive understatement. The video bounces and bobbles around as the image blurs in and out until a woman standing in an empty parking lot wearing nothing but spike high heels and a silk robe comes into focus.

A woman, of course, who happens to be me.

Jazz hands!

Honestly, it's borderline offensive that after all the time I spent in Los Angeles, all the scripts I wrote, all the internet content I produced hoping to hit my break à la Issa Rae, *this* is what has millions of views. You flip out and threaten to bury your lying, thieving ex *one time* and it goes viral?

What are the chances?

It just really sucks that instead of my brush with viral fame catapulting me to television-writing superstardom, it's what ended my career.

My phone dings with another text from my mom at the same moment the video hyperzooms in on my tearstained face. This is where it really gets good. And by *good*, of course, I mean downright horrifying.

I lift my finger to swipe away another one of her messages. I love my mom and her hopeless positivity, but after moving back into my childhood home a month ago—exactly thirty-one days after my life took a drastic turn toward the absolute worst—with no signs of getting out, I'm in the mood for self-pity.

"Collins Marie Carter!" My mom's thick midwestern lilt rings out from the other side of my much-too-thin door. "Don't you ignore that!"

I shoot out of bed and accidentally send my phone sailing through the room. "Holy shit, Mom!"

Just another perk of moving back home as a twenty-nine-year-old woman.

Privacy? Never heard of her.

"First of all, watch your language," she says, still right outside my door. "Second of all, that's the third text I've sent you this morning and you haven't responded to one."

I scramble around my room trying to find something to wear before giving up and grabbing an old T-shirt off the ground and pulling on the bike shorts busting at the seams. Because really, what's even the point of trying when your life is completely ruined?

"Mom." I throw open the door and try to harness every ounce of patience I have. "You know how much I love you, but I think with about forty percent fewer texts and fifty percent more space, we'll all be much happier."

"You need to stop watching that darn video; it's not good for you." She gives me a disapproving once-over and continues to speak as if I didn't. "Also, didn't you wear that yesterday? I know you're depressed, but you'll never feel better wearing the same dirty clothes and never brushing your hair."

If there were a chance brushing my hair and changing my clothes could turn back the cruel hands of time and convince me to never date Peter Hanson, I'd have a fresh updo and be wearing a fucking evening gown. Alas, formal wear is not the key to time travel and I'd rather be comfortable while I continue down this path of self-loathing.

"Just let me be miserable for one more week." *Or fifty-two.*

"And I promise to try to rejoin society again. It's still too fresh. I still get recognized in the streets."

Being looked down on, on the bitter, hard streets of LA is one thing, but getting the cold shoulder in the suburbs of Ohio? Absolutely not. A person can only handle so much.

"I'll give you thirty more minutes," she says, clearly not understanding the meaning of compromise. "I'm hosting Friday church group and I can't have you wandering around the house like a sad, godless puppy. Plus, I told the ladies you'd be joining us." She shoves the bedazzled Bible I didn't notice she was holding into my hands. I'm surprised I don't dissolve into a pile of ash. "Just in case you need to catch up."

"While sitting in the kitchen and gossiping under the ruse of good intentions does sound like a blast, I'm going to have to pass." I return her Bible, only slightly concerned that lying while holding it resulted in one more brick in my pathway to hell. "I promised Dad I'd help him get things for the yard today."

My dad, Anderson Carter, is perhaps the most precious human to ever human. A recently retired pharmacist, he's living his full gardener fantasy. Seeing this six-foot-two-inch, 320-pound Black man fiddling around the yard has been the only highlight of returning home. Unfortunately for me, once I told him that, he became relentless in his pursuit to recruit me into this vitamin D–filled hobby of his. I wasn't thrilled when I finally gave in, but now that it's saving me from an afternoon listening to the Karens—no shade, there are literally three different women named Karen in the group—drone on about how wonderful their boring kids are doing, I'm going to have to buy him lunch . . . if my bank account will allow it.

"Oh darn. Well, maybe next time." My mom pouts and the fine lines of aging pull on the corners of her delicate mouth, which has never muttered a single curse word. "At least Dad's going to get some quality time with you."

She may not curse, but those lips are well-versed in spewing passive-aggressive jabs.

"We watched an entire season of *House Hunters* last week; quality time doesn't get any better than that." I can almost see the wheels turning in her brain to come up with a retort, but she stays quiet because even she knows it's true. Nothing can bond two humans more than watching incompatible couples argue about a house they can't afford and screaming at a television about gray laminate floors.

"Fine, but if you're set on abandoning me and Jesus, can you at least make sure Dad doesn't forget to get the white oak tree while you're at the nursery?" She steps to the side as I squeeze past her.

She follows close behind as I try to keep my eyes trained on the carpet they replaced last year and ignore the barrage of inspirational quote art littering the walls. The collaged picture frames filled with every single one of my school pictures break up Bible verses, proof of days when I loved overly teased bangs and scrunchies working overtime to keep me humble.

As if I have any pride left.

"Sure, Mom." I pull open the cabinet and grab the "World's Best Dad" mug I gave my dad for Father's Day when I was in third grade. I pour in some of the hazelnut coffee my mom is still trying to convince me doesn't taste like sludge and hope that today will be the day I learn to love it. "Text me the name, though, because I definitely won't remember."

"The white oak." Dad's deep voice bounces off the white cabinets before he enters and drops a chaste kiss onto my mom's mouth. They celebrated their thirty-sixth wedding anniversary in February. He still kisses her every time he enters a room and my mom still blushes each time she lays eyes on him. It's sickeningly sweet. "That's what we're going to get; I had to order it. Noreen called me last night to tell me it finally came in."

"Really?" My mom's face lights up and I'm not sure if it's because she's married to a man who does thoughtful shit like special ordering her trees or because she loves landscaping that much. "You didn't tell me!"

They planted a tree in the front yard when our house was built thirty years ago. Unfortunately, two winters ago, it fell victim to a blizzard that knocked out power lines and roots alike. And while the Reserve at Horizon Creek may be a stifling hellhole put on Earth only to torture me in my lowest moments in life—let's not talk about being one of ten people of color in my middle school of more than a thousand—it's been around long enough that I can't say it's ugly. The trees planted at the inception of the neighborhood have grown into beautiful, mature trees many planned communities can't brag about.

If the opportunity presented itself, there's a ninety-eight percent chance I'd sell my soul to be back in LA. But even so, no palm tree can compare to the droopy willow tree in my backyard where I spent countless summer days losing myself between the worn pages of my favorite books. Now with my dad dedicating all his spare time to the flourishing vegetable garden and rosebushes, it's almost possible for me to pretend we're not in the middle of Ohio when I step into our fenced-in backyard.

Almost.

"Well, since it seems as if you two need a little alone time"—I hand my dad the remaining coffee, which I don't think I'll ever adjust to—"I'm going to run and get some caffeine I can actually stomach. Do either of you want a bagel or something?"

My mom opens her mouth, probably to defend her choice of hazelnut, but my dad beats her to it.

"Two everything bagels, toasted, with cream cheese." He recites the order they've shared for years. "Just make sure to drink your coffee there and take the long way home after."

He wiggles his eyebrows and my mom giggles.

My stomach turns, but I can't blame the coffee this time.

"Filthy." I grimace and shake my head in their general direction, trying to avoid direct eye contact. "And before church group, Mom? What would the Karens say?"

"Oh, honey." She swipes a stray hair out of her face, and with one glance at her expression, I regret ever getting out of bed this morning. "Trust me. The Karens and every other woman in this neighborhood would love to experience anything like I do with your father."

"La la la!" I stick my fingers in my ears and pretend to be disgusted by their overt and never-ending PDA. "I didn't hear any of that!"

I hurry to my bathroom with my parents' laughter chasing after me and make quick work of brushing my teeth and wrestling my curls into a careless bun. In LA, I never left the house without putting ample effort into my appearance. Living in the land of opportunity, I was convinced I was always one outing away from meeting someone who'd change my life.

I needed to be prepared.

So of course the one time I was caught slipping in public happened to be the one time everyone witnessed. Life is rude like that.

I contemplate putting on a bra before heading to the chain coffee shop down the road before deciding against it.

Standards? Don't even know her!

This is Ohio. The only two people I actually liked from high school left this town as soon as the opportunity presented itself. I don't have anyone to impress anymore.

Not even myself.

It's just too bad my mom won't agree.

And sure, nearing thirty should mean I don't have to sneak out of the house anymore. However, according to the laws of Kimberly Carter, I'll never be too old to be told to change my outfit and put on lipstick. Which is why, at twenty-nine and three-quarters years old, I tiptoe down the hallway and run out the front door. I leap into the front seat of my mom's old minivan and peel out of the driveway without a backward glance.

Burning rubber out of my quiet suburban hometown may not be my finest moment, but it's not my worst either. My life right now is a total dumpster fire and while there aren't many bright sides about my current situation, at least I know I can't sink any lower.

Watch out, Ohio.

It's only up from here.

Chapter 2

I drive past a moving van as the white picket fences of the Reserve at Horizon Creek fade in the rearview mirror of the minivan I still don't understand my parents buying. I'm an only child; we would've been fine with a sedan.

I adjust the radio, turning off Dad's sports talk and finding the local station I used to listen to in high school. I'm a sucker for pop music, and the Top 100 song that blasts through the speakers soothes my soul. I've gotten lost in the mindless lyrics, tapping my fingers on the steering wheel, when my phone rings.

Ruby's name lights up the screen and I contemplate letting her go to voicemail. Today has already been a day, and as much as I appreciate the motivational speeches she's been giving me since the video hit the internet, I'm not sure I can handle any of her lawyerly logic right now.

However, I do know I can't deal with her wrath at being ignored.

"What it do?" I answer, lacking the usual enthusiasm I greet her with.

There's a long pause before her brash voice bursts through my phone. "Ew. What's wrong with you?"

"Besides the obvious?" I switch the phone to the speaker, securing it between my chest and seat belt so I can keep both hands on the wheel. Safety first and all. "Not much."

"Kim's still sending you inspirational memes and Bible verses, isn't she?" She throws out her accurate guess on the first go.

Ruby has been my best friend since middle school. When her parents divorced when we were fifteen, she practically lived at our house. That's to say that she, too, has been on the receiving end of Kimberly Carter's never-ending good-vibes-only routine.

"Kim's gonna Kim," I confirm what she already knew. "But today escalated to an invitation to join her church group."

"Oh god. The Karens?" I can hear her shudder through the phone. "Were you able to get out of it? Do you need to brainstorm excuses with me?"

The worry in her voice is the first thing to cheer me up all day. Only Ruby understands the abject torture of being trapped in a room with my mom and the Karens.

"I'm good," I reassure her. "I'm going to grab a coffee now and then I'm heading to a garden center with Dad to pick up a tree for my mom and probably more vegetable plants for him."

Our backyard has enough tomatoes to supply Olive Garden. I doubt even he knows how many he has.

"I love that for—" she starts, but then her tone changes and the sound is muffled. "Luke, are you serious? I've asked you to knock a hundred times. This is a law firm, not your buddy's place. You can't just barge in here." I hear poor Luke's faint apology in the background before Ruby cuts him off. "Not now. I'm on a very important phone call."

Before Ruby's parents divorced, she was a pageant girl to the max. Her mom was a doctor and, breaking the societal norms, her dad was the one who drove her over state lines to compete in whatever pageant she was in that weekend. She had the bright white teeth, so much hairspray it was a miracle her hair didn't fall out, and an entire room dedicated to housing her evening gowns. I would tag along sometimes, and even though she denies it now, she really loved competing. She was the reigning champ for a reason.

However, when news of her dad's infidelity came to light, something inside her snapped. She quit doing pageants and made it her mission to make every man who crosses her path pay for her father's sins. Now she's a divorce attorney who only represents women (and men or nonbinary people) divorcing their husbands. Countless therapists have told her she has displaced anger, but she still hasn't made any moves to address it.

"Sheesh." I hit the directional and turn right into the shopping center where Cool Beans is located. "You're always so hard on the poor guy."

"Oh please. I've given him ample opportunities to change his behavior." I don't even need to see her to know she's rolling her eyes. "If he did his job like I've asked, there'd be no problems. I mean, really, how hard is it to knock before entering a room?"

If this was the first time I heard her talk to an assistant like this, maybe I'd buy what she's selling. But we talk every day and I know that's a complete load of crap.

"Ruby, come on." I pull into a parking spot and put my phone back to my ear. "You've never liked a single one of your assistants. Is it possible that you're the problem?"

"First of all, how dare you? Second, fuck off. If we're talking about being our own problems, then are we going to talk about how you still haven't opened your computer since you let Peter run you out of LA? Did you at least email that Reggie guy back?"

I knew I should've let her go to voicemail.

"Hold up. How did you being mean to Luke somehow turn into an attack on me?"

"Because if you think that was mean, then I've clearly been treating you with kid gloves for way too long."

Ruby's sent me emails about remote writing opportunities and has let me vent about my broken, humiliated heart without judgment. I knew it wouldn't last forever, but I definitely wasn't prepared for her to rip into me in a strip mall parking lot.

Up until right now, she's danced around the subject of my ruined career and scumbag ex. I shouldn't have told her about Reggie emailing me. He's the only person from the industry who's reached out to me, but the cynic in me can't tell if he's reaching out from genuine concern or morbid curiosity. It's not fair to put that on him; he was the first showrunner I ever worked with and has never been anything but wonderful to me, but I'm still too nervous to email him and find out. It would be a hit I'm not sure I could handle to find out he's not the person I thought he was.

"Please." I turn off the car and grab my purse. "You don't have kid gloves and you know it."

Ruby has a strong left hook and a stronger right, and each punch is laced with an uncomfortable amount of truth.

"I do too." The lawyer in her can't help but argue. "If I didn't, I would've already told you that it doesn't matter that Peter screwed you over; you can't just wallow in fucking *Ohio* and watch Little Mix reaction videos on YouTube all day. We got out of there as soon as we could for a reason. If you don't get your crap together, who are you going to end up like?"

I'm about to launch a full-out defense of my Little Mix obsession—they should have hit it huge in America and I will never forgive the music industry—but it all disappears the moment my feet hit the sidewalk and I set eyes on the last person I ever thought I'd see today.

Scratch that.

The last person I *wanted* to see. Ever.

"Oh my god, Nate."

"Exactly!" Ruby yells into the phone, obviously not grasping the severity of this situation. "You could end up like Nate the Snake! I wonder what he's doing. Didn't he say he wanted to be an accountant? What kind of teenager dreams of being an accountant?"

"No, Ruby!" I hiss into the phone, spinning out of view and plastering my back to a brick wall. "I mean Nate, here. At the coffee shop."

"Oh shit." She whispers into the phone as if he could hear her. "What's he doing there?"

Admittedly, I don't have any friends left here. But just because I don't have friends doesn't mean I don't have archenemies.

I do.

And his name is Nathanial Adams.

I don't need to explain why he's the worst. The name says it all. Everything about him is stuck-up and overly serious.

"It's a coffee shop; he's getting coffee." Because of course he is. God forbid one thing in my life not turn into a total, utter disaster.

"Well? How's he look?" she whisper-shouts into the phone.

"Seriously, Ruby? That's what you're asking me right now?" The heat from the brick exterior is seeping through the thin cotton shirt I threw on before I left the house and people passing by are starting to stare.

"What? He was an arrogant jerk, but he was also super cute." She may hate men, but she still very much appreciates them—to look at, not to talk to, she always tells me. "He's not on social media and curious minds want to know how he's held up over the years."

"You're ridiculous, and curious minds are going to have to stay curious," I inform her. "I'm waiting out here until he leaves."

"Let me get this straight. You're hiding outside of a coffee shop to avoid a guy you didn't like in high school and I'm the ridiculous one?"

Well, when she says it like that . . .

"Fine, I'll go in." I push off the wall and the slight breeze in the air instantly relieves my burning back. "But only because I'm starting to get a migraine from my lack of caffeine."

"Tell yourself whatever you need."

For a split second, I consider driving back home and settling for hazelnut sludge, but then I remember my parents' need for alone time. *Gross.*

I shake away thoughts of what might be happening on the kitchen counters and draw in a deep breath before breaching the corner.

And because the universe absolutely fucking despises me, I run right into Nate.

"I'm so sor—" His deep voice ignites a fire in my veins. My body remembers him even though my mind has fought to forget everything about him. "Collins?"

"Nate." The soles of my feet itch with the need to run, but I stand firm. Unfortunately for me, my stubbornness outweighs my desire for self-preservation. "Hi."

"Oh my fucking god," Ruby screams into the phone and nearly shatters my eardrum.

"Gotta go, bye." I hang up before she can scream some more and pray to all that is holy that he didn't hear her. But if the condescending smirk on Nate's face is indicative of anything, he heard more than enough.

Have I mentioned how much I hate Ohio?

"Ruby?" He nods his chin in the direction of my phone. "Sounds like not much has changed."

I tuck my phone into my purse even though I want to throw it at him.

You'd think after ten years apart from someone, they'd lose the ability to bring you to violence with a simple nod. But not Nathanial Adams. No, everything about his stupid, symmetrical face is utterly punchable.

I'm not sure if it's because he's wearing a cable-knit sweater in June or because he's aiming the same smug smile he tortured me with in high school at me, but all of a sudden my mind is empty save for every single wrong he's ever done me. And why, if I hate Peter with the fire of the sun, I hate Nate with the power of two.

I guess that's what happens when the guy you thought was your best friend goes away one summer and completely ghosts you when he gets back.

Time, in fact, does not heal all wounds.

"A lot has changed, actually." I try to present an air of confidence I most definitely do not feel. "But she's still Ruby."

"I bet." He steps to the side as an older man sidles by. "I can't imagine either one of you ever changing too much."

Poison laces the innocuous words. Nate thinks he's smarter than everyone around him and has somehow tricked the masses into going along with it. He's the type of person who can insult people with such ease, they end up thanking him. Whereas I struggled to make friends growing up, people naturally gravitated toward Nate.

The urge to tell him to fuck off is on the tip of my tongue, but my mom has eyes and ears everywhere. The last thing I need is one of the Karens bringing hot gossip about me causing a scene outside Cool Beans to Bible study.

"Yeah, unfortunately, we can't all experience such radical growth." I let my eyes travel the length of his body—which looks better than it has the right to, encapsulated in khakis and a pullover—before meeting his stare. "Accountant chic, living in the burbs? Who would've thought?"

Bullseye.

His hazel eyes narrow and the tips of his ears flame red. It's so much more fun to go head-to-head with a person when you're aware of their tells.

"And you? Are you finally visiting your parents? I know you couldn't be bothered to come to Mr. Carter's retirement party." He leans in, his voice dropping despite having nobody near us. "Or did you have to move back home because you couldn't hack it in LA?"

The wound is still too fresh. I flinch as his words slice straight through the oozing hole I've been trying to fill with tequila shooters and Netflix movies.

He knows he hit his mark, and much like my reaction, his sadistic grin widens.

The really messed-up part is that I'm not even mad about his jab; I'm angry I let him see that his words affected me. Pissed I reacted.

I've gotten soft.

I blame Mom's love of inspirational quotes.

But this is a wake-up call. If I'm going to be living in my own literal hell, I have to be prepared for the devil to strike at any moment. And by *the devil*, I mean Nate.

Obviously.

"Well." I push past him and pull open the glass door to Cool Beans. "As much as I'm enjoying standing around and pretending like it's good to see you, I'd rather be doing literally anything else."

"Real nice, Collins." He reaches into his pocket and pulls out a key fob. "Classy as ever."

He clicks a button on the fob and the lights on a midsized sedan blink.

"Really? A Buick?" I yell with one foot in the coffee shop. "Are you eighty?"

His steps don't even falter as he crosses the pothole-riddled parking lot and tosses his parting shot over his shoulder. "At least I have a car."

Quick and effective.

Just like he was when he changed his number and pretended like he didn't know me when I saw him at the movies with his new cool friends.

I forget all about my mom's church friends. I lift my middle finger straight into the air and hold it steady for him to see as he drives away.

I knew coming back home wasn't going to be fun, but not even being the internet's favorite tragedy could have prepared me for this. Nathanial Adams is the one person I didn't account for, and I'm now realizing what a grave mistake that was.

Chapter 3

I planned on drinking my coffee at Cool Beans, but that quickly changed once I sat down. The familiar burn of humiliation as judgmental gazes lingered my way thanks to my little show with Nate was too much to handle. Even though things aren't as bad as they were in LA when the video first came out, I'm not sure the feeling that comes with everyone staring and laughing at you ever fades.

I try to take the long way home, but there are only so many detours you can take in our tiny subdivision. I pull into my parents' driveway and grab my iced coffee from one of multiple cup holders in the minivan. The melting ice has diluted the espresso-and-milk concoction, but the bitter aftertaste is still notable. It's the perfect pairing for my attitude after my run-in with Nate . . . and my life in general.

I've known Nate since I was in sixth grade and he transferred into my class during the middle of the semester. Everyone always wants to meet the new kid, but there was something different about him. He stood out for many reasons—his clothes weren't as nice and he lived with his single dad—but he never seemed to care. At eleven, the arrogance I hate so much now seemed like a quiet confidence so elusive to most middle school kids.

And I wanted it.

I just didn't know that he'd eventually turn on me. I didn't realize one day I'd regret experiencing the warmth and contentment being near him caused. That I'd feel so stupid and betrayed, I'd still be reeling from it more than a decade later.

I check the clock, not sure if I've been gone long enough for my parents, and decide to stay in the car for a few extra minutes. Even though gas prices are a bazillion dollars and the only thing I'm contributing to the house is my winning personality, I crank up the AC and leave the engine running as I try to forget my entire interaction with Nate.

Reclining the seat, I take stock of my surroundings.

It's wild. I moved away years ago, yet at first glance, so much of the neighborhood is still frighteningly familiar. The houses I grew up riding my bike past have barely changed. The white shutters Mr. Johnson paints every spring still adorn his beige house. The American flag Mrs. Fowler hung the day her son joined the army still waves proudly outside her front door. Even my parents haven't replaced the swing they installed on our front porch when I was in third grade. It's like this little bubble in the middle of Ohio is safe from change. Stuck in time for better or worse.

But when you look a little closer, the differences can't be ignored or overstated. Whereas the buildings don't age, the same can't be said for the people.

The elderly couple that lived across the street and always gave me Popsicles passed away a couple of summers ago. Their children didn't hesitate before conducting an estate sale and putting the home on the market. My mom called me every day for a week, filling me in on neighborhood gossip I wasn't even remotely interested in. The kids I babysat for to make a little money during the summer are now speeding through the neighborhood, on their way to graduating. Mr. and Mrs. Welch sold their house a month ago—ditching Ohio for Arizona—and now the moving van I passed earlier is parked in their driveway.

I watch with bored interest as a constant stream of moving men work together to unload the truck. If I thought I looked miserable, I don't even hold a candle to these poor men. There's one house between us, but even with the distance, I swear I can still see the sweat dripping down their foreheads. Each box looks heavier than the last, but the manual labor doesn't seem as intense as the blond woman standing by, shouting out directions.

Wearing platform wedges with jeans so bedazzled they've almost blinded me twice, she's gesturing like the leader of a marching band with her free hand and holding on to an oversized tumbler—that I'd bet money was filled with wine—with the other. She looks familiar, but I can't tell if it's because I actually recognize her or because she looks exactly like every other twenty- to forty-year-old woman who lives in this godforsaken subdivision.

I don't know how long I watch. I'm so transfixed by her bright smile and sharp tone that I lose track of time. It's not until she takes a long gulp from her tumbler and her eyes meet mine across the distance that I snap back into it. Panic makes my stomach turn as she aims her white teeth my way, waving her long, thin arm over her head, and moves in my direction. I look over my shoulder, praying that I'm reading this wrong and she's looking at someone else. Alas, my luck has not changed in the last hour and I'm the only person in sight.

She moves deceptively fast for someone in such high shoes. By the time I manage to fumble with my coffee, my parents' bagels, and keys, she's already standing next to the car as I exit. She'd be taller than me even without her wedges—which are even higher up close—but she towers over me now.

"Oh my goodness!" Her high-pitched squeal ricochets off the cookie-cutter houses lining the street. "Collins Carter! I knew it was you!"

I stand stiff as a board as she wraps her arms around me, forcing more physical contact upon me than I've experienced in more than a month.

"Ummm . . ." I draw out the word, trying to figure out what in the fresh hell is happening. "Hi?"

She must hear the question in my tone because she loosens her freakishly tight grip and takes a small step back.

"It's me, Ashleigh. Remember?" She narrows her cornflower blue eyes, watching as I try to place her among the countless names I tried very hard to forget. "Ashleigh Whittington? We were both in Yearbook together at Central . . ."

Finally recognition dawns on me and I remember her so vividly it's like someone shoved me straight into Mr. Frank's second-period class, listening to his nasal voice as he lectured me about my aversion to social interaction. When I told him it wasn't social interaction I had an aversion to, it was assholes, he almost kicked me out of Yearbook. Instead, he punished me by making me interview the basketball players, and Ashleigh was my photographer.

Fun times.

"Oh, of course." I feign excitement. "From the basketball piece. How could I forget?"

It's not like it's been a decade or anything.

"Right? It was so much fun." Her smile returns to its full-blown glory and the teeth she must have professionally whitened every month nearly blind me. "Wasn't high school the best?"

I try to think of a response that won't encourage a further walk down memory lane or require me to explain why I'd rather get daily Brazilian waxes over ever going back to Central High. "It was something."

"Wasn't your reunion last year?" she asks. "I was a couple of years under you and I just started a Facebook group to start planning ours."

I look to my house, wondering why of all times my mom isn't standing in the front window, ready to join in on neighborhood gossip. The twenty feet to the front door never seemed more insurmountable and all I want to do is escape.

It's at this hopeless moment that I remember something. While my life has been spiraling out of control, sending me on a twirly, whirly ride down the sewer that is reality, there's one thing I know will never change: other people's desire to talk about themselves. I'm always only one question away from becoming a head-bobbing observer. And if the glossy veneer of Ashleigh Whittington tells me anything, it's that she's dying to talk about herself.

"You've always been so organized," I compliment her, trying anything to avoid discussing my dark high school days. "And it looks like it's paid off." I turn around and point to the house, where the moving men look like they are racing to finish before she returns. "A homeowner already? What an accomplishment!"

Even though being tethered to central Ohio is adjacent to a life in purgatory to me, it's not a lie. Homeownership is major. I can't even afford rent. Being stable enough that a bank trusts you with hundreds of thousands of dollars is so far out of the realm of possibility for me that I can't even fathom it.

"Thank you so much! It's our first home. Grant and I," she clarifies without me asking. I know I've successfully shifted any and all attention away from myself. "We just got married in April. So I'm not actually Ashleigh Whittington anymore; I'm Ashleigh Barnes now."

"Congratulations, a lot of milestones happening for you." My face is starting to ache from smiling. As a devoted follower of resting bitch face, my muscles aren't used to this much strain.

She must not notice my discomfort though. Instead of ending the conversation like I was hoping, she lifts her hand and shoves her giant diamond in my face.

"Thank you!" She looks down at her ring and lets out a dreamy sigh. "He's a dentist."

I've never heard anybody make dentistry sound so romantic.

"Oh wow."

"I know, a doctor's wife. Can you even?"

She forgets about her giant diamond and wraps her long, thin fingers around my wrist while the other hand is still clenching the tumbler I'm now doubly convinced is housing chilled Pinot Grigio. She lets out a high-pitched squeal I'm sure will send dogs running and begins to jump up and down.

And it is *wild*.

I try to match her energy but fail massively.

Thankfully, before she notices my lack of enthusiasm, a nice-looking gentleman wearing a polo drenched in sweat approaches.

"All of the boxes are in, Mrs. Barnes." His deep voice is a welcome change after the long burst of her whistle-tone screaming. "We're ready to start bringing in the furniture but need you to tell us where everything goes."

This poor man looks miserable. I wouldn't be surprised if today is the day he decides to change careers. The dread in his voice is unmistakable, but Ashleigh either is the most oblivious person in the world or ignores it. Either is plausible.

"Thank you so much, Mark. Let me just say goodbye to my friend and I'll be right there," she says.

I don't know what's more shocking: that she called me a friend or that her tone was devoid of the condescending tone most people around here have when speaking to hired help. Ever since I've moved back, I've kept to myself, not even remotely interested in forming any new bonds or friendships. But even with her ultra-bubbly personality and zest for reminiscing, I feel like Ashleigh is creeping past my defenses.

Mark, my grumpy soul brother, grumbles something that sounds like "thanks" before turning on his well-worn tennis shoe.

"Well, it was nice running into you." I start the goodbyes, ready to retreat into the fortress that is my childhood bedroom and reinforce my no-new-friends policy. "Congratulations again on everything."

"Before we go, are you back for good or just visiting?" she asks, and I freeze beneath her kind, curious gaze.

I want more than anything to say I'm on my way out, but the hard truth is that I'm stuck here until further notice.

"I'm staying for a little bit, just not sure how long." Even if all my prospects are dry and I haven't opened my computer in weeks, I can't bring myself to say this move is permanent. Somewhere deep down, I'm still holding on to the glimmer of hope that all's not quite lost.

"Well . . ." She drags out the word and her blue eyes sparkle with an excitement that both terrifies and intrigues me. "We're hosting a housewarming party soon and I'd love for you to come. You can meet Grant and, not to brag, but I make the world's best cocktails and even though people tell me it's not a real skill, I'm an expert at building cheese boards."

I know I should decline. Ashleigh one thousand percent makes her guests play icebreaker games. But somehow, some of her friendliness has rubbed off on me and caused my usual ability to say no with ease to drift into the ether.

Plus, I really freaking love cheese *and* cocktails!

Could this woman with white teeth, wedge sandals, and a penchant for joy be the Enid Sinclair to my Wednesday Addams?

"How can I say no to that?"

"Oh yay!" She bounces and strands of her blond hair fall free of the messy bun that—unlike mine—probably took tons of effort to create. "Do you have your phone?"

Wordlessly, I reach into my purse and unlock my phone before handing it to her. When she returns it, the name Ashleigh Barnes is on my screen sandwiched between rainbow and unicorn emojis. I hate that it makes me like her more.

"Thanks." I lock my phone and drop it into my purse. "I'll text you later so you'll have mine."

"Perfect! It was so great running into you," she says before wrapping her long arms around my shoulders and pulling me in for another hug. Since physical touch is my absolute least favorite love language, I go stiff as a board in her embrace. "I'm even more excited about this move now. We're going to have so much fun together!"

Her genuine enthusiasm is so disarming that for some reason I'm excited about her move too. Not mine, of course, but still. If I have to be stuck in Ohio, it will be nice to talk to someone besides my parents and the Karens.

She starts to walk away but turns around at the last minute. "Oh my goodness. I almost forgot. You know who else we'll have to invite?"

"Who?" I rack my brain for literally any person other than Ruby to name but come up empty.

"Nate Adams!" She seems almost jubilant saying the one name I never wanted to hear again.

I try my hardest not to let her see me react. Things were going so well and I can't ruin it at the last minute. Causing a scene at Cool Beans was bad enough; having a meltdown in front of my parents' house isn't even an option. And considering freaking out in front of my previous residence is what kickstarted my demise, it's a mistake I refuse to repeat.

"Nate Adams?" I attempt to play dumb. "I'm not sure I remember him."

"Really? I could've sworn you two were friends at Central." Ashleigh's gorgeous face twists with confusion. "Well, shoot, he was just here. I could've introduced you."

"I'm sorry? What?" I ask sharply—too sharply to be talking about someone I'm claiming I don't remember. Alarm bells are blaring in my head and my instincts are screaming at me to run. "He was just where?"

"At my house. He lives down the street." Although I can see the questions in Ashleigh's eyes wondering why I'm so shaken about a person I said I didn't remember, she's kind enough not to call me out on my now very obvious lie. "He was our Realtor, and I think he's on the HOA board or something. He stopped by to welcome us to the neighborhood."

He's a Realtor? And part of the HOA?

The shock of discovering someone below the age of fifty is a willing and active participant in the HOA is almost enough to distract me from the very terrible, no good, awful news that Nathanial Adams, enemy of my heart and soul, is practically my next-door neighbor.

Almost.

Anger, irritation, and—worst of all—fear claw into every part of my body. Even my toes curl with indignation as I try to process what this means and the fact that my mom, who has practically force-fed me every morsel of neighborhood gossip for the last two years, somehow managed to skip over this piece of very important information. I inhale through my nose, exhaling long and slow the way my therapist taught me during our last Zoom session, and will my body to relax.

"Well, who needs high school reunions when you live in the Reserve, right?" I let out a shaky laugh that rings false even to my own ears. "But I know you have moving to get to. I won't hold you up any longer."

"Okay . . ." She hesitates a moment and panic that she's not going to leave begins to set in. "Don't forget to send that text later so we can make plans to get together soon. I'll stock up on snacks and we can watch mindless TV."

Mindless TV and snacks?

Another offer I can't resist! How does she know all my weak spots? Witchcraft.

"I'd actually really love that." Sincerity rings through in my words. Her bright smile softens before she gives a final wave and makes the short trek back to her driveway.

I stare after her in disbelief.

When I moved back, I was positive that I wouldn't make any friends while I was home. After all, not only was I returning to the scene of all my running nightmares, but this was going to be temporary. There was no need to put in the effort to socialize. I had Ruby, and this is what FaceTime was invented for. But in this very moment, I break my no-new-friends oath and decide that

Ashleigh—despite our unfortunate shared history at Central High and her apparent extroverted ways—is one of the good ones.

My mom, on the other hand, is in for quite the mouthful the second I see her. Unfortunately for me, before I can give her a piece of my mind, the garage door rumbles to life and reveals my dad's tall form stalking toward me.

"In the car, Collins." He points to the passenger-side door of the van. "The tree isn't going to plant itself."

I want to object. But, seeing as he's been my dad my entire life and I've lost this battle more times than I could possibly count, I concede. Plus, now that I know Nate is probably lurking nearby, thinking of new ways to infuriate me, getting away for a little while sounds better than ever.

Plus, if I have to pick one parent to glean intel from, Anderson Carter is my best bet.

"So, Dad . . ." I pull his bagel out of the Cool Beans bag and hand it to him. "Want to fill me in on Nathanial Adams being our next-door neighbor?"

Chapter 4

*Y*ou know how when you're thinking of buying a new car, all of a sudden you start seeing that exact car everywhere you go? Or you finally learn the name of an actor you saw once and then he's on your TV all the time?

Turns out, it's not just the universe haunting you with your thoughts, but instead literal, actual brain science. I might have gone to school for writing, but occasionally I paid attention in my other classes and for some reason, the frequency illusion is one of the few things that stuck with me. Basically all it says is that the frequency of seeing these things hasn't changed at all, but that once your brain is aware of something, it influences where your attention goes.

It's really simple and pretty funny.

Or at least, I used to think it was funny until my brain decided to become hyperaware of Nathanial Adams.

In the days since running into Nate, I've seen him or something that reminded me of him everywhere I look, and I'm *this close* to losing what's left of my ever-loving mind. When Ashleigh told me he was her Realtor, I didn't realize what she was really telling me was that he's pretty much in charge of selling every single house in the neighborhood. I can't drive down the street now without literally seeing his face on all the FOR SALE signs scattered through the neighborhood.

"Ughhhh." I take a sip of my (non-hazelnut) coffee and aim my eyes out the kitchen window. "Could Nate be more ridiculous? I mean, who does he think he's fooling?"

"What's he doing this time?" my mom asks without looking up from the grocery store ad she's been inspecting for the last five minutes. "Oh, honey!" She nudges my dad sitting next to her. "Did you see that steaks are on sale at Meijer? We should host a barbecue this weekend! You grill and I'll make my famous potato salad and sangria."

My dad looks at me and the silent threat comes through loud and clear in his narrowed mahogany eyes.

While my mom has been married to a Black man for thirty-six years, it has not deterred her from adding raisins to her potato salad. While there are many potential reasons for this, it's likely because my dad is a giant teddy bear who doesn't have it in him to let her know her recipe is a travesty. Whenever we visit his side of the family, the poor man works overtime to make sure we're never involved in any sort of potluck situation.

"A barbecue sounds great." He gives in to Kimberly Carter as always. "I'll run to the store tomorrow."

"Mom. Focus!" While my parents being marriage goals is adorable and all, it doesn't distract from the way they both totally dismissed my latest problem with Nate. "Why is Nate walking with Mrs. Mullens and Mrs. Potts? What's he up to?"

"He's just a nice boy," Mom says. I'm pretty sure she's trying to piss me off at this point. "He goes on walks with them every Tuesday and Thursday."

"He takes old ladies on walks? Twice a week?" I ask incredulously. The levels this man will sink to have no bounds. "Has anyone checked his basement for bodies lately? I'm just going to put it out there, but there's gotta be, like, a ninety-eight percent chance he's a serial killer. No normal twenty-nine-year-old man buys a house alone in the suburbs, joins the HOA, and volunteers for morning walks unless he's hiding a freezer full of fingers in his house."

"Honey." My mom's voice turns as sweet as the term of endearment and she places the ad she's been so enthralled with on the table before slowly removing her reading glasses. None of these things bodes well for me. "You and Nate used to get along so well. I always thought you'd end up dating one day. I still don't understand what happened to the two of you."

"Nothing happened." I take a long sip of my coffee, trying to push away the onslaught of memories—and hurt—that comes with reminiscing. "He cared about being popular and I didn't. We grew apart."

"Sure," my dad's deep voice cuts through the room. "Because hating a person you haven't seen in ten years over nothing makes total sense."

I thought internet trolls filling up the comment section were brutal, but they have nothing on my middle-aged parents. Sheesh.

"If you want me to go, just say that." I walk over to the coffee machine and top off my cup before finding a lid to screw on.

"Well, since you offered . . ." My dad turns in his chair and gestures toward the front door. "Could you go water the flowers and the tree out front? I'll order a soaker hose later this week, but it needs to be watered before that."

If I was adding anything of value to the house, maybe I'd attempt to talk my way out of this chore that will force me into the sun. I'm still recovering from the sunburn I got while planting the dang tree. But my dad's back has been bothering him since he ignored my sage advice to pick up the tree with his legs instead of his back and now I'm in charge of all gardening responsibilities.

"Fine." I pretend to be put out, but there's no power behind it. "But let me put on sunscreen first this time."

"And a bra . . . and a clean shirt!" my mom shouts, unable to help herself. The midwestern motherly urge to nag and/or criticize one's child cannot be tamed.

After finding clothing that will both please my mother and be appropriate for yard work, I grab my AirPods and turn on my favorite podcast as I get to work.

Before I know it, I lose myself in the simple activity, soaking up some much-needed vitamin D while the cool mist of the garden hose keeps me from getting too hot. I'm wrapped up in the host's story, my writer's mind busy anticipating what happens next and laughing at their over-the-top jokes, when a hand on my shoulder startles me half to death.

I scream out loud and spin on my three-dollar Old Navy flip-flops, never losing my grip on the spray nozzle. It all happens so fast that by the time my mind catches up to what's happening, Nate is standing in front of me soaking wet.

"Oh my god!" I lower the hose and push up the lever on the back of the nozzle to stop it from spraying. "I'm so sorry."

Nate shakes his head and water droplets explode off his slightly-too-long hair. I wish I could say he looks like a wet poodle, but he manages to look like a fucking ad for *Realtors Gone Wild*. It's not that he's jacked and his T-shirt has now molded to six-pack abs or anything. In fact, he's softened up since high school. I don't know if it's because in LA, everyone was so obsessed with having the perfect body or because it's so different from Peter's, but I love a freaking dad bod.

And of course Nate "Single in the Suburbs" Adams is rocking the shit out of his.

"What the hell, Collins?" Nate growls, forcing my attention away from his physique and up to his face. The hazel eyes I spent so many summers staring into lack all the warmth I remember. A stark reminder that this isn't a man I want to know. "What's wrong with you?"

"What's wrong with me?" My spine snaps straight and adrenaline pumps through my veins, preparing me for the fight ahead. I've been villainized enough in the last couple of months and I'm not taking it anymore. Especially not over something so freaking stupid. "You snuck up on me while I was holding a hose! What did you think was going to happen? There's no way you're going to flip this to make me the bad guy here."

The tips of his ears turn bright red, just like they did in debate class when I completely decimated his argument. If I remember correctly, it was so bad that he stuttered through his entire rebuttal and knocked his grade from an A to a B. While I may have tried to block out most of my high school experience, moments like those will stay with me until my dying breath.

I can tell he's revving up to explode.

The Nate I used to know prided himself on never losing control. It's what made him so popular in high school. He was this enigma who seemed utterly disinterested, yet totally involved. He did debate and played chess but was still the captain of the baseball team and, eventually, prom king. His clothes were thrift store chic before thrifting was cool, but he still managed to make everyone envious of his well-worn Chucks and faded tees . . . a far cry from the stuffy style he now has.

With my kinky curls and bronze skin among a sea of silky straight hair and rosy cheeks, I never felt like I fit in. He was my lifeboat in the storm. We felt like kindred spirits.

Until we didn't.

Thankfully, before Nate can lose his cool and affect his standing in the neighborhood hierarchy, a woman I haven't met approaches pushing a stroller that looks like it may have been designed by NASA.

"Good morning, Angela." Nate's peppy voice is unrecognizable from the deep, gravelly tone he had only moments ago. "How's Mr. Liam doing today?"

What a freaking phony.

"Oh my goodness, Nate!" Angela engages the brake on her stroller. "You're soaking wet! Are you okay?"

I don't even attempt to resist the urge to roll my eyes. I mean, calm down, Angela. It's June. Poor, precious Nate isn't going to catch a chill.

"I'm fine. It's only water." He waves her off. "Just a little misunderstanding between me and Collins."

Up until that point, I'm pretty sure Angela didn't even notice I was standing there. She trains her eyes on me, taking her time to measure me up from head to toe and dismissing me just as quickly. It's not a new experience for me in this town, being made to feel as if I'm invisible, not worthy of anything, but it's still triggering AF.

The only thing worse than feeling like an outcast is feeling like nothing at all.

"Are you sure?" She bends over and reaches into the basket beneath the stroller. "I have a—"

"Thank you, but I'm sure." Nate cuts her off. "I don't want to hold you up any longer. Liam needs to get his walk in before it gets too hot outside."

Now, if I didn't hate Nate and he didn't hate me, I might think he not only noticed the way Angela dismissed me but didn't like it either. I might think that he very politely sent her on her way not because he's concerned for Liam's walk but because he's concerned for me.

It's a good thing I know better.

"So . . ." Nate says once Angela is out of earshot. "You're a gardener now?"

"Small talk? Really?" I'm so not in the mood for this. He can fool everyone else, but he won't fool me. Not again. "What do you want, Nate?"

He drags a hand through his thick black hair and groans. The low, deep rumble sends vibrations running through the ground and the worn-out rubber on my feet. I'm ashamed to admit that I feel it between my thighs.

"Listen, Collins. I don't like you and you don't like me. That's fine," he starts, and I have no idea where he's going with this. "But I respect your parents and if you're going to be my neighbor, the least we could do is figure out how to be civil toward one another. At least enough that we're not spraying each other with water."

God.

Even when he's trying to make a truce, he's still an arrogant, insufferable asshole.

"First of all, you know I didn't spray you on purpose. Please stop trying to twist this into something that didn't happen." I stop and draw in a long inhale through my nose when I feel my pulse beginning to race. "Second, I have no problem being civil. Not sure you noticed, but I was minding my own business. You're the one that chose to come over here and bother me, not the other way around."

"I see civility is off the table," he mumbles beneath his breath, which only further pisses me off. "So you planted this tree? What kind is it?"

I feel a little whiplash at the rapid change in topic, but I answer in hopes that it will send him on his way faster.

"I did." I omit that I'm only doing this because my mom has

banned my dad from all garden work for a week. It's none of his business and it will only prolong this conversation. "It's a white oak. I never got to garden in LA, so I'm going all out while I'm home."

"That makes sense. Starving artists don't typically have the space or funds to do stuff like this, huh?"

"Yup." I know he's trying to get a rise out of me. This is how Nate operates. I might've played into his games at the coffee shop, but I'm not giving him the satisfaction today. "I totally starved myself through Hollywood events and pitching my shows to execs. I should've joined the HOA like you."

"That's a nice way of saying you've been failing for ten years. Opportunity after opportunity, and yet—" He gestures to the space around us. "Here you are. Back at Mommy and Daddy's house."

It takes every ounce of self-control I possess not to react to hearing my negative self-talk coming out of someone else's mouth, but I manage.

Barely.

"And to think, my fallback plan is your first choice." I hit him where I know it hurts. Once upon a time we were best friends; it's how we're able to take each other down with such brutal accuracy. "It's easy to seem like a success when you aim low. Am I right?"

"Screw you, Collins." The mask he wears for everyone else slips and the real Nate reveals himself. "You were right to leave. Now, get over whatever hissy fit you're throwing so you can hurry up and abandon the only people that care about you. Again."

He turns to leave, not wanting to give me the chance to have the last word. But as he marches away, my blood feels like lava sifting through my veins. The heat and pressure swelling inside me make it impossible to contain my temper any longer.

"Hey, Nate." I reach down for the hose I'd forgotten about as he takes his time to turn and face me. "Just so we're clear, this time? It's on purpose."

I push the lever all the way up, aiming the nozzle and hitting my target dead-on. Nate barely flinches as the cold water rains down on him.

I don't know how long we stand there, both glaring and silently shouting everything we could never say out loud before he finally turns to leave.

"You're going to regret that, Collins Carter!" he shouts over his shoulder, not looking back once.

Instead of the fear I'm sure he was intending, petty giddiness makes my skin tingle with anticipation of battles to be fought.

"Bring it on, Nathanial Adams!"

He doesn't know it yet, but I'm going to bring him to his fucking knees.

Chapter 5

*W*hile Mom's potato salad isn't famous, her gatherings are. Nobody strives to be the perfect hostess more than Kimberly Carter.

She woke me up at six o'clock this morning to prepare the backyard. Not only did I have to mow the lawn—something I will gladly never do again—but she pulled out the ladder so I could string lights and lanterns from the trees. The folding tables stacked in the basement are scattered about the space, covered in fabric tablecloths because she would never use tacky plastic (her words, not mine) even though this is a literal barbecue and they'll probably be ruined by the end of the night.

What started out as a small gathering with some of her church friends and my dad's golfing buddies has morphed into a completely different beast. My mom told me to invite Ashleigh and Grant, whom she then directed to invite their neighbors, and so on and so on. Steaks from Meijer turned out to be steaks, chicken, hot dogs, and burgers and five pitchers of sangria. Neighbors I remember from before I moved to LA mingle with neighbors I've never seen before. There's constant motion at the gate entrance as people come and go, each person bringing a new casserole dish with them.

The good news is that we now have ample potato salads to choose from and only three of them have raisins, dried cranberries, and/or walnuts. The bad news is that someone brought creamy pineapple fluff salad and Karen D. brought "creamy overnight fruit salad" that she's been trying to force me to eat for the last hour. I've been gone for too long. I forgot how distinctly midwestern it is to throw a bunch of random junk into a bowl, toss in whipped cream or mayo, and call it a salad.

Nineties country and hip-hop alternate on the speaker system my dad installed last year. Voices blend together, bursts of laughter ringing out like an orchestra. Toddlers run freely as their parents chase after them, muttering rushed apologies to the innocent bystanders they almost take out. And even though I'm what one could call an intense introvert, I'm enjoying the energy buzzing in the backyard. Which is why it's so noticeable when a chill sweeps through the air and good vibes turn toxic.

I look over my shoulder just in time to see Nate saunter through the gate. I don't like to admit how attuned my body is to him, that it always remembers what I've worked for years to forget. While the other people in attendance have come in regular old jeans and T-shirts, he's wearing khaki shorts, tennis shoes—not the same ones I sprayed him in—and a button-up Hawaiian-print shirt. On anyone else, it would look ridiculous, but somehow, he makes it work.

The cockiness in his steps as he walks through the crowd.

The confidence in his voice as he greets his neighbors.

The way his forearms flex when he offers an enthusiastic handshake.

Nate owns the room. And dislike him as I may, even I can't deny that his presence is electric.

"He was always such a handsome boy." My mom sneaks up behind me and scares the bejesus out of me. "Go say hello."

"Oh no. I don't think that's necessary." I try to object, but she's already linked her arm through mine and is dragging me through the grass.

"Nonsense." She shushes me just like she did when I was a child. "This is your home and you're a host too. Don't be rude."

I want to ask where this energy was for the multiple other people she let me ignore, but she offers a strong shove between my shoulder blades before I have the chance. I turn and glare, but I still acquiesce.

Our backyard is a decent size, not huge by any means, but also not small. However, as the distance between myself and Nate vanishes, it feels downright claustrophobic. Unwelcome nerves blossom in the bottom of my belly. The fear of causing a potential scene at my parents' perfect barbecue is in direct opposition to the excitement of going head-to-head with my favorite adversary.

"Collins." Nate steps away from a group of middle-aged dads and greets me as I approach. "Wish I could say it was nice to see you, but a liar I am not."

"Oh, I'm so sorry. Can you please repeat that?" I lean in closer, cupping my hand around my ear. "I couldn't hear you over your shirt."

"Bazinga!" one of the dads I've yet to meet shouts. He angles toward me, lifting his hand in the air for a high five. "She got you there, Adams!"

I slap my hand against his with a little too much enthusiasm. Nate's cheeks flush red on his cleanly shaven face. Warmth flows through my veins at the sight. Not much brings me more pleasure than knocking Nate down a peg or two.

"Shut up, Ben." Nate glowers at his maybe friend. "And she didn't get me. These shirts are made by native Hawaiians and part of the proceeds go toward helping them offset the effects of tourism and colonization. Where's your shirt from, Old Navy?"

Oh fuck.

That actually is really cool. I wonder if I can get him to share the website with me for when I have money to buy things again . . .

"What's wrong with Old Navy, bro?" Ben asks, clearly taken aback by the force of Nate's frustration.

As someone who has placed myself firmly in the line of Nate's wrath, I can say it's definitely not for the weak of heart. And no offense to Ben, but no way is he prepared for this fight.

Nate dismisses Ben with a roll of the eyes before shifting his attention back to me.

"Can we talk?" He doesn't wait for a response before turning his back on me and heading in the direction of the only quiet spot in the yard.

Considering I didn't want to talk to him in the first place, I contemplate letting him go off on his own and rejoining the party. But when I see Karen walking around holding a plate of creamy banana slop, I decide messing with Nate a little longer couldn't hurt.

As I approach the secluded area behind the willow tree, I fight back the memories of summer days spent beneath the tree, spilling my guts to Nate about my fears, dreams, and everything in between. I wish I could go back in time and scoop that little girl up, hugging her tight for the hard times coming her way.

"Just so you're aware, I already told my mom that I think you may be a serial killer," I warn as I get closer. "If you murder me, your basement will be the first place they'll check."

His eyes go wide and his head jerks back. He looks horrified. "You told your mom what?"

"I'm kidding." I try to calm him down without laughing. "I mean, I did really voice my serial killer concerns with her, but she didn't believe me. She thinks you're nice for some reason."

"Jesus, Collins." He drags his hand across his face. He's already exhausted and we've barely exchanged five sentences. "What's wrong with you? Why do you have to act like this?"

Is he serious? The audacity of this man.

"Oh, no you don't." My palm itches for the garden hose again. "You dealt the first blow tonight. You don't get to pretend to be the victim because I'm better at this game than you. If you want to keep it pleasant, you'd be wise to listen to the ancient philosopher who once stated, 'Don't start none, won't be none.'"

I didn't realize rolling your eyes had a sound, but I swear I can hear Nate's eyeballs hit the back of his skull. I shouldn't be amused, but he's just so much fun when he gets worked up. And after months of reading comment after comment on the internet from nameless and faceless bullies judging or mocking me, it's nice to be able to fight back. Especially with something as low stakes as old high school grudges. I mean really, how bad could this get? He talks shit about me with people I already hate?

Whoop-de-freaking-do.

"So you're sure you want to keep doing this? You really think you can beat me in this game?" The semi-ominous undertone in his words almost makes me chuckle.

Now I'm the one rolling my eyes. "Yeah, Nate. I'm sure."

"Well then"—he pulls an unaddressed envelope out of his back pocket—"don't say I didn't warn you."

"Seriously? What is this, a strongly worded letter?"

I snatch the envelope out of his hands and rip it open. I pull out the letter, and as I read, my amusement quickly transforms into barely concealed rage.

"What the fuck is this?" I ask as I read through words like *HOA violation* and *tree removal* and *unapproved landscaping*, but it's when I see the fine that I truly lose my mind. "Two hundred dollars? Are you kidding me?"

Sure, I sprayed him with the hose and called his shirt loud, but this escalation of offenses is as ridiculous as it is unwarranted.

"Actually . . ." He leans in closer, clearly not valuing his life, as he points out the text near the bottom of the letter. "If you read right here, you'll see that the *first* fine is two hundred dollars. But if you don't remove the tree by the date listed, the HOA will be forced to issue another fine at a greater value."

"Nate," I try to reason with him. I know he doesn't like me, but he's the one who said he respected my parents, and they're who this will affect in the long run. "My dad had me plant that tree for my mom. You cannot ask me to dig it up. She'll be devastated. Don't do this to them."

"It's not me." He feigns innocence and the condescending smirk on his face widens. "I'm just presenting this to you on behalf of the homeowners' association."

"You came to my parents' barbecue for official HOA business?" The hold on my temper finally slips. "How about you take this letter and shove it up your H-O-A-hole!"

I scrunch up the letter into a ball and aim it at his face, but he easily dodges it.

"Tsk, tsk, tsk. I wouldn't do that if I were you." He bends over and picks up the paper, taking his time to straighten it out before handing it back to me. "But I have a deal to make with you, should you choose to accept."

I don't want to play into his stupid little game, but I also don't have spare money lying around to keep paying fines. Plus, I already feel like such a burden on my poor parents, I can't be responsible for costing them more money or losing the tree.

"What?" I look around, grateful to see nobody's bearing witness to this exchange. "Spit it out already."

He was always as dramatic as he was pompous. It's too bad certain things don't change with time.

"Move," he says like this is some small and easy request. "I've made a life for myself here. I've created a community that values me and my contributions. I don't need some bitter girl from high school causing scenes everywhere I go and making others question my character."

"Hold on one second. Let me get this straight." I raise my hand in front of me and close my eyes. I inhale through my nose and exhale through my mouth just like my therapist taught me, only to find out the bitch lied because I'm still mad as hell. When I open my eyes and see Nate still standing there, looking like he won something, red colors my vision. "You can't handle running into me on your little walks and your precious ego is worried some people won't like you? So you're blackmailing me through the freaking HOA?"

It's so absurd that I almost laugh. As a screenwriter, I worked tirelessly to come up with plots and ideas that would make people laugh or cry or scream. But never, and I mean never, could I come up with something as truly and utterly ridiculous as this.

Some of the cockiness fades from his demeanor, but because he's Nate, he doesn't back down.

"It's obvious you hate it here," he says. "You've always thought you were better than us. So why don't you just take this as your next excuse to leave?"

Now, if I were thinking clearly—which I'm not—or concerned in the slightest about Nate's feelings—which I'm also not—I might notice the way his angry words could be masking a deeper hurt and insecurities. But I don't, and Nate is in large part to thank for that.

"You think I want to be here?" The rhetorical question drips with acid as it falls out of my mouth. "You think I left for LA as soon as possible only to return at nearly thirty to live with my parents for fun? Do you really think if I had literally *any other options,* I'd be standing in the backyard of my childhood home, arguing with *you*? Come on, Nate. I may not like you, but even I know you're smarter than that."

"Well then, it looks like you have quite the dilemma in front of you." He shoves his hands into his khaki pockets, rocking back onto the heels of his shoes. "But what was that advice you gave me earlier? Oh, that's right. Don't start none, won't be none?" He pauses, taking a step closer. "Looks like round two goes to me."

He aims his bright smile at me, winking once before walking away. My hands curl into fists so tight, I can feel the sharp sting as my nails break the skin of my palms. I watch him walk away, trying to think of anything at all to say so that he doesn't get the last word, but I come up empty-handed.

He may have won this round, but that was because I didn't know we were playing dirty. Now that I know his game? He better watch out. Because unlike my queen, Michelle Obama, there's nothing stopping me from going as low as I can.

Chapter 6

*H*e's leveraging the HOA against me!" I shout in the middle of Ashleigh's sparsely decorated living room with Ruby on speakerphone. "Who even does that?"

As soon as Nate left, I abandoned the barbecue and spent the entire night staring at the HOA violation notice, frantically googling the consequences of not paying. I mean, really, it's a made-up system for bored, power-hungry people to feel a slight sense of superiority. What could they really do?

Well, as it turns out, a lot.

Beyond the amount of fees piling up, I found horror stories of liens being put on houses, and—in some cases—forcing homes into foreclosure. Between this news, the steak, two different potato salads, cupcakes, and three glasses of sangria I had at the barbecue, I thought I was going to vomit. I stayed up all night doomscrolling and plotting all the ways I would seek revenge against Nate.

He really thought he had me.

But luckily for me, my best friend is a kick-ass lawyer who's willing to roll around in the mud with me.

"He's not leveraging the HOA against you," Ruby's semi-distracted voice bursts through the speaker. "He's blackmailing you and that is a *literal* crime."

"Are we sure this isn't some big misunderstanding?" Ashleigh asks from the kitchen. Her calm and sweet voice is a nice change of pace from the warpaths Ruby and I are on. "Maybe he was just joking and trying to get a rise out of you. I can't see him really taking this feud of yours to the HOA. It doesn't seem like him."

"You don't know him the way I know him. Trust me, this is exactly like him. He'll do whatever it takes to win." I tell her the god-awful truth before I redirect my attention. "But back to what Ruby was saying: When you say *literal crime*, does that mean he could go to jail?"

Glee I didn't think was possible to feel on two hours of sleep spikes my adrenaline as I picture Nate being escorted out of his two-story house with the entire neighborhood watching.

"It's possible," she says, spurring my fantasy on. "But he'd more than likely just have to pay a fine."

I deflate on Ashleigh's couch, which may or may not be more comfortable than my bed. "Boo. That's not nearly as fun."

"Awww, Ruby." Ashleigh sits down next to me and places little glass roller tubes on the coffee table. "You should see her face. It looks like you just kicked her puppy."

When Ashleigh and I exchanged numbers, I did plan on calling her eventually . . . just not this soon. But after working myself into a frenzy, I knew I had to talk about Nate to somebody and I couldn't let my parents hear. I considered taking a drive and calling Ruby in the car, but I realized that in this situation, Nate totally has the upper hand. I needed somebody on my side. Someone on the ground. Someone local.

Thank god Ashleigh is so friendly and outgoing, because while meeting new people may come easy to some people, I really struggle with it. I've never been the most popular person. I mean, besides Ruby, Nate was one of my closest friends, and we saw how that worked out. Then in LA, I made some friends at school, but because we were all in the same industry, the relationships felt very conditional. Like people were only ever friends if they could get something out of it.

And then, of course, there was Peter.

I met Peter my sophomore year. He was the graduate teaching assistant in my creative writing class. I'll never forget walking into the lecture hall and seeing him for the first time. All tall, tanned skin, and whiskey-brown eyes I swear you could see from space. He was my California dream in human form.

And I wish I'd never laid eyes on him.

"Sorry to crush your dreams, Colls. But you know, we can always— Luke!" Ruby shouts at her assistant and startles Ashleigh. "Why is Mrs. Grayson complaining that I'm not returning her messages? What messages is she talking about?" She stops yelling and gives poor Luke a second to defend himself. "No, taking messages only works if you deliver them to me. How am I supposed to know to call her back if you're hoarding them on your desk? This isn't rocket science."

While I usually try to defend Ruby's assistants, I can't help him out this time. I'm sure he's afraid to bring them to her because she's always yelling, but even I know he needs to pass the messages along. Luke has been her assistant for a whopping four months. Unfortunately—or fortunately—for him, I have a sneaking suspicion he won't make it to five.

"Please excuse her," I say to Ashleigh, who's staring at the phone with wide-eyed horror. "She's a monster to all of her assistants."

"I'm not a monster." Ruby rejoins our conversation and I assume she's sent Luke off to cry in a corner somewhere. "Expecting my assistant to deliver the messages he takes is literally the bare minimum for his position, and thanks to him, I have to go. Apparently my client has been trying to get in touch with me for the last four days because her jackass husband has decided he doesn't have to abide by the parenting schedule."

"Oh no!" sweet, innocent, angelic Ashleigh gasps. "That's horrible!"

"It's typical," Ruby says. "And I know I shouldn't generalize, but men are trash."

"Exactly!" I pipe up, needing everyone to remember why we're on this phone call in the first place. "Which is why we need to figure out how to strike back at Nate. Men can't win again!"

I'm not quite sure how I've turned my petty neighborhood rivalry into a case of misogyny, but now that I have, it feels right. I'm not backing down and I know Ruby won't either.

"You and Ashleigh think of some plans and we'll reconvene later tonight," Ruby says. "And if worse comes to worst, I can draft a cease and desist that'll make him shit his pants."

Reason 2,000,001 why Ruby will always and forever be my best fucking friend.

"You're the best." I tell her something she's already acutely aware of. "Talk later."

"Bye, Ruby!" Ashleigh shouts at the phone, but there's a little tremor of fear in her voice. "Nice chatting with you."

Ruby doesn't respond before hanging up. She's probably in a rush to yell at Luke one more time before she has to be professional and levelheaded while she talks to her client.

"Wow." Ashleigh stares at me with wide, horrified eyes. "Ruby is . . . she's intense."

That's maybe the understatement of the century. Ruby is fully fucking unhinged, but, if she's on your side, she will go to the ends of the earth for you. It's why she stays booked and busy. Her clients know she's willing to do whatever she can for them, even if it means sinking into the mud.

"She is," I agree. "But her bark is worse than her bite."

That might be a lie, but I say it anyway because Ashleigh looks like she could use a little reassurance.

"Oh good." She releases a heavy exhale and laughs quietly. "I was nervous for her assistant for a second there."

Worried my expression will give away the fact that Luke will be unemployed in the very near future, I attempt to change the subject. "What are those?"

I point to the amber roller tubes she brought over earlier and feel immediate regret. I already had an idea of what they are, but the way her blue eyes gloss over and her perfect smile turns slightly deranged, I know exactly what's inside.

"Oh my goodness!" She claps her manicured hands together before snatching the tubes off the table and handing one to me. "I made you an essential oil blend. I know you're feeling a little stressed, so I combined my favorite calming oils to make the perfect blend for you."

I fight back my groan, watching as she ticks off her fingers, naming all the oils she used.

"There's lavender, vetiver, frankincense, and just a touch of jasmine. I mixed them with coconut oil, so all you have to do is roll that on the insides of your wrists, down the back of your neck, and behind your ears whenever you're feeling stressed, and it will calm you right down."

It takes every single ounce of self-control I have not to pick up the glass roller and hurtle it across the room. Not only was I raised by a pharmacist who always praised and valued the importance science has in our society, but before I quit all social media, I watched as many of the girls I went to high school with fell into the cult that is essential oils. One day they were posting funny memes and cute videos of their kids, the next day they were ranting about conspiracy theories, homeschooling, and breeding chickens.

It was entertaining at first, but as they fell deeper into the cult or came out of the other side sad, disillusioned, and not to mention broke, it was just depressing. And I know that Ashleigh, as a young, beautiful white woman preparing to start a family, is the prime target for any and all MLM schemes.

"This is really sweet of you." I take the roller and have to admit that while I do doubt its magical healing power, it does smell amazing. "But I have a therapist and a Xanax prescription at home for when my anxiety gets totally out of control. I'm okay."

I can see how my ranting and raving today could make it seem like I'm already out of control, but my therapist has been encouraging me to voice my feelings instead of pushing them away. I want to feel my anger today. It's the only thing fueling my determination to get back at Nate rather than folding to his demands.

"If you're sure, then that's all I need to hear." She sounds doubtful but doesn't push it. One more reason for me to like this woman.

Plus, now I feel content knowing that even if she does join MLMs, she's much too gentle and kind to get totally invested. I'll just have to distract her with my endless drama and keep her too busy to fall prey to the boss babes and hustle-harder girlies who would, no doubt, eat her alive. It's my duty as a dedicated friend and civil servant to be as petty as humanly possible.

"So, about Nate . . ." I bring the conversation back to the topic at hand. "You know him better than I do. How do we get him to back down?"

I'll save my revenge fantasies for Ruby. I don't want to pervert Ashleigh's pure mind with the many ways I want to make Nate cry.

"I don't know," she says. "I'm still surprised he's doing this to you. He was so nice when we worked with him to find this house. I didn't think he had something like this in him."

I contemplate filling her in on my serial killer theory, but Ruby warned me against it. Something about libel and defamation if I warned the neighborhood to stay alert.

Blah blah blah.

Whatever.

"Oh, he definitely has it in him."

I've known it since I was sixteen. Nate's always had this facade of being some laid-back guy who doesn't care what people think of him, when in reality, he's consumed by it. And he's willing to do anything, to use anyone, to get where he wants to go. I just don't understand how that place is living alone in the suburbs and on the homeowners' association board.

"Ruby said what he's doing is illegal. Are you considering taking it to the authorities?" She bites her lip as if even thinking about the ramifications is making her nervous. I almost hand her my miracle roller to help her relax.

"No," I answer without hesitation. "Nate might be a giant asshole, but not even I'm willing to escalate our feud to that level. I want to embarrass him, not ruin his life."

He's gone way too far by bringing my parents' home into it, but if I'm honest, I still have my doubts that he'll act on it. All I need to do is push him and force him to admit that he's full of shit.

"He made it seem like he was so invested in making this community feel like a family. He said it was why he joined the HOA, to make sure everything was open and easily accessible in case anyone had any concerns. I can't believe I fell for that," Ashleigh says. "Ugh. What a jerk."

As the light dawns on Ashleigh about Nate's true character, an idea starts to form in the back of my mind.

"What did he want to make open and accessible?" I ask. "The HOA?"

"Um . . . yeah." She nods and her brows furrow together.

"Most HOA boards only have a few meetings and nobody ever knows about them. Nate convinced the other members to host monthly meetings. They post the schedule in the Reserve at Horizon Creek Facebook group."

There really is a Facebook group for everything.

"Can you check and see when the next meeting is?"

"Sure," she says.

She grabs her phone and starts tapping around on the screen. As I wait, my skin begins to buzz the way it used to when the first embers of a new story idea started to burn. My brain spins and turns, plotting out endless possibilities while I wait for Ashleigh to find any information.

"Oh!" She shoves her phone in my face, pointing to the screen with her pink polished nail. "There's one coming up soon!"

I take my time reading through the post, scanning over all the comments and rolling my eyes at Nate's pompous replies. His skill for well-placed snark is truly remarkable.

I hand Ashleigh back her phone when I'm finished. My shoulders, which had been aching from hunching over my laptop, feel fantastic. The stress headache pounding away at my skull for the last four hours magically disappears. Any ailment can be cured by the simple pleasure of a well-formed plan and the potential of publicly humiliating my enemy.

Who needs essential oils when you have bad intentions and vengeful ideations?

"I hope you don't have plans this Friday," I say to my new friend, "because we have an HOA board meeting to crash."

Chapter 7

When I moved to Los Angeles, I did my best to avoid the sun whenever possible. This means I frequently skipped out on beach days and if I did manage to be coerced to hang poolside, I made sure not only to slather my body in sunscreen, but also to wear a hat so large it was mistaken for an umbrella a time or two.

Sure, they may say Black don't crack, but that doesn't mean that Black can't get skin cancer. Plus, my Black has been cut in half and I don't want to test the strength of my Irish genes.

So it's safe to assume that if I avoided the stunning waterscapes in California, I for damn sure wasn't spending my summer days lounging by the pool at the Reserve at Horizon Creek. In fact, aside from the one time my mom forced me to go to a bridal shower for one of her church friend's daughters, I've stepped foot in the clubhouse approximately two, maybe three, times tops.

"Wow." I take in the space, which is a far cry from the dingy carpet and beige walls of my memories. The hardwood floors gleam beneath modern light fixtures with large area rugs sectioning off the space. A coffee bar with a mini fridge filled with creamers sits along the far wall, and now I know where I'll be the next time my mom tries to force hazelnut coffee on me. "At least now I know where the HOA fees are going."

"It's so nice, isn't it? You should come with me to the pool," Ashleigh suggests, oblivious to my disdain for UV rays. "I go on weekday mornings after Grant goes to the office, after swim practice, but before it gets too crowded."

"As much fun as that sounds—" I start, but I am distracted by the booming laughter I hate to admit I remember so clearly.

I turn toward the sound just in time to see Nate with his head thrown back, a huge smile making him seem years younger spread across his face. I don't mean to stare, but I can't look away.

While I might be here on a revenge mission, my heart squeezes with regret and fondness for the boy I once cared for so deeply. I stand frozen, overcome by memories of sitting in my backyard with him and the way my skin would tingle with pleasure when I managed to make him laugh. Even when we were kids, his laughter was elusive, like there was so much hiding beneath his too-cool persona. But before I could figure him out, he upgraded his style . . . and friends.

I turn my attention back to Ashleigh before he can catch me staring.

"Hey." Ashleigh drops her voice to a whisper. "Are you okay? What he did was really messed up, but you don't have to do this if you don't want."

"Thank you, but I definitely want to do this." I shake my head free of silly childhood memories and prepare myself for the battle ahead of me. "He's not going to know what hit him when I'm done with him."

Bullies bank on silence.

But if Nate thinks he can do whatever he wants while I sit back and allow him to step all over me, he's made a gross miscalculation. People don't up and abandon the life they've spent ten years building to move in with their parents because they're winning at life.

No, no, no.

When choosing an opponent, it's wise to find someone with something to lose. It makes it easier to predict their next move. Nate didn't do that when he decided to mess with me. Because me? Well, I hit rock bottom weeks ago, and unlike Nate and his carefully crafted life, I don't have anything to lose.

"So . . ." She drops her voice and glances over her shoulder to make sure none of our neighbors are within earshot. "What's the plan again?"

I can tell she's nervous, but much to her credit, she's hiding it well. Her smile is the only thing giving her away. It's vaguely reminiscent of Ruby's from her pageant days. Gorgeous, but strained at the corners and a smidge too big to be natural.

"We're going to watch and gauge the crowd at first, then we'll act according to them. If they hate the HOA as much as everybody on the internet says, I'll go with straight heckling. Add on to everybody else's complaints and fan the flames of anger. If it's more laid-back and polite, then I'll have to be the chaos creator." It's a title I'd like engraved on my tombstone one day. I reach into my purse and pull out the letter Nate gave me along with a list of tough questions that will "stump your HOA every time" that I found on Reddit. "I'll start going through the questions one by one until Nate looks like he's ready to explode. No matter what, I'll gently toss in little comments about blackmail just to watch him squirm. He's banked on his stand-up, good-guy act. He'll freak if he thinks I'm going to blow his cover."

"And what do I need to do exactly?" Ashleigh asks before huffing the amber roller bottle she's clutching in her hand.

"Nothing," I reassure her. "You're here to keep me company if this is as boring as I expect it to be and to make sure I don't sleep through my moment."

"Oh good." The tension finally leaves her shoulders and color returns to her rosy cheeks. "I can definitely do that. I'm great company and I need like five melatonins and a hot bath before bed. No way will I drift off."

I can't tell if that's a weird humblebrag or a cry for help, but before I can figure it out, her blue eyes drift over my shoulders and her eyes widen with unconcealed panic. A superspy she is not. However, I didn't need to see her face to know Nate was coming.

Because while my brain is set on hating him, my stupid body is refusing to hop on board.

It's almost as if the more he does to make me hate him, the more my physical awareness of him grows. Shivers trail down my spine while the hairs at the nape of my neck stand tall. My stomach flips while my thighs tighten, and I wonder if this is how it feels to lose the little that's left of my mind. This man is driving me crazy, and the worst part about it is, I'm enjoying every single minute.

"Ashleigh, I'm so glad you decided to come." Nate greets her from right behind me, the heat of his breath tracing the shell of my ear. "Would you mind if I stole Collins from you for a second?"

Ashleigh, the poor, sweet girl, looks between Nate and me like a deer caught in the headlights. As a reformed people pleaser, I recognize her expression all too well.

"It's okay." I smile, squeezing her hand in mine. "Why don't you go save our seats and I'll find you later?"

"All right. If you're sure . . ." She still seems unsure about what to do, and for the first time, guilt begins to gnaw at my conscience for dragging this innocent bystander into my shit.

"I'm sure," I tell her with confidence I don't quite feel. "I'm not privy to HOA meeting etiquette, but he is the vice president of the board, and that might mean something in between these walls."

I don't know what's wrong with me, but I'm physically incapable of not insulting Nate anytime he's near. Thankfully, my snark seems to get through to Ashleigh and a real smile pulls at her line-free face.

She pivots on a sky-high heel and struts down the hallway. Every person she passes stops what they're doing to watch her go. It's mesmerizing. I wonder what I'd be capable of doing if I possessed a power that strong.

"What are you doing here?" Nate's terse voice pulls my attention back to the matter at hand.

I spin to face him, and long gone is the happy-go-lucky Nate from moments ago. No signs of laughter linger on his hard face, and his strong jaw is set as he awaits my answer. It's hard to believe he's the same person I used to consider my best friend. As much as I've tried to figure it out, I have no idea what happened to cause us to go from friends to enemies. All I know is that tonight won't be the night we mend fences.

"Who? Me?" I bring my hands to my chest, almost missing it when his eyes follow the movement and linger on my cleavage for just a second too long. "I'm just a concerned neighbor. I don't know if you know this or not, but . . ." I lean in and drop my voice to an exaggerated whisper. "Some of the board members are blackmailing residents."

Fire lights in his hazel eyes and I know I have him right where I want him. Like putty in my hands.

Sucker.

"Don't do this here." His words are slow and quiet, like he's speaking to a small child and not a contemporary. "This is not the time or the place for you to throw a temper tantrum."

He may be trying to get me to see reason and leave, but he doesn't realize that with a few simple words, he's unintentionally triggered the absolute crap out of me.

Peter always accused me of throwing temper tantrums. Anytime I stuck up for myself or demanded answers he avoided giving, he'd manage to flip the situation in his favor. The last time he told me I was throwing one was in the parking lot outside our apartment. Right after I found out that he not only used me for years, but he'd also stolen and taken credit for my dream.

It was the last time I saw him.

It was the moment that caused my world to explode.

"Excuse me?" Anger not meant for Nate clouds my vision. "I am *not* throwing a temper tantrum. Children throw temper tantrums and I am not a child."

"I mean, you did spray me with a water hose." He pauses before adding, "Twice."

"The first time was an accident!" If I knew it wouldn't bring my parents shame, there'd be no stopping me from leaping across the space separating us and throttling the man in front of me. Peter was a liar and a cheater, yet somehow, Nate is still more infuriating. "And no matter how you cut it, the letter was a massive and unnecessary escalation."

"I think it was the perfect level of escalation with a perfect outcome for all parties involved. Your parents get to keep their landscaping, you get to leave Ohio, and I get to go back to my normal, peaceful life."

I don't want the playful glint in his eye to distract me from my rage, but as he lists his reasons, I can't help the way my temper cools down.

"Normal and peaceful, huh?" I repeat his words back to him, fighting to keep the glare on my face. "That's one way to say boring."

"Ha ha. Very funny." His voice is deadpan, but it still doesn't hide the humor lurking behind his words. "Now can you go home, please?"

"You want me to leave? Let me think about that . . ." I tap my pointer finger on my chin, pretending to contemplate the thought. "I think I'll stay. What is it that you said in the Facebook group? That the key to turning community into family is involvement? I'm here to be involved, Vice President Adams."

Even if we did resolve our issues, there's not a chance I'm leaving. Not only did I tame my curls into a presentable updo, but

I also put on makeup *and* a bra. I'm here to stay. That kind of effort does not get to go to waste. Regardless if it means sitting through a boring HOA meeting.

His cheeks puff out and the tips of his ears burn bright red. I can't tell if he's pissed or scared, but both are pleasing to my eyes and heart. The best part is I wasn't even expecting this! I was planning on saving my mischief for once the meeting started. Getting to mess with him this early in the night is icing on the already very delicious cake.

Plus, I may or may not have drawn a mustache on his face on a couple of the FOR SALE signs I passed walking to the meeting tonight.

What's that old saying again? Oh yes, all's fair in love and war. Just this time, it's easy on the love, heavy on the war.

"Fine." Any of the levity that had worked its way into his miserable demeanor is gone, any semblance of joy has been overridden by the desperation of a man who overplayed his hand. "But even though you may not think about anybody other than yourself, the people in that room really do care. Don't make a mockery of the meeting in order to make yourself feel better. Your parents deserve better than to be embarrassed like that."

"Funny of you to worry about my parents when you dragging them into this is *literally* the only reason I'm here." I keep my voice as carefree as I can manage and make sure not to let my smile falter. "But don't you worry, someone will leave this meeting embarrassed tonight. It just sure as hell isn't going to be any of the Carters."

With that fantastic fucking parting shot—that I didn't even plan!!—I pat him on the back and take my merry behind to go find Ashleigh.

And to think, he thought he had me beat.

God, I love it when people underestimate me.

Chapter 8

*L*isten.

It's not like I expected community theater when I decided to crash the HOA, but even the lowest of expectations couldn't have prepared me for what an absolute snoozefest these meetings are.

The meeting is held in a room about the size of a classroom, and unlike the space we first entered, this room is devoid of art unless you count the American flag tacked up on the far wall. They set up a long table at the front for the board members and scattered a handful of chairs for the audience. I will say, I'm impressed—and disturbed—by the surprisingly high turnout. I mean, I know Ohio is boring, but even I can't get over the number of people who had nothing better to do than attend an HOA meeting. At least Ashleigh and I came for revenge. What's everyone else's excuse?

The beginning of the meeting lasts nineteen hours.

Fine.

Ten minutes.

But time is relative. And trapped in the beige room, reciting the Pledge of Allegiance with AC that I'm sure is two days away from breaking, it feels as though time completely stops.

The board files into the room, taking their seats behind the table, and my jaw falls open. I already knew there was one person on the board I couldn't stand, but I'm shocked when I realize he's not the only one. Mr. Bridgewerth sits front and center with his wrinkled fingers clenched around an old wooden gavel, with Nate as his right-hand man. The Reserve at Horizon Creek HOA board president—and my former English teacher—seems very content with his position at the top of the most power-hungry, irrelevant group in the history of the world.

Seeing them sitting next to each other, quite literally rubbing elbows, I almost wash my hands of the entire plan. I mean truly, if Nate's life consists of Ohio real estate and sitting on an HOA board with the worst, most misogynistic, racist teacher I ever had the displeasure of being taught by, is there anything I could do to bring him lower? I don't think so.

But never one to back down from a challenge, I get my head in the game and give it the good old college try.

It's called *determination*. Look it up.

See also *petty* and *spiteful* . . .

Anyways.

After Janice, the secretary, introduces the rest of the board, she reads through minutes from the last meeting and presents the agenda for tonight. When she hands the microphone—metaphorically, of course—to Mr. Bridgewerth, my eyelids begin to droop.

I'm transported back to Central High, sitting in the back of the classroom struggling to focus as Mr. Bridgewerth bores us to death. His monotone voice reads through the management report and with every nasal word, I realize that the chances of me not dozing off during the meeting are slim to none. Facebook told me this meeting would last around an hour and a half and I'm not sure even my well-thought-out plan for revenge is enough to fuel me.

When they move on to the budget, my eyes gloss over.

"We should've brought the wine with us," Ashleigh whispers into my ear, "or maybe even tequila."

She's not wrong.

"I think some people come to complain about the HOA being a bunch of tyrants"—or at least that's what YouTube showed me when I googled what to expect—"but we have to get through the boring stuff before the fireworks can start."

I'm gonna have to buy a damn essential oil to thank her for sitting through this with me.

I feel myself begin to nod off as Mr. Bridgewerth lists out the costs for potential projects. I probably would've fallen asleep completely if I hadn't caught Nate's look of triumph. It's the shot of espresso I need. No way am I missing out on my opportunity to publicly shame him because my distaste for a reasonable bedtime finally caught up to me.

After what feels like a millennium, the numbers stop and we move on to the juicy stuff . . . well, as juicy as an HOA meeting can be. But I'll take it.

"And while I understand that children are looking forward to summer activities, we urge you to keep your neighbors in mind and rinse the chalk off your driveway," Mr. Bridgewerth says to the room. "While we appreciate that parents love their children, not everyone wants to see little Johnny's 'art.'" He uses air quotes as he says *art* like only a true and practiced asshole would. "If chalk remains for more than five days, it's a violation and you can expect to receive a fine."

The world keeps spinning, but some things never change. It will never make sense to me why Mr. Bridgewerth, a man who seems to despise children, became a teacher. Besides the whole being-a-social-outcast thing, his class was one of the most hated parts of my high school experience. The memory of him pulling me to the side and suggesting that I set my sights on more "attainable" universities will forever live rent-free in my mind.

I think his exact words were something like, "When you shove diversity in your writing for no reason, it's as if you're intent on creating characters readers can't connect with. If your work in this class is an accurate representation of your writing, then I hope you've applied to more realistic and attainable schools."

Thankfully I got into USC and was able to rub my acceptance in his miserable face for the rest of the school year, but still. Remembering the hell he put me through causes my blood to boil all over again.

And people wonder why I left this place the second I could.

I glance around the room, trying to gauge how the other people in attendance are feeling. I came into tonight assuming everyone shared my opinions of the HOA—that they are a bunch of bored jerks, looking for any place to grasp on to the teeniest bit of power. I may not have a ton of pride left, but the little that I do have would dissipate in an instant if I was booed in a suburban clubhouse conference room.

"During the summer, we also see an uptick in flag violations," Mr. Bridgewerth says, much to the dismay of the audience, who begin to whisper around me. "Please keep in mind that the only flags approved for display are American flags and flags for sports teams . . . just not Michigan."

A good Michigan joke always lands in Ohio. I'm pretty sure it's the state's unofficial icebreaker. So when not a single person chuckles—outside of the brownnoses on the board (cough Nate cough)—I know these are my people. We're all sick of the HOA's shit and they're going to be eating out of the palm of my hand by the time I'm finished with them tonight.

Of course, Mr. Bridgewerth is not deterred. I have to imagine, with a personality like his, he's well accustomed to open hostility and resentment.

"Most importantly, I know gardening is all the rage, according to the internet." His words drip with condescension and the whispers turn to groans. "But the Instagram doesn't dictate the Reserve at Horizon Creek. If you'd like to alter the aesthetic of your home in any manner, including landscaping, you must first seek board approval by going through the steps we have laid out on the HOA website."

At this point, an older gentleman a couple of rows in front of us can't hold back his frustration anymore.

"Oh, for cryin' out loud! When I bought this house, we didn't even have an HOA!" He doesn't stand up, but Mr. Griffin's wild hand gesturing allows everyone in the room an easy view of who's speaking. "Carol, God rest her soul, assured us that if we approved an HOA, you'd just increase amenities and keep the community organized. We were told you'd never try this Big Brother government crap you're always pulling on us. Now, pardon my language, but if my Alice wants to plant new flowers, she should damn well be able to without asking for *your* permission."

Applause explodes around us and the previously sleepy room is bursting with energy only shared anger can provide. Now, this is what I came for!

Mr. Bridgewerth doesn't react, but Nate begins to nervously fidget beside him. His eyes shift around the room but never meet mine.

"That's right!" a familiar face I can't quite put a name to shouts, waving a piece of paper over his head. "I got this letter last week because I washed my car in the driveway."

"And I was fined because my daughter spent the weekend with me and her car was parked in the street for too long," Mrs. Long complains.

I don't attempt to hide my gleeful smile. The louder the crowd grows, the more uncomfortable Nate becomes. At this point, he looks like he wants to crawl out of his own skin. It's glorious.

"Order!" Mr. Bridgewerth slams the gavel against the table. "If you want to speak, you will be given time at the end of the meeting to raise your concerns in an orderly and organized manner. However, before we get to that portion of the meeting, I have something to announce that wasn't on the agenda."

Since this is my first—and likely last—HOA meeting, I don't

realize going off the agenda is a big deal until I see the heads of the other board members snap toward Mr. Bridgewerth with wide eyes and matching confused expressions.

Nate's bright-red ears can be seen from my spot across the room, and even Janice's permanently pinched face seems tighter than normal. Curiosity causes me to lean forward in my chair, anticipating what Mr. Bridgewerth could possibly say.

"As you all know, I took on the position of the homeowners' association board president with the utmost dedication and commitment." He places the gavel on the table before pushing out his chair and standing up to address the room. "However, it's with both great sadness and excitement that I inform you that I'm moving to sunny Florida at the end of the week. And so, it's with a heavy heart that I must announce my resignation from the board, effective immediately."

"Oh shit!" I don't mean to swear, but talk about a twist I didn't see coming.

Luckily for me, my mom won't get an earful about my language because I'm not the only one unable to contain my reaction. The room erupts in a flurry of commotion.

Ashleigh and I sit, gobsmacked, as everyone around us shoots out of their seats, hurling question after question to the front of the room. Mr. Bridgewerth is still standing, motioning for the crowd to relax, while the rest of the board stares at him with undisguised confusion and frustration.

After who knows how many minutes of continuous yelling and bordering-on-obscene hand gestures, Mr. Bridgewerth has had enough.

He grabs the weathered gavel and slams it against the table so hard, I'm shocked it doesn't splinter.

"Enough!" His voice cuts through the room. "One at a time or not at all! This isn't elementary school. Please, use some decorum or this meeting will end now."

When I told Ashleigh there'd be fireworks, even I didn't think it would be this eventful. Nobody seems prepared for the wild turn of events tonight, least of all the involved community members filling up Conference Room 2 in the Reserve at Horizon Creek clubhouse.

While my neighbors aren't pleased, his warning takes hold. The yelling over one another comes to an end. Those with questions, concerns, or both take turns standing up and airing their grievances to the room.

"The letter I received said I needed to bring it to the board within two weeks in order to dispute," a middle-aged woman with fantastic highlights says from behind us. "If your resignation is effective immediately, then will there be a pause on our 'violations'?" She uses air quotes around the word *violations* and I automatically appreciate her and her artistic choices. "How will things be decided until a new president is appointed?"

Echoes of "yeah" and very earnest murmurs of "what she said" travel around the room. I attended tonight with the sole desire to heckle Nate and cause him to squirm in front of an audience, but I can't help but feel bad for him. It's obvious that he was completely taken by surprise with this announcement. I'd be furious if I was on the receiving end of all this vitriol because Mr. freaking Bridgewerth didn't communicate his plans with me.

"Thank you for your question," Mr. Bridgewerth starts before settling into his seat. "After tonight, Nathanial Adams will be the interim board president. Because of certain bylaws, we must hold an election before that can be made official. You will all receive information on how to cast your vote soon."

I'm not sure if being a writer with a minimal amount of friends failed to tip anyone off, but I'm not big on peopling. I much prefer the sheets to the streets and would happily spend all my days curled up in bed with a good book or binge-watching my new favorite show.

My involvement in causes I care about usually ends at a standard donation of funds. Tonight is the closest I've ever come to participating in an uprising. Sitting in a room as mild-mannered suburbanites unleash their wrath has made me feel more alive than I've felt since my world came crashing down around me.

So maybe that's why, upon hearing that Nate—the person least in need of extra power—is going to get promoted to president, I'm on my feet before I can think better of it.

"Will you also be sending out information on how to run for HOA president?" I ask into the madness.

The room goes silent as all attention shifts to me.

Including Nate's. He scowls.

"Miss Carter," Nate says, "while we appreciate your interest in our community, I'm not sure this a commitment you've given proper thought to."

If he could've managed not to be such a patronizing jerk for two seconds, maybe I would've reconsidered this rash decision.

But since Nate is incapable of not being a total jackass, he only adds fuel to my fire.

"On the contrary." I lift my chin and put my hands on my hips—the most lethal of stances. "I've been sitting here all night, listening as our neighbors have come to you with clear and serious concerns. They're telling you that they are unhappy with the leadership and, quite frankly, the overreach of the current HOA board. You've had all night to stand up for our neighbors, but you've sat silently until now. Why is that? Can you please explain why you're more concerned about having an opponent for the position of president than you are about helping Mr. Griffin and Mrs. Long?"

The energy in the room, which had only begun to settle moments ago, amps right back up.

"She's right," Mr. Griffin shouts, still gesturing wildly. "Why don't you want her to run? Isn't this America?"

Never has "isn't this America" been used in my defense, and I'd be lying if I said I wasn't basking in it. It's impossible to beat back my smug smile as Nate works to deflect the crowd's growing ire.

"No, Mr. Griffin, I mean . . . yes." Nate stumbles over his words. "This is America. I don't mind Miss Carter running, but—"

"But what?" Mrs. Long yells in my defense. "You don't think she can do a good job? That you care more? Isn't that what elections are for?"

"You're absolutely correct. I misspoke and I would love nothing more than to encourage anyone who cares about our community to be as involved as they'd like." Nate's tone is properly apologetic, but if the firm set of his jaw says anything, it's that beneath the surface, he's absolutely stewing. "I'm very sorry, Miss Carter."

"Thank you, Mr. Adams." I pause for a moment to swallow the laughter bubbling up in the back of my throat before I respond. "I'm sure you will make a formidable opponent."

"Well then." Mr. Bridgewerth takes back control of the meeting. "Miss Carter and anyone else looking to run for the position of board president, please locate me after the meeting and I'll give you the information you need for the election. The rest of you, please keep an eye out in your mailbox for voting instructions in the coming weeks."

As polite applause rattles around us and the meeting moves forward, Nate and I maintain eye contact, neither wanting to be the first to look away. We may seem cordial to everyone watching, but between Nate and me? We both know what we're really saying.

The small smiles on our faces and glimmers in our eyes declare war. And this time it's not going to end quietly. With an unspoken promise, we're vowing to do whatever it takes.

Because this time, the winner takes all.

Or at least the HOA.

Chapter 9

Part of me expected a parking lot showdown with Nate after I announced my candidacy for HOA president. I was a little disappointed after I left from filling out the paperwork and was only met with a jubilant Ashleigh. Sparring with Nate was ninety-nine percent of the reason I signed up. If he was going to retreat peacefully into the night, what even was the point of all this?

My closed laptop mocked me from my desk as I tossed and turned all night long. The reality of what I just volunteered myself for came crashing down on me before I could reach my REM cycle. As if I don't have a thousand more pressing issues to tackle, now I get to add learning neighborhood bylaws to my plate.

"Collins!" My dad shouts from somewhere in the house. "The plants aren't going to water themselves!"

I roll over and grab my phone. Seven o'clock in the morning.

Retirement is ruining my father.

"Coming!" I yell back even though I want to snuggle deeper into the duvet they bought me for college.

I open my morning text message from my mom to see what Bible verse she sent me today. Philippians.

Classic.

Pulling on my favorite sweatshirt, I opt to go braless again before slipping into my most worn-in leggings, where the thread is *just* hanging on at the seams, before heading downstairs.

When I enter the kitchen, I'm met with the familiar sight of Anderson and Kimberly sitting at the kitchen table, one hand on their coffee cups, the other entangled with each other. Gross.

"Good morning, parentals," I greet them both, trying to ignore the growing void of loneliness threatening to swallow me whole. Who cares if my future only includes my mom's wall art, cats, and monthly HOA meetings? Not me.

"Good morning, sweetheart," my mom says. "There's coffee on the counter if you want any. I bought that creamer you like; it's on the second shelf in the fridge."

"Thanks, Mom." Getting my favorite creamer from the store is a small gesture, but unbidden tears spring to my eyes. "That was really thoughtful."

When I dated Peter, I was so distracted by his gorgeous eyes and thick head of hair, I didn't even notice that he never did small things like this. I was always going out of my way to let him know I cared, but instead of expecting the same treatment, I accepted crumbs.

Less than crumbs, actually.

Peter gave me nothing for years. He used me and abused the trust I had in him. And worse? I allowed it, not even thinking to demand better until he turned my world upside down.

My parents may wake me up at seven and force me to watch *Survivor* with them every week, but it's nice to be reminded what it feels like to be loved and appreciated.

"Oh please, it's just creamer." She waves me off, not even a tiny bit aware of how moved I am. "Though, I did have to have quite the conversation with the woman at checkout. She was asking if I was lactose intolerant. She couldn't understand why I was getting almond milk creamer instead of the real stuff."

I pour more than I should into the medium-roast coffee my mom brewed this morning. "Gotta love the Midwest's commitment to the dairy industry."

'Murica.

"So . . ." My dad levels me with the same look he used when he found out Ruby and I put instant mashed potatoes on Reggie Braftly's lawn in sixth grade. "What's this I hear about you running for HOA president, and why is Jack telling me instead of my own daughter?"

"You were in bed when I got home last night and I just woke up." I knew this wouldn't stay a secret, but I'm still surprised by the speed at which gossip travels in this neighborhood. "I didn't think news would get around before sunrise."

"Does this mean you're planning on staying longer?" my mom asks.

This was one of about a million things I wasn't thinking about when I opened my big mouth last night. I've been trying to plot my escape from the Reserve at Hell's Creek since I moved back, and with one careless moment, I tethered myself to this place for even longer.

Alexa Martin

"I guess so." I take a deep gulp of my coffee and avoid my dad's disapproving glare.

It's not me staying longer that he's objecting to. He loves having me here, that much I know. It's just that I'm an avoider. I always have been. And even though the logic has proven faulty time and time again, I probably always will be. My dad knows—maybe even more than me—that this new HOA scheme is an attempt to distract myself from the upcoming pilot season where I should be rejoicing in the script that I worked my ass off on getting recognized.

"Mm-hmm." The deep tenor that resonates in his throat says more than any number of words ever could.

"I think this is wonderful," my sunny, ever-the-optimist mom says. "What does running for the HOA even entail? Is there anything we can help you with?"

"I'm not totally sure yet," I say, instead of admitting that I only signed up out of revenge and have no idea what I got myself into. "I'm going over to Ashleigh's later to start researching and planning my campaign strategy."

Mom looks very impressed. Dad looks . . . skeptical.

"Well, before you go figure out how to take over the neighborhood, don't forget to take care of the garden." He slides a little piece of paper across the table that I know is a checklist. "The compost is due for a turn today and the grass needs to be mowed."

The good news is that if I ever do gather the courage (and funds) to return to LA, I can always fall back on my newly acquired landscaping skills to help pay the bills when times get hard.

"Ten-four, Papa-roo." I pull out the name I called him when I was younger and watch as his face instantly softens. He's such a teddy bear. "And I know you said you didn't trust me with the edger last time, but I really think I'm ready now."

My fatal flaw is thinking I can do anything after watching approximately one and a half YouTube videos on any given subject. Fix the leaky sink? No problem. Work potentially deadly equipment? Easy-peasy. Win a homeowners' association election for a neighborhood I vehemently dislike and haven't lived in for ten years? Piece of cake.

He doesn't even pretend to consider it. "Absolutely not."

"Fine." I pout. "But don't complain to me when your lawn is looking disheveled because you don't have faith in your daughter."

"I'll manage." His deep chuckle blends with my mom's light giggle. Even their laughter is in perfect harmony. It's unnecessarily adorable.

"Whatever," I say once I've drained what's left in my mug. "While you two are in here laughing and holding hands, your daughter will be outside, doing tough labor with no appreciation."

My martyr act has never been successful, and ten years out of the house hasn't changed that.

"Sounds good," my mom says.

"Enjoy yourself." Dad smirks over the rim of his coffee cup.

I almost respond, but my parents thrive in the morning. I'm no match for their abundance of comebacks and burns.

Plus, I have a plethora of yard work to do before going to Ashleigh's house to start planning how to bring Nate to his knees . . . I mean, my campaign strategy.

I don't know how long I've been outside, but the sun is high in the sky as I finish pushing the lawnmower across the grass. My T-shirt is sticking to my back and my curls are growing frizzier by the second, reminding me how much I hate humidity.

Summers in LA are hot. If you live in the Valley, between the traffic and the extreme heat, it's basically like living in hell. But at least it's a dry hell. There's nothing worse than feeling damp all the time. Disgusting.

Pieces of grass fly from the mower and stick to my legs and arms as I move back and forth across the yard. I can feel the grime layered onto my skin: sweat, dirt, grass, repeat. A thousand showers won't be enough to make me feel clean after this.

But even with all that, I'm not miserable. The mower is so loud, it drowns out all my thoughts. And trust me, my mind is a much more peaceful place without the constant stream of negativity and self-doubt trying to bring me down.

So I might be dirty and stinky, but I'm also calm.

And obviously that can't last.

"A fair way away from the glamour of Hollywood, aren't we?" Nate's grating voice breaks my Zen with the efficiency of a baseball bat against a car windshield.

I turn to face him and my palms itch with the urge to slap the smug smirk off his face. Of course, where I look like a hot dumpster in my years-old workout gear, Nate looks fantastic.

It only makes me hate him more.

He should be very grateful my dad didn't hand over the edger after all.

"Well, as the future homeowners' association president, it's crucial that my neighbors see how dedicated I am to landscaping."

The second thoughts I had about running against him this morning are cut down faster than the blades of grass sticking to my legs. I was considering taking up needlepoint with my mom, but after watching Nate's grin falter and eyes narrow? It's clear that needling Nate is more than enough for me.

"You made your point. You were able to make your little scene," he says. "Now can you drop this whole charade? There's no way you actually want to be on the HOA. You're just wasting everyone's time if you keep this up."

"Are you ever not a condescending ass?" I mean really? If he asked nicely or—god forbid—apologized, I might back out of this. Probably not—I like messing with him way too much—but the chances would be much higher. He's a smart person. I don't understand how he doesn't realize his reactions only spur on my questionable behavior. "You're not concerned about me wasting people's time. You're afraid you're going to lose."

"Lose to you?" His bark of laughter should offend me, but instead it draws me closer. "You're delusional. You don't even like it here. How are you going to convince people to vote for you, a person who ran away from this place as soon as she got the chance, over me, the person who never left and has been on the HOA board for four years?"

"Are you on drugs?" There's no way a person can be this delusional. Between the sweaters in summer and choosing to live in an Ohio suburb as a young and single man, he has to be on something. It's the only explanation.

"Of course not!" The color drains from his affronted face. "Why would you say that?"

"Because if you think that people like HOA members, you have to be on something." It only takes one second to glance at Reddit to see how hated HOAs across the nation are. "I basically already have you beat for the simple fact that I wasn't on the board before. I hate to break it to you, but the people are not on your side here."

As a woman in politics, there aren't many times that I'd have a leg up on a man, but this is definitely one of them. And it is glorious.

"You're not even a homeowner." He's trying to seem calm, but the vein in his forehead is starting to protrude. "Are you even eligible to run?"

"This rule shit is why people hate the HOA. Between this conversation and your threat to fine my parents over their oak tree, my folder of dirt is bursting at the seams."

His hazel eyes go wide at my not-so-implied threat. "You wouldn't."

I laugh at the thought of keeping this election civil, aka boring. I mean, has he even met me before?

"Obviously I would. Playing dirty is the only reason I'm running."

His eyes narrow to slits. My skin tingles and electricity shoots through my veins. I'm primed and ready to go head-to-head with my favorite opponent.

"Oh my goodness gracious." My mom's sweet-as-sugar voice cuts through the air and extinguishes the fire in Nate's eyes. "Nathanial Adams, is that you?"

"Mrs. Carter." He closes the space separating them and wraps her in a giant bear hug. "How are you?"

When Nate and I stopped being friends in high school, my mom grieved the relationship maybe even more than I did. From the time Nate and I became friends until the summer we stopped, he was at my house more than his own. He never really told me much about his mom, but whenever anyone brought her up, you couldn't miss the way his eyes would gloss over and his jaw would tighten. From the little he did tell me, she called on occasion—always from someplace new—but he hadn't seen her since he was two or three. I know she wanted to be a singer or something, and from what I could gather, having a family was never her goal or priority.

His dad, on the other hand, only wanted a family. It's just that the family he wanted mainly consisted of a wife. He was so desperate for someone to love him—and if we're being honest, take care of him—that he ignored the amazing family he had in front of him. He was such a flake, always forgetting Nate's sports and parent-teacher conferences because of a blind date or worrying about impressing the newest woman in his life. We invited his dad over for dinner with us often, but I think he only took us up on the offer once. Nate tried to make excuses, claiming he was a hopeless romantic, but really, he was just hopeless.

And Nate paid the price.

They lived at the apartments on the edge of the neighborhood.

Close enough in distance that we rode the same bus, but far enough that it felt like he lived in a different universe. It wasn't long before my mom reached out to his dad and insisted that Nate spend the afternoons at our house. There'd always be two snacks waiting for us when we walked through the door. She helped him with his homework and took him shopping to get supplies for his science fair projects. And until his grandparents started sending for him to spend the summers with them, we spent more days than I'd like to remember in the stands cheering at his baseball tournaments.

"I'd be better if you ever stopped by to see me." Her smile widens past the point of natural. "I was coming out to see if Collins wanted some lemonade. But since you're here now, why don't you two chat and I'll bring you both a glass? Like the old days."

"Oh, I don't know. I—" Nate starts.

"Nonsense." My mom, never one to be denied, cuts him off before directing her attention to me. "Collins, honey, you and Nate go sit on the porch and I'll be there in a second with some drinks."

I want to object, to offer a resounding *hell no*, but it's pointless. What Kimberly Carter wants, Kimberly Carter gets. Plus, I need to save all my energy for fighting Nate.

"Okay, Mom."

I don't question if he's following me. I know he is. He might love to give me a hard time, but there's a good chance he's more eager to please my mom than I am.

Although my parents have updated many of the things around the house, the porch still feels remarkably similar to when I was a kid. The planters are updated, but still in the same places. The old rug has been replaced with something slightly more modern, and the swing that my grandparents gave us is still bolted to the exact same spot I remember it being my entire life. As Nate follows me onto the blissfully shaded area, it's almost as if by instinct we fall into the same pattern we did all those years ago.

He grabs on to the chain holding up the swing as I plop down, giving it one gentle shove before taking a seat on his side. I tuck my ankles crisscross-applesauce while his long legs use the carpet-covered concrete to keep the swing moving slow and steady. Memories come rushing back of us, young and innocent, sharing secrets and snacks as we rocked back and forth on these same hot summer days. The thick echo of our childish giggles swirls around me, shrouding my bitterness in the sweetness of moments I'm incapable of forgetting.

"Wow," Nate whispers, his voice as soft and tender as I remember it being all those years ago. "Never thought we'd be here again."

"Me neither." I keep my eyes trained on the empty sidewalk in front of me, too afraid to look at him. "Leave it to Kimberly to get us here."

We might not have much in common anymore, but falling victim to my mom's tenacious drive will keep us bonded forever.

"Seriously. Your mom is a formidable opponent. I have a feeling your dad has never won an argument against her."

His deep chuckle, both bone-achingly familiar and deeply foreign, washes over me.

"I honestly don't even know if they argue." I mean, I'm sure they do; all couples argue. But I've never witnessed it. "When I walked into the kitchen this morning, they were holding hands while they drank their coffee. It's sick."

"It's nice," he corrects with a bite in his voice that wasn't there seconds ago. "You're lucky."

I am lucky.

Kimberly and Anderson Carter are my touchstone. When it felt as though the world was crumbling around me, I still knew I'd be okay. There's a safety that comes from knowing, no matter what is happening, you have a support system who will love you through everything. It gives you the confidence to conquer the world and the grace to regroup when you don't.

Even if you have to go to Ohio to do it.

"I know," I say simply.

I can tell Nate was expecting me to say more, but my family is the one thing I don't feel the need to argue about or prove.

"I'm back!" My mom bursts through the front door with the subtlety of a rhinoceros. She's holding a tray with two glasses of lemonade and a plate of snacks, but it doesn't distract from her blond hair, which has been brushed, or the fresh pink lip gloss that wasn't there before.

She's so extra. I love her so much.

"Ooooh!" I forget about any and all tension and awkwardness lingering between Nate and me when I set my eyes on the cheese plate my mom threw together. "I didn't know we had all of these cheeses. And cashews!"

I scoot over to make room as my mom sets the tray between Nate and me. I'm giddy. If I could have charcuterie for dinner every single night, I would.

"Glad to see at least this hasn't changed, huh, Mouse?" Nate says.

It's a throwaway comment. One I'm not sure he even realizes he's said until my gaze shifts from the tasty tray to his face. For as much as I've enjoyed harping on Nate's worst qualities and the demise of our friendship, it only takes a moment—a single syllable—for my defenses to crumble to the ground. My chest aches with a yearning so deep, I didn't know it was possible.

All because of that stupid nickname I didn't realize I missed.

It's been twelve years since our friendship fell to pieces and I'm still not sure how it happened. It started like all other summers. I went over to his house and talked his ear off while he packed up for a month at his grandparents' farm. He'd be back in the middle of July and I had big plans for making my mom drive us to Cincinnati for the weekend to go to Kings Island and a Reds baseball game. I hated baseball, but he loved it, and even as a teenager I knew anything could be made bearable with giant hot dogs and cinnamon-sugar-covered soft pretzels. He seemed really excited too. He loved getting away from his dad and spending time with my family. A trip to Cinci and a couple of nights in a hotel? I didn't have to twist his arm to get him to agree.

Not surprisingly, his grandparents' farm wasn't the most technologically advanced place to be and it was in the middle of nowhere. So when he wasn't responding to texts or answering my calls, I assumed it was an issue of service. I never thought he was avoiding me. But then the day he was supposed to come home came and went and I never heard from him. When I went to his dad's to look for him, Mr. Adams always had an excuse. Ruby ended up going with me to Cincinnati. We had a blast, but there was a cloud looming over the entire trip. I was worried about him, and at the same time, I was frantically trying to recall what I could've said to make him so mad at me.

When the first day of school came, we still hadn't talked. And when I saw him huddled up with all the popular kids he claimed to hate so much, holding hands with the girl who'd made my life hell, everything became crystal clear. I'd been ditched. He found a new group of friends who were more popular and had more money.

He didn't need me anymore, and I didn't need him.

"Oh, Mouse. I forgot all about that." Mom looks at me with a wistful smile, her eyes shiny beneath the bright afternoon sun. "What did you call Nathanial?"

This feels like a trap.

Part of me wants to lie, pretend I don't remember. But the other part of me can't deny that, even if it had a bad ending, once upon a time, Nate and I meant a lot to each other.

I look to my mom and drop my voice to a whisper. "Bear."

I avoid looking at Nate, but I can feel the heat of his gaze burning a hole through the side of my face.

"Oh, that's right! Mouse and Bear, together again. How wonderful." She clasps her hands together and looks at Nate and me like we're the most precious beings on planet Earth. "You two catch up and enjoy. And don't be a stranger, Nathanial. I expect to see you much more often now."

"Of course, Mrs. Carter. It was nice to see you." Nate stands up and hugs my mom once more.

It's cute.

I hate it.

My mom finally turns to leave, but my appetite has already been ruined. *Stupid Nate and his stupid nickname. How dare he taint this perfect spread?*

I grab a cashew anyway, popping it into my mouth and chewing it, just not with the joy it usually brings.

"So . . ." The word lingers. I try to think of anything to say that won't make me remember how much I hate him. Or worse . . . how much I don't. "Do you like cheese yet?"

He started calling me Mouse because I liked cheese plates way before they were all the craze on social media. He would nibble on it when my mom was around, but he hated cheese with a passion— that should've been my first red flag. I mean, who doesn't like cheese? He wouldn't even eat cheesecake!

"I don't pull it off my pizza anymore, but I'm still not a fan."

So not a complete monster, but the potential still stands.

"Well, that's good, I guess . . ."

Although the air between us is never particularly pleasant, it hasn't been awkward either. The promise of an impending insult always fills the void. But now, with old memories resurfaced, Nate whistles a tune I've never heard before while I manically munch on nuts. It's wildly uncomfortable, but neither of us wants to be the first to tap out.

Me?

A quitter?

I don't think so!

After what feels like a millennium, Nate finally gives in.

"Oh, you know what?" He checks his watch knowing that I damn well do not. "I forgot I have to show a house soon. Tell your mom I said thanks for the drink."

He doesn't wait for a response before running down our walkway without sparing a backward glance. Unlike my previous victories against Nate, this one feels more than a little lackluster. The usual satisfaction is missing and a deep sense of longing is there instead.

And tragically, it's at this moment, with my attention focused directly on my mortal enemy, that inspiration strikes for the first time in months.

I leap off the swing, leaving an offensive amount of untouched cheese in my wake, and sprint into the house, taking the stairs two at a time until I reach my room and throw open my computer.

HOA**holes

Written by

Collins Carter

Chapter 10

I know my script is fiction, but nothing could have invigorated my drive to pulverize Nate more than re-creating him in fictional form. Art imitating life and all that jazz.

After I finished writing the first scene—faster than I've ever written a scene before, may I add—I hopped into the swagger wagon and sped over to the local craft store. I wasn't going to let this inspiration fade for even a millisecond.

I take my time wandering through the aisles and filling my cart with obscene amounts of glitter, paint, poster board, and the crowning jewel of it all: a massive bag of wiggle eyes.

I throw the bags overflowing with art supplies in the trunk but tuck the bag of eyes into my purse so they're easily accessible. And instead of driving straight home, I take the minivan on a little detour.

I drive down each street of the Reserve, blasting my Little Mix playlist and stopping beside every FOR SALE sign with Nate's obnoxious smile. I look out the windows and check my mirrors before I get out. I'm not ashamed of my behavior, but the fewer witnesses, the better. When I'm sure the coast is clear, I exit my car with my wiggle eyes in hand and cover Nate's stupid hazel eyes with a pair of much more fitting googly ones.

Will some people say I'm being childish? Possibly.

But those people don't have a sense of humor and I don't care what they have to say anyway.

So there.

I've covered about fifty percent of the neighborhood when I see my beige-enthusiast opponent going door-to-door a few blocks away from my house and table my mission for a later date.

I speed home and don't even bother saying hi to my parents before grabbing my art supplies and racing straight to Ashleigh's house.

"Knock, knock, biotch!" I pound on her door with my free hand, and it's only a matter of seconds before I hear the lock turn. "Nate's definitely up to something but I brought—" I stop mid-sentence when the door opens and reveals Ashleigh in the most wild outfit I've ever seen. "What's going on here? Are those . . ." I squint my eyes and look closer at her seizure-inducing leggings. "Neon wine bottles?"

"Aren't they so cute?" She kicks her leg up for me to get a better look. "Wait until you see all the different designs they have! They're in the guest room."

The searing in my eyes makes it hard for me to comprehend what she's saying.

"I'm sorry." I blink slowly, trying to clear my eyesight. It's like

I was looking directly into the sun. "Did you say you have more of these . . . in your guest room?"

"Yes! Come look!" She grabs my free hand and yanks me into her house, pulling me behind her with a strength that, quite honestly, frightens me.

However, nothing—and I mean nothing—is as scary as the sight I'm met with when we walk into her guest room. It's like I've walked into a fun-house closet. Slasher music plays in my head as I take in the bedroom, which has been taken over by neon, pastel, and patterned fabric. Garment racks filled to the brim with floral and striped dresses line the walls, and empty boxes are scattered across the carpeted floor.

"Ummm . . . wow." I look around the room, but there's too much going on for my eyes to focus. "This is a lot of clothes."

"My inventory came in last night! You're the first one to see." She jumps up and down, clapping her hands. "Don't you love it?"

I've never heard anyone sound so excited about anything . . . and a couple of my friends in LA were nominated for Emmys.

"You know . . ." While I normally shout the first thing that comes to mind, I pause for a moment to think through my response. And I'm not positive, but I think that's what people call growth. "I can honestly say I've never seen anything quite like this."

"I know! I'm so excited!" She tells me something I'm already very aware of. "You were so right about those oils. It just wasn't for me. But this? Selling adorable clothes? I think I've found the perfect fit."

I laugh at her pun, unsure of what else to say.

I've heard of many MLMs, but an MLM selling leggings? I

would've happily gone the rest of my life not knowing about this nightmare. Supporting Ashleigh by purchasing lavender oil was one thing, but I will not be seen wearing pizza pants. No way.

That's taking it too far.

"Do you have anything to drink?" I'm not really thirsty, but I am desperate for an excuse to escape this room.

"Of course! I made sangria last night and it should be perfect by now." Ashleigh jumps at the opportunity to show off the crystal pitcher she received for her wedding. "I know it's early, but it's five o'clock somewhere, right?"

I'd be willing to bet she has a kitchen towel and a glass or two that say the exact same thing. Boozy quotes are the millennial's version of Bible wall art. Not exactly sure what that says about my generation, but I don't think it's good.

"It's never too early for sangria." In the olden days, sangria is literally how people drank water. This is historical appreciation. Plus, with the way politics have been going, it feels as if we're heading straight to the dark ages. It's only fair that we get to indulge in the boozy parts too. "We'll just have to double-check our spelling if we have more than one glass."

Equipped with glitter pens, poster boards, a plethora of stickers, and a freshly topped-off glass of sangria, I and my newly appointed campaign manager are ready to tear shit up.

"First things first," Ashleigh says, getting to work. "You need a campaign slogan."

"See! I knew you were the right choice for the job!" I lean

across the blank poster board to pull her in for a hug. I may or may not be feeling the effects of the sangria already . . .

"Thank you." She laughs once I've released my grip on her. "What about 'Collins Carter for homeowners' rights' or something like that?"

"Oooh. That's good, but I was thinking of something a little jazzier. Something along the lines of"—I pause for dramatic impact, holding my hands in the air as if to frame my words—"'Collins Carter. Because Nathanial Adams is a power-hungry douchebag who will ruin everything.'"

I think it has a nice ring to it.

I'd definitely put that sign in my yard.

"Well, that's . . . that's definitely one direction." Ashleigh tries to keep a straight face, but she only lasts for a second before she breaks into uncontrollable laughter. I join in soon after.

"Okay, fine! No name-calling on the signs." I wipe the tears off my face. "What about 'The right person for homeowners' rights'? Or something like that?"

This time when Ashleigh's face lights up, it's not from barely restrained laughter.

"Now you're thinking!" She flips open the notebook next to her and starts writing. "What else can you come up with?"

For the next hour, we sit on her rug, bouncing ideas back and forth. Some are better than others and I still throw out a few more inappropriate slogans. But in my defense, "Collins Carter, because fuck that other guy" is perfect marketing and I will die on that hill.

"All right." Ashleigh looks down at her notebook with a sparkle in her eyes. "I think we finally have them!"

"Me too. I kind of love them." Even though I may have decided to run purely to drive Nate crazy, excitement and pride I didn't expect to feel cause my stomach to flip.

Or maybe that's the three glasses of sangria.

"'Collins Carter,'" Ashleigh recites the line we've workshopped to death. "'Your home. Your needs. Your president.'"

"It's the perfect balance with 'Collins Carter. Get your HOA bylaws off my lawn.'"

Humor, heart, and seriousness? Nate's going to have a freaking coronary.

Even though I've taken this pledge to ruin him with the utmost dedication, I don't think he believes I'm going to go through with this campaign. What he doesn't realize is that after you've been publicly humiliated on a national scale, making yourself look silly in a tiny Ohio suburb is small fries. I could—and will—do this all day.

"They're perfect." And they are.

I grab a pencil and fresh poster board and get to sketching the first yard sign. I don't mean to toot my own horn, but when I was living in LA, I took a few calligraphy classes with my friends. Not only is my penmanship, quite frankly, fucking regal, but handlettering is also one of the most soothing activities I've ever done. With every loop of the letter and flourish of the pen, my worries begin to melt away. By the time I put the pencil down and grab the glitter, I'm not even thinking about Nate anymore.

But of course, that peace can't last too long, can it? The loud sound of Ashleigh's doorbell breaks us out of our happy arts and crafts bubble.

Thanks to the beauty of technology, Ashleigh doesn't have to move to see who it is. She pulls her phone out of her pocket and opens her doorbell app.

"Oh shit." Ashleigh, unlike me, doesn't have a vocabulary as filthy as the sewers, so this outburst garners my full attention.

I drop the glitter pen, keeping my eyes trained on the visibly anxious woman in front of me. "What? Is everything okay?"

Maybe I've watched too many Housewives get arrested on camera, but I'm about ninety percent sure she's staring at images of FBI agents outside her door, ready to bring her in for her part in some nefarious pyramid scheme.

She worries her bottom lip for a moment longer before looking away from her phone and filling me in. "It's Nate."

Of freaking course it's Nate.

I mean, stalk much? Is there anywhere in the godforsaken neighborhood that's safe from him?

"I saw him slithering from house to house earlier." I can't tell if annoyance or panic is more prevalent in my voice. "What's he up to?"

"How am I supposed to know?" Her eyes go wide. "Maybe he's hard up for a new pair of leggings?"

"Oh my god. Could you imagine?" The only thing more horrifying than some of those prints is some of those prints on Nate.

The doorbell rings again and I add being impatient to the never-ending list of gripes I have with Nate. Everything about him is the worst.

"Should I answer?" Ashleigh looks between me and the door, her features curled up with indecision. "My car's in the driveway. He knows I'm home; I can't just ignore him."

I may have no problem being rude to Nate, but I don't think Ashleigh has it in her to disregard someone's feelings. Which I guess might be one of the things I like best about her? I'm pretty sure if I ask her to not answer the door, she won't. But considering she's my only friend in the state of Ohio, I won't do that to her.

"Answer," I say. "I know he's up to something and this way we can know what. You're going to have to play a double agent and I'll hide in the kitchen until he leaves."

I think Ashleigh is too nice to play a double agent, but I'm hoping she can at least keep it together for a few minutes.

"Perfect," she whispers even though we're too far away from the door for him to hear us. "I'll see what he wants and then report back. Hopefully there'll be something useful for our campaign."

Did I underestimate my new neon-legging-wearing bestie?

"Yes! That's what I'm talking about!" I lift my hand in the air for a high five. "I knew hiring you on a strictly volunteer salary was a fantastic idea."

I scurry into the kitchen as her long legs carry her to the front door. Even though we've already had more than a socially acceptable amount of sangria, I pour myself another glass as I attempt to eavesdrop.

"Hey, Nate! What brings you here today?" I can hear Ashleigh loud and clear. On a scale of one to ten of volume, one being a whisper, ten being a stadium announcer, Ashleigh lands at a solid eight point five. Nate, on the other hand, is much better at discretion and has always been about a three.

I add *quiet talker* to my rapidly growing list of grievances.

"Oh really? At what time?" Even from across the house, I can hear the uncertainty in her voice. "Ummm. Okay, yeah. Let me check my calendar and I'll get back to you."

No matter how much I strain my ears, I can't hear what Nate says, and by the time Ashleigh closes the door and comes into the kitchen, I'm practically climbing out of my skin.

"So?" I ask as soon as I see her. "Why was he here? What did he say?"

Instead of answering, she grabs the crystal pitcher sitting on the counter in front of me and pours the remaining sangria up to the rim of her glass.

As far as stall tactics go, it's pretty effective.

"Well . . ." She take a long sip of her drink, still processing whatever Nate threw her way. "That was unexpected."

"Oh god. What'd the asshole say this time?"

I already think so poorly of him that unless he came to tell her he was dropping out of the race or doing something altruistic, I'm not sure anything he could say would surprise me.

"Well, it's kind of less what he said and more what he's doing," she says.

The poor thing looks so nervous. A kinder person would let her off the hook. Nate and I are grown-ups; there's no reason I shouldn't walk down the street and get answers for myself. But I'm not all that kind and I need to know what the hell Nate has up his sleeve this time.

I don't say anything, and after a moment, Ashleigh crumbles beneath the silence.

"He has a petition and is holding a private meeting next week to get you off of the ballot." She says it so fast, I have trouble separating the words. But *petition* and *private meeting* both stand out. "He said that since you don't own a home, you're not eligible for the position."

Ugh.

What a freaking nerd!

Who tries to win the HOA presidency on a technicality? I should've known he'd try to weasel his way out of this fight. And if I wasn't so annoyed, I'd rejoice in knowing just how nervous I make him.

I stop for a breath, careful not to shoot the very anxious messenger in front of me.

I saw him hours ago; he could've said this to my face. But it's good to know that even after all these years, Nate is the same spineless jerk who ran off that summer and pretended I didn't exist. He has passive-aggressive on lock, but when it comes to actual confrontation and handling things like a mature human, he's completely incapable.

"Well then, it's a good thing we've figured out our campaign slogan," I say to Ashleigh, who has long since finished her sangria. "Because we'll have to be prepared when we crash yet another meeting."

I knew this election was going to be more than glitter signs, shaking hands, and neighborhood meet and greets, but Nate is stooping to levels I never imagined.

But I have no problem matching his energy.

If Nate wants to get dirty, he has no idea how messy I can get.

Chapter 11

*T*he problem with being unemployed—besides the obvious—is that it becomes really easy to conflate a hobby with an actual, paying job.

Like, say, hypothetically of course, you decided to run in your neighborhood's HOA election, and soon what started as a bit to rile up your sworn enemy becomes an all-consuming, time-sucking, and money-draining activity. One day you're making tiny signs with glitter pens for shits and giggles and the next you're making red, white, and blue statement lawn flamingos to share with all your neighbors.

"I'm still not sure I understand." My mom's eyes flicker between me and the giant piles of plastic flamingos. "What are you going to do with all of these flamingos? And why are they patriotic?"

I add one of the blue flamingos I've painted with white stars into the wagon I pulled out of the garage.

"Because this is Ohio, Mom." I don't understand what she's

not getting. "If I'm going to win, I have to be in touch with what my constituents want."

In a stroke of genius I'm still amazed I came up with, I decided that plain old yard signs simply wouldn't do.

No, no, no.

I needed something bigger.

Something with pizzazz.

A statement!

With one quick trip to an internet conglomerate I shall not name, I was one click and free overnight shipping away from not only bulk red, white, and blue flamingos, but also a ten-foot-tall inflatable Ben Franklin. And you tell me, what's a better way to prove I'm for homeowners' rights and freedoms than a giant inflatable of a slave-owning turned abolitionist founding father?

That's right. Nothing.

Added bonus? Nate's going to fucking hate it.

"Oh! I almost forgot." I grab the handle of the wagon piled high with yard signs and flamingos and pull it behind me. "I made one especially for you. I already put it in front though."

We make it through the gate, and even though I set everything up, I'm still taken aback by the intense display my parents allowed me to put in front of their house.

The not-so-quiet hum of the motor filling Ben Franklin and his American flag kite is noticeable even over the few cars driving by. Campaign signs and graffitied flamingos litter the lawn. It's like Uncle Sam threw up in front of the house.

It's glorious.

I hit the back brake on the wagon and park it on the sidewalk.

I take my mom's hand, leading her through the flamboyance of flamingos until I get to the one I made for her.

"Ta-da!" I gesture to her flamingo with the flourish of a *Price Is Right* model presenting a new car.

"Oh, I love it, Collins!" Be it an oak tree, latte, or plastic lawn tchotchke, Kimberly Carter loves a gift. And to be fair, this one is really cute.

Her flamingo is more sparkly than the rest. I glittered its beak and superglued rhinestones for eyeballs. However, the true pièce de résistance is the quote art I painstakingly hand-lettered across its wings.

"What does that say?" She's not wearing her glasses and her eyes aren't what they used to be. She leans closer and reads out loud. "Live. Laugh. Flamingle. Oh my goodness, I love it!"

See?

Do I know my audience or do I know my freaking audience?

"I knew you'd like that." I point to a flamingo that I painted with tomatoes and put a mini gardening hat on. "That one's for Dad."

Just a guess, but I don't think he'll be as excited to see his.

"They're so cute! And the signs are wonderful." She fawns over everything with the same enthusiasm she had when I was in elementary school. "I'm so impressed with how seriously you're taking this."

We make our way out of the yard and I disengage the brake on my childhood wagon.

"Thanks, Mom." I can't decide if I'm impressed with myself or have reached a level of self-loathing so deep that I can't tell up from down. But I have been working really hard, and honestly? At this point, I'll take any compliment I can get. "Now, wish me luck. I have a campaign to win."

And an enemy to destroy.

*B*y the time I made it to house number four, I figured out that not only is the internet's read on homeowners' feelings toward HOAs correct, but that my campaign promise of doing the absolute least is exactly what people want to hear.

Also, while my mom was impressed with my craft skills, the rest of the neighborhood couldn't care one way or the other. If I offer to set the flamingos up for them though? That changes everything. My neighbors give me carte blanche to do whatever I want as long as I guarantee that I won't pull any "Big Brother crap" if they vote for me. I tell them I won't even watch it on CBS, they chuckle, I chuckle, and that's that.

Now two blocks are covered in flamingos and glittered yard signs and my wagon is topped with fresh supplies to take over a third. To make things even better, when I leave my backyard, I see my favorite opponent walking my way.

And he looks furious!

"Well, Benji-boy," I say to the giant inflatable that is equal parts hilarious and terrifying as I wait for Nate to approach. "Time to let the fun and games ensue."

"Wow." Nate doesn't miss a beat before going in. He stares up into Ben's eyes before turning his incredulous stare to me. "So this is what we're doing now?"

"I'm sorry?" I ask. "I don't know what you're talking about."

I know exactly what he's talking about.

"Really?" He gestures to Ben and my wagon full of flamingos. "You have no idea what I'm talking about?"

"Not a clue." I shrug, knowing damn well that people feigning ignorance is one of his biggest pet peeves. "Now, if you don't mind, I have neighbors to talk to, signs to distribute, and issues about the current HOA leadership to discuss."

The last is total BS, but he doesn't need to know that. It's fun watching his pale skin turn hot pink. Messing with him is too damn easy.

Instead of turning around and heading home like I assumed he'd do, he steps in front of me, effectively preventing me from getting back on the campaign trail.

"You need to stop," he whispers, and I know it's to keep himself from screaming. "This is starting to get ridiculous."

"Starting to get ridiculous? Seriously?" He attempted to blackmail me through the HOA at my parents' barbecue. This has been ridiculous from the beginning! "You're hilarious."

"I'm failing to find the humor here." He takes a step closer and I can practically feel the heat of his ire radiating off him.

"Nate, come on. Pull the stick out for a second and look around." I drop the handle to my wagon and gesture to my parents' front yard. "I spent two days decorating flamingos and making yard signs to run against you for the HOA. There's a giant inflatable of Benjamin Franklin holding an American flag kite on my parents' front lawn. Everything about this is hilarious."

"To you!" he shouts, finally losing his temper and what's left of his mind. "Everything's a joke to you! You don't take anything seriously. You can't even take care of yourself. How are you going to run an HOA?"

"Get over yourself!" I step into his space, yelling right back. "Look around, Nate. It's the fucking HOA! Nobody cares about it. In fact, most of the neighborhood wants it abolished."

"That's what they think they want until it happens and our property values decrease by five to six percent!"

"Are..." I trail off, momentarily dumbfounded by what's happening here. "Are you shouting statistics at me?"

He inches toward me, closing the remaining space separating us, his face as red as my dad's tomatoes. "I'm shouting facts!"

"Oh my god." I throw my hands in the air. He's impossible. "You even argue like a freaking nerd."

"I'd rather be a nerd than whatever the hell this is." He grabs one of my flamingos out of the wagon and waves it around like a madman. "Who paints flamingos? These aren't even HOA approved."

"Duh, Nate." I roll my eyes knowing the effect is lost behind my sunglasses. "That's the entire point. I'm not some megalomaniac out to rule over them with all my imaginary power. Collins Carter is for homeowners' rights."

"Collins Carter isn't even a homeowner," he snips back without hesitation. "And Collins Carter shouldn't be in the race."

"Just admit that you know I'm going to beat you and you're scared." I reach for my flamingo, but his grip tightens around its neck. "Maybe then I'll drop out."

"Please," he scoffs in the cocky way only he can manage.

"There's no way you're going to beat me. If anything, you covering the neighborhood in these tacky flamingos will prove how much they need me."

My jaw falls to the ground. I'm overwhelmed by the bloody audacity of this man. It's one thing to come to my house and talk shit to me, but to bring my flamingos into it? Absolutely not.

"How dare you." I pull on the flamingo he's still holding. "Give it back."

"No, these aren't HOA compliant." He tugs even harder. "You can't keep putting them everywhere."

I latch on to the head with both hands, using my entire body to get it back. "The fuck I can't."

"You kiss your mother with that mouth?" He sneers and his knuckles turn white.

"Sure do." The plastic neck starts to crumple beneath the pressure as I struggle to hold on. "But you're welcome to use yours to kiss my ass!"

"Classy, Collins."

"Please." My palms are starting to burn as my grip loosens. "Like you have any room to talk."

All he had to do was not. Not give me the HOA letter. Not walk his ass over here. Not be a jerk.

But instead, he had to insert himself into a situation where he wasn't needed and cause an unnecessary scene. Now we both look out of our minds, arguing in front of giant Ben Franklin and playing tug-of-war over a flamingo painted with fireworks. Until finally, with vivid clarity I don't often get, I realize I don't have to do this shit.

"Fine," I say. "Take it."

It's out of character for me to give up on anything . . . especially something as deliciously petty as this, and I'm not sure Nate comprehends what's happening.

Because when I let go of the flamingo, Nate pulls harder.

And without my equal and opposite force holding on to the other side, Nate and the flamingo go flying.

It feels like everything moves in slow motion.

I watch, cemented to my spot on the sidewalk, as Nate stumbles backward, trying to catch himself, and the flamingo takes flight. Considering I've only seen these majestic birds at the zoo, this might be the closest I ever come to seeing one fly in real life. It soars across the yard, the painted fireworks winking beneath the bright afternoon sun and its metal spoke legs aiming straight for the heart of our founding father.

The moment of impact is not nearly as explosive as I anticipated, but the small pop and whooshing sound of escaping air blare in my ears. Poor Ben rocks back on his feet before swiveling side to side with a flamingo lodged in his chest. He shrinks in front of my eyes, going from an imposing ten feet tall to a devastating rippling puddle of nothingness in the middle of my dad's bright green lawn.

Calm on the outside but irate inside, I slowly turn to Nate, who, to his credit, looks properly horrified.

"Are you happy?" I whisper the rhetorical question before my voice turns shrill. "You murdered Benjamin Franklin!"

"Collins—" He starts what I'm assuming is a meaningless apology that I want to hear none of.

"Save it." I cut him off, ready to take this fight to the next level. "You'll have a lot of explaining to do once I tell the Karens how much you hate democracy."

His eyes widen, and pure, unadulterated fear darkens his hazel eyes, proving that not even mild-mannered real estate agents are immune to the destruction three Karens can wreak.

Chapter 12

While I've seen Nate out and about, being a general thorn in my side, I didn't know exactly where he lived until Ashleigh and I arrived for the meeting.

"This is it?" I ask Ashleigh as I look at what is, begrudgingly, one of the nicest houses in the neighborhood.

Part of me—the practically homeless, constantly-feels-like-a-failure part—wants to turn tail and run home. I don't even care about the damn HOA and I'm not sure it's worth subjugating myself to seeing how well Nate seems to be doing for himself. But the other part of me, the bigger, pettier, more stubborn part, can't let him win. Even if it comes at the expense of the minuscule amount of pride I have left.

"Twenty-two fifty-three Elm Street." She reads the address off her phone one more time. "This is it."

I should've known. "Of course it is."

While I find him to be completely intolerable at best, I guess the tedious, obsessive, and controlling aspects of his personality do have their perks. His landscaping is impeccable. My dad has done an amazing job with our garden and the rosebushes in front are flourishing, but it definitely looks like it was done by my dad. Our flowers are imperfect, overgrown in some places, struggling in others. Our shutters have been painted a few times, my mom taking the time to test color swatches from Home Depot every few years before inevitably going with the same shade of gray. The house looks lived-in and loved, but not perfect. Like a house in a quaint Ohio neighborhood should look.

Nate's house, on the other hand, looks ready to be photographed for a magazine. Like the cover house for *Best of Suburban Central Ohio* or something that would declare him the best of the worst.

His walkway stands out from the poured concrete the rest of the neighbors have. Bricks laid out in a gorgeous herringbone pattern lead to a front door that's the perfect blend of modern and traditional. Symmetrical hedges sit between the shutters that he probably touches up every other week. The old light fixtures have been replaced with ones that I know from my mom showing me in design magazines cost a pretty penny. It's clear to anyone who passes by that the person who owns this home not only cares about it, but spends more time than the average homeowner tending to it.

And it's glaringly obvious that he chose his home as the location for this "secret" meeting not out of convenience, but to show everyone who comes tonight how much better he is than me. It's smart. But it's not enough.

He's still underestimating not only me but how much people love an underdog.

"Are you sure you want to do this?" Ashleigh rubs her palms against the abstract-print purple-and-black leggings she changed into before we left. She hasn't said anything, but I know she's a nervous wreck that I'm going to cause a scene at Nate's house. "We can go back to my place and work on more signs . . . Oh! Or we can get all dressed up and head into C-bus! I heard a new bar just opened up that's so cu—"

"I'm sorry." I cut her off because, while I can see that she's still talking and getting really excited, I can only focus on one thing. "Did you just say C-bus?"

I hope I heard wrong.

I had to have heard it wrong.

"C-bus? Yeah, it's the nickname we all call it. Columbus . . . C-bus. It's fun," she explains, like any of the words she is saying make it less cringe.

Fun fact: they do not.

"A nickname? It's fun?" I repeat her words, struggling to find any of my own.

"Yeah, you know, it's like the JLo of Ohio," she says with a straight face.

She has to be trolling me.

She's definitely trolling.

"The JLo of Ohio? You're fucking with me, right?" Because I've written a lot of ridiculous things during my tenure as a writer, but not even I could muster up the audacity to write something this absurd.

"Not at all." She shakes her head and, in the plot twist I didn't see coming, looks at me like I'm the one not making sense! "I think the mayor or somebody said it. I remember reading it in the newspaper and it stuck."

Okay.

Somebody kill me.

Unless somebody already has and this is actually hell. Which, at this moment, doesn't feel too far-fetched.

"Ashleigh." I grab both of her hands in mine. "I say this with love, but I'm going to need you to never say that again. Okay?"

"Oh, just you wait." Her light and bubbly laughter falls carelessly out of her lips like I wasn't being drop-dead serious. "You'll be calling it C-bus soon too."

"Yeah, I think I'm gonna pass on that trend."

I know people talk about the economic divide, but this right here might be the truest division between people.

Ashleigh not only *intentionally* left the house in the most hideous leggings I've ever seen, but she also brushed off my very serious linguistic recommendation without so much as a second thought. The differences between the confident and the insecure seem immeasurable. I wonder what I could've accomplished if I took Ashleigh's approach to life. What could I have achieved by now if I didn't doubt every move I made? While I don't know for sure, I have to imagine that I wouldn't be crashing a secret HOA meeting in freaking Ohio.

"So . . ." I look up the walkway, which feels more daunting than I'm willing to admit. "Are you ready?"

Ashleigh's gaze follows mine and she inhales deeply. "I guess so."

We start up the brick pathway. It's like the saddest version of *The Wizard of Oz* to ever exist. My stomach twists into knots with every step toward the imposing door. My mask of nonchalance threatens to fall as thoughts of what waits on the other side begin to set in. I don't know what Nate has told these people about me, and I'm about to barge—uninvited—into his home. If this goes badly, the Karens are going to have a field day and my mom is going to murder me.

I hesitate outside the door. My hand hovers over the doorknob as I give myself one final second to come to my senses. Of course, my senses have been on the fritz ever since my brush with viral fame, so instead of turning tail and heading back home, I take a deep breath and push open the door.

Quiet conversation drifts from the back room into the entryway.

I try not to stare as I take in the inside of Nate's home. After seeing the exterior, I'm not surprised to see the interior also looks magazine ready. From the framed prints on the wall to the various shades of beige rugs protecting the hardwood floors, it looks as if his home was decorated by Average Interiors USA. It's all very nice, but nothing is personal. There's not a single family photo to be found. Nothing in this space gives even the slightest hint of Nate's personality.

When I lived in LA, my apartment definitely wasn't photoshoot ready. Most of my decorations came from flea markets and estate sales, but every single piece meant something to me. I didn't bring it into my home if it didn't bring me joy or express something about myself. Even though I might not love my mom's style, at least our home is warm and lived-in. Nate's place feels like a hotel. It's beautiful, but it's cold.

It's sad.

Nate's dad had an endless trail of women going in and out of his life, but nobody stayed long enough to turn his house into a home. Looking around his house, all I see is the sad little boy who loved family sitcoms and dreamt of marriage and becoming an accountant. And in a rush of very unwelcome emotions, sadness for the child who wanted to fit in more than anything causes my eyes to water.

Luckily, before I can fall victim to my stupid emotions, his grating voice rises above the whispered conversations.

"I know we're all looking for a change. I want that too." He sounds more politician than next-door neighbor. I don't even have to see him to know he's wearing his khakis and a button-up shirt. "When I purchased this house, I did it knowing the potential this neighborhood has. To be one where families new and old come together, where we support and look after one another."

"We all want that. What we don't want is someone driving around, nitpicking the flowers they plant or where our car is parked, sending us fines and violations for the homes we paid for," someone in the crowded living room says and is followed by echoed murmurs of "yeah" and "exactly."

"I'm not here to—" he starts, losing his train of thought when his eyes meet with mine in the back of the room. "I'm not here to monitor the way you live. My goal is to become the person you all feel you can come to with all matters of this neighborhood in order to create a community where we feel safe and our property values increase."

Dammit.

Even I have to admit that's a good answer.

A smug smile tugs at the corners of his full lips. He looks over the crowd before deliberately meeting my stare.

Now, it could be said that my tendency to react without thinking could be one of my more toxic traits. However, it could also be argued that my ability to act without fear is one of the best things about me. I like to think the latter is true.

"If that's true and your overall goal is building community, then why are you hosting this meeting with so many people missing?" I school my features, not wanting to let anyone see how much joy I feel in getting a rise out of Nate. "I know there wasn't anything posted in the Facebook group, and my parents, Anderson and Kim Carter, who have been homeowners in this neighborhood for thirty years, had no idea about this meeting. Maybe I'm missing something, but that doesn't seem very conducive to your supposed 'building a stronger community' mission."

His face turns bright red beneath the recessed lighting when I use air quotes while talking. My toes curl in my sneakers as I watch his feelings play across his face.

Pissing off Nathanial Adams is my kink.

"She's right," an older woman I recognize from Nate's morning walks says. "It is important to have everyone involved. Why weren't they invited?"

"I can answer that one for you," I say before Nate can respond.

I weave through the small crowd until I'm standing beside him at the front of the room. We're shoulder to shoulder and the heat radiating off him elevates my body temperature. "I think my good friend Nate here is hosting tonight in order to keep me off of the ballot for HOA president. I grew up in this neighborhood, but because I moved out for a few years, he's worried I'm not qualified for the job."

Nate shifts beside me. His anxiety is practically tangible.

"No, no. That's not it at all." He raises his hands in front of him. "What my old friend here is leaving out is that as we've reconnected, she's mentioned more than once that her time in the Reserve is temporary. Mr. Bridgewerth leaving was a surprise to everyone, and we don't want something like this to reoccur. Since she's not a homeowner or a renter and is only sleeping in her childhood bedroom for the time being, we can't be sure she's dedicated to staying at all."

As far as digs go, calling me a loser stuck in my parents' house is pretty fucking effective. I even see Ashleigh flinch from the impact of it.

"Well, do you have to be a homeowner to run for the HOA? If so, I think that makes all of this meeting nonsense pretty unnecessary." Mr. Stanley, who hasn't aged a day since I graduated from high school, asks from a chair in the corner. "Also, what's all this I keep hearing about you hating the founding fathers? Are you some kind of communist or something?"

I bite my tongue so hard I taste blood and it's a testament to my self-control.

Not only did I tell the Karens about Nate killing my Ben

Franklin, I also stuffed every mailbox full of flyers that may or may not claim that Nate thinks the Declaration of Independence is a hoax and that Ben Franklin never existed.

It's almost scary how many people didn't even question that it was the truth.

"I do not hate the founding fathers, nor do I believe the Declaration of Independence is a conspiracy created by the deep state. I've seen the flyers going around and I can guarantee that they are just someone's idea of a joke. It's unequivocally false," Nate says to Mr. Stanley before aiming a scathing glare my way. "Now, on to your other question—"

Nate begins, but I quickly cut him off. If there was one thing I was prepared for tonight, it was this question. And I'm not letting Nate put his negative spin on it.

"No, Mr. Stanley, you don't have to be a homeowner to be part of the board. You can be a renter or even live with a family member." I recite what I read online before I came. "All you need to be a member of the HOA is dedication and the desire to serve. As someone who has lived in this neighborhood since the day my parents brought me home from the hospital, nobody is more dedicated to seeing this community thrive. I'm running because I'm for less overreach and more homeowners' rights. Just like the founding fathers envisioned."

"Me too! That's what I'm for too!" Nate tries to steal my thunder before shifting the conversation. "Now that we have all of that figured out, I have drinks and snacks in the kitchen for everyone. Please feel free to help yourself."

Nobody needs further encouragement. Everyone leaps out of

their seats and heads toward the aforementioned food and drinks. I start to follow, thinking Nate probably splurged on good wine to impress everyone, but before I can make it, his fingers wrap around my wrist.

"Collins?" Something in his voice tamps down my irritation. "Would you mind staying after everyone leaves?"

It sounds like a setup and my serial killer theory is beginning to feel more and more plausible, but I'm nothing if not a glutton for punishment.

"Sure," I agree, my curiosity more than a little bit piqued.

Plus, if all else fails, I'm pretty sure I can trick him into saying something else incriminating enough to put on my next flyer.

Chapter 13

As the last two women leave Nate's house, leveling me with a final glare before the door shuts behind them, a heavy silence falls over the now-empty space. It's later than I thought it would be. Apparently, suburban folks love a good spread on a weeknight. There's not a single scrap of food left over on the many platters scattered across his kitchen. Empty wine bottles and glasses litter every surface in sight.

"So . . ." Nerves I didn't expect come out of nowhere. "What a night, am I right?"

His back is toward me as he finishes locking up and I take a moment to stare without him knowing. I was right when I guessed his outfit earlier. His khaki pants mold to the backs of his thighs, which have grown thicker since our high school days. As the night wore on, he undid the buttons on his sleeves and rolled them up. He's always so uptight, so polished, that the barest sight of his forearms sent a few of his guests scrambling.

"That's one way to put it." He runs his hand through his

slightly overgrown hair. He sounds tired, run-down even, and I can't help but wonder if he's regretting asking me to stay. "You were a hit though."

Much to my shock and awe, he's not wrong.

After I said goodbye to Ashleigh with promises to text her when I got home and meet her for lunch to debrief tomorrow, I was forced to mingle with Nate's other guests. I tapped into my extrovert reserves and made my way around the room.

I made sure to say hi to the neighbors I've known throughout the years, asking how their spouses and children were doing, but also made sure to introduce myself to the attendees I hadn't yet met. I even managed to wrangle an invitation from Mrs. Morris to join her and Nate on their morning walks. Nate's eyes almost popped out of his head when she offered, and although agreeing was on the tip of my tongue, I politely declined.

I also fell in love with Caroline and Hank Sanders. They bought their house the year I left for college. I've seen them out and about over the years, but tonight was the first time we'd ever spoken. They're both in their late thirties; she works from home as a part-time psychologist, and he runs a construction company in Columbus—which he absolutely didn't refer to as C-bus. They have two kids who go to the local middle school and are getting too cool to hang out with them anymore. She went to school in NYC and even though she moved out here kicking and screaming, she's really come to enjoy the quiet peacefulness our suburban town offers. We have the same taste in food, shows, and books, and before she left, she invited me to her next book club meeting. Something I agreed to with no hesitation whatsoever.

Actually, I got along with pretty much everyone. The only people who were noticeably cold toward me happened to be the same women who lingered next to Nate all evening long, giggling at everything he said and ignoring the diamonds adorning their ring fingers.

"Well, duh." I infuse my words with a heady dose of sarcasm. "I'm a freaking delight. I don't know why you sound so surprised."

"No. It's not that," he says. "I'm not surprised people liked you as much as I'm surprised that you seemed to like them."

I think that if I dig around deep enough, there might have been a compliment rolled up in there. "Ummm, thanks?"

"Welcome." He turns away from the door, and I can't help but notice the circles beneath his eyes or how slow and heavy his steps are.

"Are you okay?" I ask.

He may be my sworn mortal enemy, but it's only fun to destroy him when he's at his best. I'm not a monster; I don't enjoy kicking people when they're already down. If I'm going to spend my days working on campaign signs and my evenings mingling with my constituents, I need to know if my competition is up to par.

"Am I . . . yeah. I'm fine." His steps and his words falter. "Thanks."

I'm not sure if he's being sarcastic, and for some reason, it's a kick to the stomach.

For a few years, I knew him better than I knew anyone. I could tell what he was thinking with a single glance. I could decipher what he meant by the tilt of his lips or the subtle inflections in his speech.

Now his face is marred with lines and I don't know whether they came from laughing or frowning. He's a stranger, and as much as I want to deny it, I hate it.

"Umm . . ." I fiddle with a loose thread on my sweater, unsure of what to do with my hands. "Can I help you clean up the kitchen?"

This is so fucking awkward.

"Sure," he says, but it sounds more like a question.

I push off the stool and head to the sink anyway, rolling up my sleeves before I turn on the water. Suspicion dances behind his eyes and I can tell he doesn't trust my motives.

"I still hate sitting idly and awkward tension," I explain in another uncharacteristic move. "I'm not offering to be helpful; this is a fully self-serving activity."

Once I got to sixth grade, my anxiety during tests became so bad that my mom had to go to the school and ask the teachers to either allow me to stand or let me sit on a bouncy ball. To this day, the only reason you'll ever find me exercising is because I'm literally buzzing with anxiety.

"I forgot about that." An almost wistful smile crosses his face. It makes him look years younger, and for a second, I catch a glimpse of the Nate I once loved.

It should be all I need to turn the water off and run straight back to my parents' house. I've played this game with him before and I was left burned. But the stupid nostalgic part of me I like to pretend doesn't exist wants to keep that look on his face for as long as possible.

"Do you remember that one time we walked around the neighborhood charging people for the worst car washes in the history of car washes?" I pump dish soap onto the sponge as the memory I buried deep in the corners of my mind resurfaces.

We stole a bucket and rags from my dad's garage, not knowing the towels we were using to dry with were so dusty that they left the cars dirtier than when we began.

"Damn. I forgot about that," he says. "Didn't your mom trace our steps and issue refunds?"

"She absolutely did." And even though she didn't let me forget what she'd done for almost a full calendar year, she never once asked us to give the money back.

"Your mom's the best," he says mindlessly, and I can tell he regrets it the second it leaves his mouth.

"She is," I agree, unsure of where to go from here.

Grateful for the task at hand, I keep my eyes down, watching as the iridescent bubbles lather on the glasses.

Nate moves around the kitchen, clearing the counters and table until he's collected all the empty dishes. He puts them in the sink, taking up the space beside me. We work in silence, moving in tandem as I rinse and he transfers them to his state-of-the-art dishwasher.

It's weird, but it's not uncomfortable. In fact, it's the first time I've felt completely at ease in months.

Not that I'll ever admit that out loud.

When the sink is empty and the washer is fully loaded, Nate hands me a hand towel devoid of a kitschy phrase. I nod in thanks, too nervous that speaking will somehow break the spell we both seem to be under.

I take my time folding the towel and rest it on the counter

before following him back into his living room. He sits on the oversized sectional that only an hour ago was seating at least six of our neighbors. There's more than enough room for me, but I can't even think about sitting right now.

"Thanks for helping clean up. That was . . . that was nice of you." It's clear he's not accustomed to thanking me. The words definitely don't roll off his tongue.

I shift on my heels and wish I had pockets I could shove my hands into so I could stop fidgeting. "I can be nice . . . sometimes."

"I know you can. I'm just not used to being on the receiving end of Collins Carter's kindness."

"Well, I'm glad I was able to refresh your memory." The stress I've been trying to ignore begins to melt away and my shoulders relax. "Your house is really nice, by the way."

If we're doling out compliments, I might as well get that one out of the way. Plus, it gives me an opportunity to openly gawk at the space.

Without the people crowding the living room, I'm able to look closer at the details scattered throughout the space, but it still feels impersonal. It lacks the warmth it's trying so hard to portray. The art prints framed on the wall are lovely, but I could see them in any department store. There's a set of ceramic vases on the mid-century coffee table that are gorgeous, but none of it screams Nate.

Not that I even know who he is anymore.

I wander toward the built-in shelves at the far side of the room stuffed with books, frames, and a few knickknacks that might finally give me more insight into the man across from me. I scan through the titles on the shelf, not seeing any of the sci-fi books he loved when we were younger or a single book on baseball. I'd be hard-pressed to believe he's ever opened a single book here. I might be wrong, but I don't get the sense he was dying to explore the colors in the Pantone book.

I get to the frame and chuckle when I realize he hasn't even replaced the placeholder photo. The blond woman inside is smiling brightly at whoever's taking her picture. She clearly understood the assignment when she booked this modeling job.

"Really?" I lift the frame up and turn to Nate. "You can't even stick a picture in this frame? You do know that the ones that come from the store aren't meant to be kept in here, right? If you need a picture, I'm sure my mom could help you out."

There was an unfortunate portion of my life when my mom was at one-hour photo every other day. The amount of film she went through was criminal. I bet she has the boxes stacked up in the attic and she's waiting for an excuse to bring them back down.

I expect him to laugh, or at least smile, at the memory of my mom posing us in the garden as she tried to find the perfect light. But instead, I watch as his back goes ramrod straight and he loses the little color he has.

"I'm sorry." I don't know what I'm apologizing for, but I put the frame back where I found it. "I was just giving you a hard time. I didn't mean anything by it."

He sits for a moment longer before his jaw ticks and a look of determination crosses his stoic face. He unfolds his long body from the couch and slowly closes the space between us. When he picks up the frame, the air in the room goes static. The hairs on my arms rise as I watch him study the picture with a look of longing I've never seen on him before.

"That's Elizabeth," he says, his eyes never leaving the photo. "My fiancée."

My stomach crashes through the floor.

"Your fiancée? Wow." I blink rapidly and try to regain my composure as I struggle to process this information I shouldn't care about. "Congratulations."

He doesn't respond.

He doesn't even move.

I'm not even sure if he breathes.

He stands next to me, staring at the picture for what feels like a millennium.

"Sorry." He shakes his head and places the frame facedown on the empty spot on the shelf. "She's not my fiancée anymore. It's been about a year actually."

When I came to his house tonight, I was prepared for an all-out brawl—with words, of course. I spent the afternoon envisioning the many comebacks I'd throw at him and the way his skin would burn with embarrassment when I owned him in front of his guests. I prepared for every possible scenario.

But I can say, with one thousand percent certainty, that I did not prepare for this.

"Oh my god, Nate," I say, all bad history between the two of us forgotten in a moment. "I'm so sorry. I had no idea."

"Of course you didn't." He lets out a humorless laugh. "How could you?"

Resentment colors his words, but for once, I don't think it's directed at me.

"What happened?"

The question slips out before I think better of it. I'm sure I'm the last person he'd want to confide in about this, but for some reason I can't put a finger on, I can't let it go.

He walks back to the couch, and for a moment, I think he's not going to tell me. I don't like it, but I understand it. We aren't friends.

The quiet whoosh of the dishwasher punctuates the uncomfortable silence looming over us. But just as I open my mouth to change the subject and pretend this never happened, Nate's hoarse voice cuts through the room.

"She called everything off the morning of the wedding," he says, and I'm sure I heard him wrong. "Her maid of honor came to tell me. I was already in my tux. She wasn't ready to settle down and didn't think we wanted the same things. She didn't want the kids and suburbs. Which is fine. I just wish she would've figured that out sooner. I haven't heard from her since. Not even an email. That part hurts."

Despite the way things ended with us and the joy I find in pissing him off, a fire ignites inside me at the idea of someone other than me hurting him. My heart breaks for the kid I knew who wanted nothing more than a family of his own and the thought of him losing it when he was so close to having it all.

"Are you fucking kidding me?" The urge to go track this bitch down and give her a piece of my mind is almost too much to handle. "The *day* of the wedding?"

He nods but doesn't say anything. He leans back in his seat, his gaze trained on me as I try to process this information.

It's a familiar feeling, this dynamic between the two of us. Nate sitting quietly, taking in everything and carefully observing while I shoot off the handle. He was always the calm one of the two of us. My body is physically incapable of holding emotions back. Even if I manage to stay silent for a moment, it all comes rushing out sooner rather than later. For better or worse, I wear my mangled, battered, and partially black heart on my sleeve.

"I don't know her and maybe she's a very nice human, but I really hope she gets a mosquito bite on the bottom of her foot every day for the rest of her life and that every restaurant she goes to is out of her favorite item."

Some people believe in good vibes only, but I don't subscribe to that BS. I believe in all vibes at all times. There are a lot of garbage humans on this planet who deserve nothing more than a truckload of negative energy sent their way in the form of the smallest, most annoying punishments possible.

Petty vengeance is one of my greatest strengths . . . something the man sitting across from me can vouch for.

"It's okay." Nate attempts to wave off my curse, obviously not privy to how they work. "It's probably for the best anyways. This house was going to be my gift to her, but since we weren't married yet, I was able to keep it. It might not be everything I assumed it'd be, but I joined the HOA, made friends with my neighbors, and I'm still loving living here."

"It's not okay, though, Nate. She can't just change plans and break your heart like that," I tell him, more upset for him than he seems to be. "What's wrong with these people who think they can walk all over us? Why are we supposed to be grateful for the scraps they throw us?"

I don't realize I'm yelling until Nate approaches me and, with a painstaking gentleness, takes my hand in his like I'm some wild animal to be tamed.

"I appreciate your passion." His eyes never leave mine as he speaks. "But why am I getting the feeling that this isn't about me and Elizabeth anymore?"

I clamp my mouth shut.

My skin heats as Peter's face flashes in my mind. The way he looked down at me—literally and figuratively—as he broke the news. Approximately ten million strangers have watched the video of me freaking out in the run-down parking lot outside my apartment, but other than Ruby, I haven't told anybody what happened that night. The story is on the tip of my tongue. The anger and resentment have spent so much time building up inside me, they're begging for a release.

I just don't know if Nate is the person I can trust to hold my pain.

"Are you okay?"

I know this should be the moment I pack it all in and head back to my childhood bedroom, go lie down and pretend that everything is normal. But instead, looking at Nate, I remember all those times I confided in him sitting beneath the willow tree in my backyard, and the way, as he'd listen so intently, no problem felt too big. With him by my side, nothing was insurmountable.

"You really don't know why I came back home?" I know he

has this entire act of being above social media and everything that the rest of society seems to enjoy, but I'm having a hard time believing that of the millions of people who watched my downfall, he wasn't first in line for the show.

"Hand to god." He lets go of my hand, holding it over his heart and raising the other in the air. "I have no idea."

I'm still not sure this is a good idea, but I also don't care anymore.

What can I say? Self-preservation has never been my thing.

"I didn't want to leave LA," I tell him. "I had to leave."

Nate's eyes snap to mine and his mouth opens and closes before he decides against saying anything at all. He did this when we were kids, always allowing me to vent and rant without interruption.

"I doubt you know much about my time in LA, but I met my ex-boyfriend, Peter, when I was in school." I start at the beginning of my story. If I'm going to tell it, I'm going to tell it all. "He was the teaching assistant in my writing class. He was older, smarter, and so freaking handsome. Everyone had a crush on him in that class. He, she, them, didn't matter. He was just so damn charismatic that everybody was drawn to him. When he started directing his attention to me, it was like the sun was shining all its light on me."

All my friends had been so jealous. Not only did he think I was an exceptional writer, but he also made it more than a little obvious that he liked me for more than that. It sounds desperate and stupid, but I wasn't used to this attention. Almost all of my friends modeled for extra money and two of them ended up dropping out of school because they became so successful at it. It's not that I don't think I'm pretty—I very much like myself—but when I was with them, people weren't tripping over themselves to ask me out.

"He gave me special attention. Giving me extra feedback on my scripts. He was always willing to meet me before class if I had questions, which was a key part in my getting an A in that class. And the second he was no longer my teacher, he asked me out."

He took me to *Back to the Future* in concert at the Hollywood Bowl. It was the nicest date I'd ever been on. Looking back, I think he had me ensnared in his trap the moment we sat in our seats and the opening chords played from the stage. He made me feel special . . . worthy.

"He got staffed in writers' rooms for some of my favorite shows and was always working on the next best movie script. I was graduating and trying to break into the industry he seemed to be conquering. When he passed along a few of my samples and helped me land my agent, a part of me started to doubt that I'd be able to do anything without him. Like all the success I managed to gain was directly tied to him."

Nate, who has been silent so far, speaks up. "I don't know much—well, anything about that industry, but I have to assume that even if he showed your scripts, you'd have to have talent to get an agent. It couldn't just be because of him." He looks away from me, biting down on his lip, and I wonder if I even want to know what he's thinking. "And you know, I've given you a hard time, but you've always been really talented. I still remember the stories you used to write when we were younger."

"Thank you." It feels as if gravity dissipates and I'm floating on air. My skin tingles under his heartfelt compliment. It's one thing when my parents tell me I'm talented, but it's something else completely when a person who struggles to say anything nice about me does it. "That actually means a lot."

"It should." He smirks, and lines I'm not convinced came from smiling deepen beside his eyes. "You know I don't give out compliments often."

"How could I ever forget?" I gave him a ceramic mug I made in pottery class my freshman year. He was so free with his thoughts that I almost took it back. I think the only thing he liked was the color palette.

Jerk.

"Okay." He leans against the wall and I feel like those hazel eyes of his are trying to look straight into my soul. "What happened after he started systematically breaking you down until you were insecure and dependent on him? I'm guessing you moved in and he doubled down. Maybe tried to link your careers even deeper? As a favor, of course."

My jaw falls open because that's exactly what happened next.

"I moved into his one-bedroom apartment and he offered to put his name on the script I'd been working on." I start to feel queasy as I recount all the mistakes I made . . . how I did this to myself. "I tried to sell a few scripts on my own, but there was one I'd been working on since college. It was the project I knew had the most potential. It was fresh and fun but still had a lot of heart and a smidge of darkness. I'd been polishing it for years, holding off on it until I knew it was as perfect as it could be."

If you look around, a lot of white men in the industry will tell you they're struggling to find work because studios are only wanting diversity. However, if you only look a layer deeper, you'll realize that's not true at all. Sure, it may be easier for me to get a meeting, but a meeting isn't the same thing as a green light and funding.

Inevitably, someone would tell me that they couldn't relate to my messy biracial heroine. It was like she could either be funny and white or troubled and Black. I could never wrap my head around that, why characters of color couldn't have a full existence and problems that weren't always about their race. Like, how are they spending millions of dollars on dragon stories rife with assault, but the successful Black woman leaning into her ho phase is too risky?

"After a few of my scripts fell to the wayside because they weren't relatable enough, Peter thought to add his name to the script. At the time, it felt like a great idea. Having him take a few meetings and showing that it was already white-man approved would help skip over a few obstacles. But adding his name to this script was all he did. The concept, the characters, the dialogue, that was all me."

"Oh fuck." Nate grimaces. "I think I see where this is going and it's not good."

"Bet you ten dollars it's worse than you're thinking." I offer my hand.

Nate shakes it with wide eyes and his brows nearly touching his hairline. "That bad?"

"Oh yeah." It was an actual nightmare. I still wake up in a

cold sweat some nights. "So as I'm sure you can see very clearly, when Peter took the show out and pitched it, he didn't only add his name; he erased mine. Something he didn't tell me until I was driving home from work and started getting text messages from writers who knew the title of the show, asking if the good news was true."

Nate's face twists and his shoulders stiffen like he's bracing for impact.

"I was so excited when I saw the news that I didn't notice my name was missing or wonder why I was seeing this on the internet instead of hearing about it from my boyfriend, agent, or literally anybody." I still get angry at myself for being so naive. There were a million clues and I ignored them all. "I drove to the liquor store and splurged on the best bottle of champagne I could find. I mean, I had a paycheck coming in. I could afford it, right?"

WRONG.

"I got home, lit some candles, put the champagne on ice, maybe had a shot of tequila or two—"

"Collins, no." Nate groans. "Even I know you don't handle tequila well."

"Hey! That was one time and I didn't know how to handle my liquor yet. Plus, you know those kids were hogging the swings. If they would've just gotten off the third time I asked we wouldn't have had any problems."

I mean really. Children are assholes; it's a universal truth. You lose your temper with them one time and people never let you live it down.

"Anyways." I level him with a pointed stare and continue with the story. "I finally sit down and pull up the deal announcement. And wouldn't you know it? My name is nowhere to be found. The entire announcement lauded Peter Hanson as this longtime screenwriter who's written for some of television's best shows and is finally ready to run a writing room of his own. They credited this thirty-something white man for a coming-of-age story about a Black woman.

"I was still telling myself it was a mistake when he came home. We'd been dating for years. We lived together. We loved each other. No way would my boyfriend do this to me." I tend to think in terms of worst-case scenarios, but this was outside the realm of even my imagination. "I figured it was all a misunderstanding. So imagine my shock when I brought this up to him when he walked in and he said—and this is a direct quote—'When I open up applications for the writers' room, I'm going to look at yours first.'"

"No, he didn't." The absolute horror in Nate's voice would be enough to make me laugh if this story didn't make me want to burst into tears all over again.

"Yup." I nod, confirming that Peter Hanson does, in fact, have more audacity than any other human on the planet. "Then, when I got rightfully furious hearing this news, he told me I was over-reacting. That was not the right thing to say." I tell him something I'm sure any rational human with a brain knows. "And I'm not sure if you remember this about me or not, but I don't tend to handle these situations all that well."

"What? You? A temper? Never!" The sarcasm is so heavy, I can practically see it dripping from the corners of his mouth.

"Okay, okay. Settle down, now, Señor Realtor." I roll my eyes and bite back the smile I didn't think would be possible while telling this story. "We wouldn't want to let people know you have a sense of humor and ruin your reputation."

"Excuse me!" He rests his hands on his hips and I don't want to admit it, but he is giving *big* zaddy energy in those khakis. "I'll have you know that Mrs. Morris thinks I'm hilarious. She spends the majority of our walks in stitches."

"That's not the defense you think it is," I tell him. "But yeah, if there was a right way to handle this situation, I did the opposite of that. I grabbed the unopened bottle of two-hundred-dollar champagne and left."

"That doesn't sound too bad," he says.

"Well, after I left, I knocked on all of my neighbors' doors on the way out screaming, 'He thinks I'm overreacting! He hasn't even begun to see overreacting.' And I may or may not have still been wearing the high heels and silk robe I put on for the later part of our celebration." I admit it wasn't one of my finer moments. But rage can make you do some wild things.

Like run for HOA president . . .

"Oh. Okay, yeah." He nods and I get the feeling he wishes he had another glass of wine right about now. "That's not good."

"Nope," I agree. "And it doesn't end there."

This is the part I have nightmares about. If I would've stopped here, gathered my thoughts, and gone back to the apartment to cry my eyes out and call Ruby to plan out proper revenge, I think I'd still be in LA. But I was running on pure emotion and I wasn't thinking straight. Some people (Kim and Anderson) would argue that I wasn't thinking at all.

"I went into the parking lot and his car was just right there." The sun was setting and I swear a single ray illuminated his bright red BMW. It called to me. "He always parked right outside of our window. I shouted his name, and when he came to the patio, I shook the bottle of champagne and aimed the cork straight at his windshield. It was the first time my aim was right on. The spider-web crack exploded in the glass. Then, in my spike heels, I climbed on his hood, dancing around as I drank the champagne and screamed, 'How's this for overreacting?' And then also maybe started belting some TLC songs using the bottle as my microphone."

What?

If you're having a meltdown over your scumbag, thieving boyfriend and the legendary Lisa "Left Eye" Lopes doesn't immediately pop into your mind, what are you even doing?

"The only problem here was—"

"The only problem?" Nate cuts me off.

"Yes. *The only problem*"—I stress the words, repeating them once more—"was that the neighbor who kept shouting things like 'Yes, queen! Men are trash! You can do better!' was shouting this while she was simultaneously recording me. Then she posted my little . . . outburst . . . to the internet before I even got my ass off the car."

"Oh no." While the lighting in his living room isn't the best, it's still easy to see the exact moment realization dawns and he figures out how bad it really was.

"Oh yes." I plaster a fake smile on my face. "In my robe, dancing on my now ex's car, I went viral. So viral in fact, they songified it.

I lost my day job when my boss saw it. My agent dumped me and because Peter is now a bigwig in the television world, I've essentially been blacklisted from the entire industry. The show I thought would launch my career is what ended it. How's that for irony?"

And not Alanis Morissette ironic; actually, terribly, unforgivably ironic.

It's not a bop.

Nate doesn't say anything. He stares at me, unmoving for what feels like centuries, before he pulls his wallet out of his pocket and hands me a twenty.

"We only bet ten." I take it anyway, folding it up and tucking it inside my bra.

"Ten wasn't enough," he says.

As the person who experienced it firsthand, I must I agree.

"So that's my story." I shrug and notice that some of the tension in my shoulders doesn't feel quite as bad. "Now I'm back in freaking Ohio and running for the HOA . . . or at least I'm trying to, if the person I'm running against doesn't get me thrown out on a boring technicality."

"That was probably before your opponent knew you were capable of breaking windshields and dancing on cars if wronged."

A very unattractive snort falls out of my mouth before I can stop it. "Shut up!"

I shove his shoulder and he turns on the drama, rubbing the spot before holding both hands in front of him. "I'm sorry! Please don't attack me with a champagne bottle and your terrible singing!"

"Oh my god." I cringe remembering watching the video and

hearing my voice set to bad autotune. "I'm such a bad singer! One of the comments on the video said that I might be tone-deaf and have violent tendencies, but I had great legs and they'd still ask for my number. I really appreciated that."

Listen, when you're brought as low as I was, you accept the wins wherever you can find them.

"Elizabeth's maid of honor told me that my tux was a good look on me and I should consider still taking wedding pictures to document it."

"What is wrong with people?" I swear, staying in my room until a meteor hits or the world floods sounds more and more appealing with every passing day.

The smile on his face fades a little and I watch as his eyes flicker toward the upside-down frame on the bookshelf. "I wish I knew."

I glance down at my watch and see that it's actually really late.

"Oh shit. It's almost midnight!" I say, happy my mom's not around to scold me for my language for once.

"Really?" He pulls out his phone and double-checks in case I don't know how to read the time on my digital watch. "Wow. How'd that happen?"

"You know what they say: time flies when you're immersed in somebody else's trauma." It's a weak attempt at a joke, but I feel completely drained all of a sudden and it's all I can come up with. "But you wanted to talk about something?"

He hesitates for a moment.

Tonight was full of surprises, but the biggest of them all was how comfortable it felt confiding in him. I don't think I'll ever admit it again, but I missed this. I missed him. And even though I'm tired, part of me isn't ready for it to end.

Part of me wants him to put on a pot of coffee and for us to stay up talking for the rest of the night.

But of course that's not what happens.

"It's not important," he says instead. "We can talk about it another day."

Another day.

"Yeah, that'd be nice."

Unlike when I walked into his home earlier, this time when he smiles at me, it reaches his eyes.

Returning to Ohio and running for the HOA was never in my plan, but maybe there's a chance it won't all be so bad after all.

Chapter 14

Even though the crime rate in the Reserve at Horizon Creek is approximately negative two percent, Nate still insisted on walking me home last night. His house is on the same street as my parents', just a block down. If I squint, I can see his perfectly manicured lawn from my bedroom window.

I tried to sleep when I got home, but my mind was racing. I kept picturing Nate in his tux, getting the bad news, and then having to go share that with their friends and family. It's not on the same scale as what happened to me, but having your pain broadcast in public isn't something many people can sympathize with. Knowing that Nate and I had this in common made me feel closer to him.

Made me see him in a different light.

Instead of sleeping like I should've, I spent the rest of the night in front of my computer, creating the next scene in *HOA**holes*. My heroine gets the violation letter from the HOA, and when she arrives at the meeting, she discovers her nemesis next door is actually the president. When he doubles down on her infractions, she vows to beat him at his own game and decides to run against him for the presidency.

Is it a little too familiar to my clusterfuck of a life?

Yes.

But I'm not even a little bit sorry.

I typed until the sun came up and my eyes couldn't focus any longer. When I finally climbed into my twin-size bed and snuggled into my down comforter, my body ached and my head throbbed with an onslaught of ideas. It's the best feeling in the world, and after I left LA, it was something I feared I'd never feel again.

I just can't believe Nate is behind this creative surge.

"Collins!" my mom's voice shouts from the other side of the door. "Are you ever going to wake up? You slept through waffles and bacon. You never sleep through waffles. Are you feeling okay? Should I call the doctor? Your dad—"

"I'm fine, Mom." My voice is still thick with sleep. "I was up late writing."

I regret it as soon as I say it.

"You're writing again? Anderson!" she shouts down the stairs to my dad. "Colls just said she's writing again! Isn't that wonderful?"

I can hear my dad's muffled voice but can't make out what he's saying.

"No. No, I don't know what she's writing, just that she's

writing. I already said no! Who cares? You know that computer didn't even open for the first few weeks she was here. I was so worried. I prayed for this! Praise Jesus!"

I pull my pillow over my head, trying to drown out the one-sided conversation being shouted outside my door. Between the lack of sleep and the intense conversation with Nate, my head can't handle this. But it doesn't matter how hard I tug the pillow around my ears; it's useless against the vocal projection powers of Kimberly Carter.

"Mom." I roll over and stare at the empty ceiling that once upon a time was covered in posters. "Is there something I can help you with?"

"Oh yes, sorry. I just got so excited. You know how much I love it when you write. I was actually talking to—"

Oh my god.

"Mom. Focus, please." I cut her off. Nobody can go on side tangents like her . . . except for maybe me, but again, that's because of my mom. I claim no responsibility for that personality defect. "Did you come up for something?"

"Sheesh. Are you always this snippy after you write?" I can't see her, but I know her arms are folded and her blue eyes are doing their best attempt at shooting lasers through my door. "All I was coming to tell you was that Ashleigh stopped by. She said the two of you had plans to meet for lunch."

I roll over and grab my phone off the bedside table. It's already past noon and I have eleven unread texts and five missed calls. "Shit."

"Collins Marie!" my scandalized mom scolds me. "I'll never

understand where that mouth of yours came from. I knew LA wasn't a good place for you."

"Mom." I start typing a message to Ashleigh to see if she'll be around in fifteen minutes. "If you think that the students at Central High School didn't have the most foul, atrocious language I've ever heard, you're seriously mistaken."

I mean, the cussing, the mildly inappropriate jokes, and the downright offensive slurs I heard on a daily basis were ten times worse than anything I ever heard in LA. I wrote for daytime television and that's about as clean as you can get.

"You're exaggerating," she huffs out, and I open the door in time to see her cheeks at peak brightness.

"You're so cute when you get angry, Mom." I pull her into my arms and kiss her on the cheek. "I'm going to meet Ashleigh soon, but when I get home, I can tell you about my new project if you want. And maybe we can binge whatever show sounds good on HGTV if you're up for it?"

She hugs me back and her eyes go soft. "I'm always up for spending time with my favorite girl."

When I was in LA, I was in LA. I didn't come home to visit as much as I should have. My mom has a borderline phobia of flying, so they only came to California two or three times, and every time, my mom needed a full day of recovery to come out of her Xanax fog. I created a community in LA that I was really proud of. We had Friendsgiving every year and created a family away from family, but being home, I can't deny how much I've missed them.

How much I've missed the comfort of being around people who know everything about me and love me unconditionally. I give my mom a hard time, but being here and connecting with her as an adult has been the brightest spot of this entire ordeal.

"Don't forget to put lipstick on before you go this time." She breaks the moment with such effectiveness it's almost impressive. "And maybe let your curls breathe today. A bun for this long can't be good for your hair."

"All righty then, this was fun while it lasted." I pull out of her arms and hurry into the bathroom, locking the door behind me.

Then I let my curls breathe and put on lipstick like my mom told me to do.

I'll never admit it to any of my supercool, trendy millennial Los Angeles friends, but there's nothing I love more than a chain restaurant.

Sure, a small, local-owned, organic, vegan bakery is lovely. But you know what else is great? Southwestern egg rolls and a frozen margarita from Chili's.

"We should do this more often." I dip my egg roll into the avocado ranch before taking a larger-than-ladylike bite. "Oh, yum."

Chili's always freaking hits!

I groan as I chew; my shoulders shimmy and bounce along to the Top 40 pop hit playing quietly on the overhead speakers.

"Now that you're 'properly fed and boozed'"—Ashleigh's use of air quotes is the only thing more passive-aggressive than her deep sighs and discreet eye rolls as I inspected the menu—"are you going to tell me what happened last night?"

My stomach twists a little—but not enough to deter me from

the food at hand—as I think back on last night. I don't know if it's from nerves, excitement, or fear, but I do know I can't tell her everything. Something passed between Nate and me as we confided in each other, and as much as I've grown to like Ashleigh, I can't give her what she wants in this moment.

"Nothing really." I trace the tile design on the table to avoid her all-knowing eyes. "We talked for a little bit, caught up on a few things, then I went home."

"Oh really?" she snaps. "Is that all? You talked, caught up, did a little bit of nothing in his empty house until after midnight?"

"Okay. You know I love you, Ash." Yes, we've moved into nickname territory. You could say things are getting *pretty* serious between the two of us. "But I'm really struggling to take you seriously in that dress. You look like a kindergarten teacher who's starting her own YouTube channel."

Instead of wearing a pair of her ridiculous leggings, she stepped out of her home—into public—in a truly unhinged sundress. Don't get me wrong, it's a cute dress . . . for a child. There's a mix of flowers, geometric shapes, and primary colors. I don't know who the designer is, but I really believe it was not supposed to exceed toddler sizes.

"Well, figure it out, because you're feeding me crumbs, and as your campaign manager, I demand to know more." She picks up the unsweetened iced tea she ordered and glares at me over the rim of the mug. "This is unacceptable!"

"While I understand your thirst for good gossip, I really don't have any." I feel a tinge of guilt for lying to her, but not much since for once, I know my heart is in the right place. "We talked about things and caught up. It was actually kind of nice. I forgot that he's not always a giant douchebag."

In normal circumstances, I'd love nothing more than to spread gossip about Nate. However, as low as I claim to go, sharing what he told me about his ex is crossing a line—even for me. Now, if I had witnessed the extensive khaki collection I know he owns or walked in on him kissing a neighbor? I'd share in a heartbeat.

Also, after I got home and started writing, the annoying HOA president took a turn for the sexy. As dialogue flowed out of me, it became harder and harder to separate the fictional hero in my script from the man down the street. Traits of Nate's that worked my nerves only days ago seemed so appealing on paper. It's as if a lifetime of suppressed feelings are spilling out of me and I only have one person to blame . . .

Or thank.

"I know you're holding something back, but I guess I'll let it slide this once," she grumbles before snatching an egg roll off my plate. "No." She aims a polished nail complete with glitter and rhinestones at me before I can object. "If you won't feed me gossip, you have to feed me egg rolls. It's in the bylaws."

She chomps down and arches an eyebrow as if daring me to argue.

"If it's the law, then what can I do about it?" Plus, she ordered a Caesar salad with no croutons. She deserves a taste of happiness.

"Exactly, nothing."

We both finish our food, me with gusto, Ashleigh with obligation, and are waiting for our check when Ashleigh's phone begins to vibrate with notification after notification.

"Sheesh." I look at the influx of notifications lighting up her phone. "Popular much?"

I deleted pretty much all the apps off my phone after my life blew up. Getting tagged in different versions and hot takes of your lowest moment is not the good time you might assume. Now the only things on my phone are *Words with Friends* and *Candy Crush*. I have the home screen of a sixty-five-year-old and I'm okay with it.

"This is so weird." She unlocks her phone and starts to tap around. "Angela never texts me. And she tagged me in the HOA Facebook group?"

I'm draining the remaining drops of my margarita as she investigates this mystery when the familiar chords that have haunted my dreams for the last two months cut through the noise around us.

"What is . . ." Her words trail off as understanding dawns on her face.

I watch in abject horror as the color drains from Ashleigh's rosy cheeks. I don't have to see the video to know what she's seeing. Every frame, every second from the video is scorched into my mind. The humiliation I was beginning to put behind me rushes to the surface and I worry everything I've eaten is going to make a sudden reappearance. I don't wait for her to say anything; all I know is that I can't stay.

"I . . . I have to go." Panic finally pushes me out of my seat and out of the restaurant.

As soon as I push open the heavy door and the humid summer air hits, I start running and I don't stop until I reach the main road leading back to the Reserve at Horizon Creek. The curls I decided to let free are stuck to my forehead and the back of my neck, and my lungs burn as they fight to get enough oxygen. I put my hands on my head in a weak attempt to slow my breathing and gather my thoughts.

I don't know if I should go back to Ashleigh and try to explain what she saw, but the thought of showing my face again makes my stomach turn. The awful thing about going viral is you know there's always a chance someone you meet will stumble across one of the lowest moments of your life. A little voice in the back of my head is constantly warning me not to get too close, that I'm always a second away from being plunged back into humiliation. I know I fucked up and that vandalism is never the answer, but it feels extra shitty that I'm still being punished for my reaction to the bad behavior Peter was rewarded for.

Since there's no way to gracefully slide back into the booth and explain this away to Ashleigh—and also because I'm a coward—I continue walking the familiar path back to my parents' house. The summer sun is high in the sky and every step feels harder than the last. My slip-on sneakers are like bricks on my feet, and by the time my house comes into view, I'm dripping sweat and absolutely miserable.

But besides the sugary tequila treat I decided to drink, something else isn't sitting quite right.

I've been back in town for a while now. So long, in fact, that the internet has found more new targets than I can count. I know the video of me will never disappear, but I was hoping the times of it making its rounds on social media and having think pieces written about it had come and gone. The last time I checked, the number of views had stopped climbing and settled into a slow crawl.

So why, after all this time, is this video only now making the rounds in this sleepy suburb? How did Angela find the video to post in the HOA group?

There's only one thing that's changed, and I know exactly where to find him.

My dad's outside inspecting how the white oak is coming along when he sees me. He aims his bright smile at me, but it falls the minute he gets a good look at me.

"Oh no." Concern colors his words. "Are you okay?"

"Fantastic." I look down the street, my pace never slowing as I focus in on my target. "I just have to take care of something real fast."

You'd think that my hyperreactive ways would've changed thanks to the time they destroyed my entire life, but the opposite is true. Once the worst has happened, it loses its power. If I survived it once, I can survive it again.

Maybe.

I stomp up Nate's brick pathway not seeing any of the beauty I noticed last night. I pound on the door that I've now decided is the ugliest effing door I've ever seen and hope my fist punches a hole through it.

"Nate!" I shout, not caring who witnesses what's about to happen. "Open the door, you coward!"

I hear him before I see him.

The sound of muffled footsteps running down the stairs precedes his confused expression and tousled hair appearing through the long, rectangular window next to the door. He doesn't hesitate before swinging the door open.

"Collins?" His eyes are full of questions as they flicker back and forth from my scowling face to whatever's happening behind me. "Is everything okay? What are you doing here?"

"Is everything okay?" I practically screech from the sheer audacity of it all. "Are you kidding me?"

Before I can say anything else, he grabs me by the elbow and pulls me into his house, shutting the door behind me.

"What the hell, Collins? Why would you—"

He starts but I cut him off. I'm hot, humiliated, and my feet hurt. I'm not in the mood for his crap.

"Why would I? Why would *you*?" I step into his space and barely manage to keep my hands to myself. His neck looks like such a wonderful place to rest my hands.

He squeezes his eyes shut and drags his hands through his mess of dark hair. "I don't know what you're talking about."

For some reason, this pisses me off more than I thought possible. I'm furious I let him embarrass me, but I might be able to respect him if he owned up to being a scumbag. This *I'm such a good guy* bullshit is such a cop-out.

"Okay. Yeah, sure." I laugh even though nothing about this is funny. "So you mean to tell me that it's a coincidence that the day after I confide in you about everything that happened with Peter, the video just happens to show up in the HOA Facebook group?

And that Angela, the asshole who's constantly kissing your ass, didn't hear about it from you?"

"Wait—" He shakes his head and tries to interrupt me, but I'm so over this shit.

"No. Nope. No fucking way. I will not wait, because you know what? I went to lunch with Ashleigh today and she was begging me to share what happened last night, and you know what I told her?" I don't give him a chance to answer because the sound of his voice is liable to make me murderous. "Nothing! And even though you couldn't wait to use what I told you against me, I'm still not going to tell anyone what you told me. Because contrary to popular belief"—I pause and take a deep breath before screaming—"I'm a good fucking person!"

"Collins—" he starts.

"Don't talk, don't say my name." I'm still yelling when I fling open his front door. "You, Nathanial Adams, are the fucking worst and I will never forget this."

I've said all I needed to say and my adrenaline is starting to fade fast. I need to get out of here before I break down in tears in his goddamn foyer.

What a nightmare.

I march out of his house and down his walkway with both middle fingers raised high above my head.

When I reach the sidewalk, I notice Angela standing across the street, a bitchy smile evident from even a hundred yards away.

"Why are you here? Don't you have a family to take care of?" I scream across the street. "For the love of god, get a fucking hobby!"

The smug look disappears and her over-Botoxed face attempts

to crumple. Unfortunately for her, the only Karens I deal with aren't out here and I'm not buying tickets to this show.

I keep my head held high, and even though I want to run, I hold my pace steady as I march toward my parents' house. And much to my credit, I do a fan-freaking-tastic job of holding it together . . . until I see my parents outside.

Their concerned expressions cause their gently lined faces to crease with worry, and it undoes me.

"Inside." My voice is hoarse with unshed tears as I rush past them. "I can't let these people see me cry."

There's not much I'm feeling thankful for in this moment, but managing to keep it together until I'm safely concealed in the comfort of my parents' house is one of them. And that when I do crumble, for the second time in as many months, at least I'm not alone.

Chapter 15

When I was in high school, my mom went through a stage where she was obsessed with the show *Hoarders*. Day and night, it was always on our television. I always used to sit with her, my lips curled up in disgust as I judged these poor people. *How could they let it get this bad?* I'd ask myself, trying to figure out what in the world could be worse than living in these rodent-infested houses.

Now, as I sit in my bedroom, paper plates and empty cups piling up in the corner, wearing the same shirt and sweatpants I've had on for a week, empathy unfurls within me as understanding sets in.

My poor, sweet parents have been doing everything they can to get me out of my bed and back into the land of the living. They even made campaign flyers and handed them out to neighbors. My mom tries to sound cheerful when she knocks on my door with dinner or a piece of gossip from the Karens. But when they think I'm not listening, I hear hushed conversations through the thin walls about therapists and worst-case scenarios as they frantically try to come up with a plan.

If I was thinking clearly at all, this would be enough to get me out of the room and down to the garden with my dad or even just to the couch.

But I'm not thinking clearly.

I'm sad.

And it's a sadness so deep that my bones ache. At every moment of the day, I can feel it building in my body. My limbs feel heavy and my vision clouds with tears that fall without notice.

Logically, I know getting out of the house and moving on will help, but what's the point of moving forward if with every step forward, someone's waiting to yank me back to square one?

My doorknob starts to jiggle and temporarily distracts me from my latest doom spiral. Even though the lock is supposed to indicate a desire for privacy, it only serves as a small obstacle for my mom.

"I'm naked." I'm not, but it's the first thing that comes to mind that might give me a few more minutes of solitude.

"Don't care. It's nothing I haven't seen before," a familiar voice that's definitely not my mom's says as the flimsy door swings open. Ruby steps inside my room and her beautiful face scrunches up in disgust. "Oh holy fuck, Collins!"

"Ruby Jane Peterson!" my mom shouts from somewhere inside the house. "I don't care how old you are, you know that language is not acceptable here. You're much too beautiful to have such an ugly mouth."

Ruby pulls her lips between her teeth and her big blue eyes practically double in size.

"Sorry, Mrs. Carter!" she shouts before lowering her voice to a hushed whisper. "Oh my god! Is that what it feels like to be my assistant? I haven't been scolded since high school!"

"Welcome to my life." Faced with Ruby's effortless, blinding beauty, I sit up in my bed, acutely aware of the current rat's nest sitting atop my head. "Kimberly Carter lives to correct people. A few weeks ago, she told the checkout person at Costco that it wasn't professional to gossip about their co-workers in front of customers."

It was highly upsetting. Low-stakes gossip that doesn't affect me whatsoever is my favorite kind of gossip. Plus, my mom stopped them before I found out why Hannah kept calling out—consequence-free—and shucking their responsibilities onto poor Nick.

"Nobody has more opinions than a midwestern mom."

This is absolutely true. "No lies detected."

I watch as Ruby uses the pointed toe of her very cute flat to fling dirty laundry out of her way as she clears a path to my bed. The desire to pull the covers over my head and hide is almost too great to beat back, but Ruby is my person. If anyone can see me like this, it's her.

"Soooo . . ." She sits on the edge of the bed and gestures to my disaster of a bedroom. "This is . . . this is something."

"It's not my finest moment." Embarrassment and shame prevent me from looking her in the eyes.

"We all have low points and I can't wait to figure this out. But"—she throws the comforter off my bed and points to my bedroom door—"before that can happen, I'm going to need you to take a shower and wash your hair. Your poor curls look like they've taken the brunt of this meltdown and I wouldn't be a real friend if I didn't intervene."

If there's a day I hate most, it's wash day. My head already aches from regret; detangling the disaster I've allowed to take place will only make it worse.

"How about I—" I make the mistake of thinking I can negotiate with Ruby.

"How about you get in the shower, wash your hair, and then come tell me what the hell happened that has you ignoring my calls and your mom calling me?"

Oh fuck.

I knew my parents were worried, but I didn't think they were call-Ruby-level concerned.

"My mom called you?"

"Oh, only about twenty times a day for the last three days." She stands up, her almost-six-foot frame towering over me, and yanks me out of bed. She pushes me in the direction of my door. "Go. Shower. Then we'll talk."

"Sheesh. Bossy." I try to go for annoyed, but fail miserably. I'm so grateful to see her that I could cry. Which, because I can't fucking control it, I do.

"Hey." Ruby turns me around when she hears my voice break. "It's okay. This is all going to be okay. I promise."

She pulls me into her arms and we hug each other tight until my tears begin to subside.

"Has anyone ever told you you've got a fantastic set of boobies?" I ask as I step out of her embrace. My tears have left wet marks right on her chest. "They're perfect crying pillows."

"Wow. Nobody has ever said anything nicer! Thank you!" Her dazzling, pageant-winning smile lights up my room. "Now, I love you, but you really do stink. Please go get in the shower."

I don't make her ask again. My body still aches and I'm doubtful that I'll ever run out of tears, but for a moment, standing in front of my best friend, the clouds began to lift. It's not much, but it's enough. As I strip off my dirty sweats—which should probably be burned at this point—and step beneath the warm stream of the shower, I hold tight to the small inkling of hope and let some of my fears wash off me and down the drain.

When I walk into my room after my shower, my mom and Ruby are standing in it like the last week never happened. New sheets are on my bed, the floor is spotless, and an outfit consisting of something other than sweats is folded on top of my dresser.

"Oh, there's my beautiful girl!" Mom crosses the room with a look filled with so much relief, I almost choke on my guilt. "Ruby and I straightened up your room a bit so you can get ready and go out to lunch. Also, Ashleigh has been stopping by every day. It might be nice if you girls invite her along. If the amount of baked goods she's brought over is any indication, she's very worried about you."

"Yes, I like Ashleigh, she can come." Ruby doesn't even ask my opinion. "Is her last name Whittington? I think we did some pageants together back in the day."

"Ashleigh Barnes now," I correct her. "But yeah, that was her maiden name."

Of course Ashleigh was a pageant girl. I should've known from her perfect posture and unnerving ability to keep a smile on her face.

"She was always really sweet, and not in a phony way. How funny that she ended up being your neighbor."

"Oh good!" My mom claps her hands together. "I'll give her a call and let her know you'll be by to pick her up shortly." She starts to leave my room, but before she turns the corner, she stops and turns around. "It really is good to see you smile again, Collins. I hope you know how loved you are."

Between her soft tone and the expression on her face, which is so sincere it knocks my breath away, I struggle to fight back a new wave of tears. Before I can even open my mouth to come up with a response, she's gone.

"I love your mom." Even Ruby's steadfast voice seems a little shaky.

"She's the best."

It's fun to give her a hard time about her obsession with Matthew, Luke, John, and her bedazzled Bible, but I've never not known how incredibly lucky I am to have her as my mom. Well, maybe for like a month in seventh grade, but middle schoolers suck and I cannot be held responsible for the things my hormonal little body made me say and do.

"All righty then." Ruby, never one to get sidetracked by pesky things like feelings, bounces right back into her usual no-nonsense self. "There's an outfit on your dresser. If you even contemplate switching the denim for leggings, please be aware that I will tackle you to the ground. Also, I know all the kids are wearing them and your podiatrist told you they were a good option, but please, for your friend who flew to Ohio for you, give the Crocs a rest for the day."

"My friend who flew to Ohio?" I repeat her words back to her. She might not be a midwestern mom (yet), but she already has the guilt trips down pat. "How can I argue with that?"

"You can't." She winks. "You know arguments are how I make a living; you don't stand a chance against me."

The worst part is that I didn't stand a chance even before she decided to go to school for it. Luckily, though, we're usually on the same page and having her on my side of a debate is the best thing in the world. Looking back, I'm pretty sure it's why Peter wasn't crazy about her. All my other friends worshipped the ground he walked on, but Ruby? Ruby saw right through him. She loved to come over and debate him on whatever subject he deemed himself an expert on . . . and there were a lot.

"Speaking of flying to Ohio . . ." Segues have never been my strong point. "How long until you fly back to LA?"

"I'm here for at least a week, but maybe longer," she says. "I haven't touched my PTO since I started working. Between the time I've accrued and the ability to work via video calls, I could stay here for a month."

She might not say it outright, but I can read the subtext.

She's here until she knows I won't fall apart. And I love her even more.

"Oh my god!" I grab her hands when I realize the best, worst news ever. "Does that mean you'll help me run my HOA campaign?"

"Ughhhhh. You know I didn't like anyone when I lived here." She rolls her eyes so hard, for a minute I think they might actually get stuck in the back of her head. "I'm pretty sure I toilet-papered a few houses you're going to want votes from. Are you sure you want me on your team? Plus, you know how intense I get. Once I start, you won't be able to get me to leave."

"Of course I know! Why else do you think I'm asking? If you're there, it will be so much fun! We can pass out flyers and silently judge everyone just like the old days!" I tighten my grip on her hand, fully prepared to not let go until she says yes. "Please. You know I'm not above begging."

"Judging people does sound fun." She taps her foot as she considers it, and I can tell she's softening. "I'll do it under one condition."

"I will do literally anything. I mean, look at me." I gesture to my bedroom, which only minutes ago looked like a scene from a low-budget horror film. "I'm living with my parents, involved in the most contentious HOA campaign that has maybe ever existed, and my temper tantrum is going to haunt me until my dying days. Do you really think there's anything I won't do at this point?"

"All right . . ." She leans in with the same conspiratorial grin that used to precede all our most wild nights. I lean in, too, excited to hear whatever scheme she's concocting. "You don't ever, and I mean *ever*, ignore my calls like this again. I was out of my mind worried about you!"

"Rubes—" I start, but she cuts me off with a long finger pointed in my face.

"No, you don't get to *Rubes* me. You completely shut me out." Her eyes gloss over and her voice trembles. "That's not the kind of friends we are, Collins. You don't hide from me. We show each other everything. The good, the bad, the fucking ugly. We are there through it all. You don't ever need to hide in your stinky-ass bedroom from me. Do you understand me?"

She's talking about me, but I know she's right back to the summer when she found out her dad had been lying to her for years. He hadn't just had a series of one-night stands; he had an entire other life that he was living. I don't think I've ever seen someone so destroyed. It changed her in a way I still have trouble articulating. After that summer, her worldview changed. Where she found safety before, she now saw danger. But instead of cowering behind doors (or in her bedroom in stinky old sweats) she figured out a way to fight back. Sometimes I still wonder what path she would've gone down if her dad hadn't done what he did.

"I'm sorry." I don't try to make excuses, because there are none for shutting her out the way I did. It was selfish and maybe even cruel. "I'll never do it again. I was worried about burdening you with the same old song and dance, but you should've been my first call and I'm sorry I didn't do that."

"I can always hold space for you and you are never a burden," she says. "You're my best friend and I love you. Don't hesitate to ever ask me to help carry whatever you're going through."

"I love you too." I hug her again, this one shorter and less tearful than the last. "Also," I say as I pull away, "did you just say you can always hold space for me? Does that mean what I think it means?"

"Ughhhh. Yes, I'm seeing Monique again." She scowls at me when I can't bite back my smile any longer. "You weren't answering the fucking phone! Who else was I supposed to call?"

"Even though I can also always hold space for you, I'm not a licensed therapist. You should call Monique even when I'm not in the midst of a nervous breakdown."

I've been trying to get her into therapy ever since we graduated from high school. Her mom made her go while her parents were going through the divorce, but she hated it and refused to go after. It wasn't until I found Monique during a rough patch a couple of years ago and was relentless about singing her praises that she booked her appointment. To say it's been an on-and-off-again relationship is the understatement of the century, but knowing my latest spiral got her back into therapy is the bright spot I didn't know I needed.

"Yeah, okay. Just don't do it again." She rolls her eyes, but I can tell her heart's not in it. "Now, get dressed. I'm getting hangry."

She leaves my room and pulls the door closed behind her but pushes it back open almost immediately. She sticks her head into my room, humor dancing in her eyes again now that the heavy stuff is taken care of.

"You were right! The amount of wall art your mom has is bordering on unhinged!" she whisper-shouts. "And no offense to your childhood cuteness, but nobody needs that many pictures of one person on their walls."

"I told you!" I whisper right back, not offended in the least. There's an entire section of the hallway dedicated to my awkward tween years, and let me tell you, no adult needs a daily reminder of that period of their life. None. "Now, go. I know what you're like when you haven't been fed and I don't think sweet Ashleigh will be able to handle it."

"Good call." Her eyes go wide and she slams my door. Not even a few seconds pass before I hear her shout, "All right, Mrs. Carter, now that that's taken care of, fill me in on the Karens. You always have the best gossip."

I slip on my jeans, smiling to myself as I skip over my Crocs and opt for a pair of Ruby-approved sandals.

The heavy fog I was under begins to lift, and things don't feel so bad. Sure, last week sucked, but that was then and this is now. My best friend is in town, my family is the best, and I still have the opportunity to exact intense and painful revenge on Nathanial "the Snake" Adams.

Things are definitely looking up.

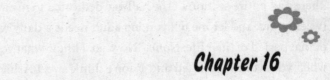

Chapter 16

C**-bus stand up!"** Ruby yells as we navigate the crowded sidewalk in downtown Columbus.

Don't ask me how we got here. I'm still not sure myself. All I know is that after a few shared appetizers and a couple of drinks down the street from my house, Ashleigh was somehow able to convince us to check out the nightlife scene in Columbus.

We hopped in an Uber and told them to drop us off at their favorite bar. Our driver, Katrina, who had a cooler in the front and a survey in the back for music selection and temperature control—ten out of ten service—told us that Short North Arts District was where we wanted to be.

She did not lie.

I wanted to hate it and bah-humbug the entire night away, but goddammit if it's not only really fucking cute but there are great drinks for prices I couldn't have even dreamt of in LA. And Ruby, my serious friend who never takes a day off and hasn't had more than a glass or two of wine in years, is on her hot-girl summer-party shit.

It. Is. Glorious!

"Oh my god!" She points to a bar across the street with a rooftop deck covered in string lights. "Can we go there next?"

Ashleigh and I look at each other and shrug.

"Sure," I say. "Wherever you want to go is fine with us."

This is Ruby's world and we're just living in it.

She shrieks so loud, she startles the group of too-cool men wearing coordinating striped button-ups and fedoras. They start to glare, but when they see Ruby, their entire demeanor changes.

"Hey, gorgeous," Fedora number one in the navy shirt says. "Where are you ladies heading off to?"

I know what's about to happen before Ruby even opens her mouth. I'd feel bad for the guys, but something about matching fedoras makes me hate them on sight. So instead, I stand to the side and enjoy the show.

"No, thank you." She pays the man dust.

"Damn, girl." He smirks and steps forward, not at all deterred by her flat-out rejection. "It's like that?"

I bite my lip as Ruby's posture gradually straightens and her hands curl into fists.

"Why are you still in front of me?" Every woman walking by can sense her annoyance, but shocking absolutely nobody, the men are still smiling like it's all fun and games. "What part of 'no, thank you' didn't you understand? Was I too polite?" She looks over her shoulder at me and Ashleigh before answering her own question. "I was too polite."

Fedora's face reddens when the realization that this isn't going to end with his intended results begins to dawn.

"Fuck you then." His chest puffs out and his face twists with anger and embarrassment—the most dangerous of feelings for the cis male ego. "You're not even that hot."

"I am though. I'm hot, successful, and smart as fuck." Ruby starts to laugh, which only acts to further piss off the guy in front of us. "You're a guy who harasses women on the street and is pissed because I don't need you to validate my worth. Which is exactly why I said no, thank you. Oh, and also because of the fedoras. You look fucking ridiculous. Take them off." She stops and points to one of the guys in the group. "Except you, you can pull it off. Congratulations, that's no easy task."

The man in front of us is practically vibrating with rage, but the guy she said could pull off the fedora could not look more pleased. "Thank you," he says at the same time his friend says, "Fucking bitch."

"Oh my god, thank you so much!" Ruby's smile turns megawatt and her eyes sparkle even beneath the dim streetlights. "I haven't had work in a couple of days and I was really missing scorned men calling me a bitch. Now I can really enjoy the rest of my night!"

It's obvious this guy has never come across anyone like Ruby before. His mouth opens and closes as he tries to come up with something to say, but after a few seconds of silence, his friends grab him by the arm and pull him away.

"Damn, Ruby," I say as I watch him walk away with his head hung in shame. "I think you just did more to prevent catcalling and street harassment than law enforcement ever has."

I hope this moment lives in his mind until his dying days and he thinks twice before approaching women on the street.

She loops both her arms through ours and starts pulling us in the direction of the rooftop bar she saw before we were so rudely interrupted. "I do what I can . . . especially if it entails arguing with entitled men."

"That was amazing. I want to be you when I grow up." Ashleigh looks at Ruby with a familiar expression of shock and awe. "I could never do that."

"That's probably because you're a well-adjusted human who doesn't have an unhealthy hatred of men due to unresolved daddy issues," Ruby says.

I can tell Ashleigh doesn't know if she's being serious or not, but before I can clear it up, we get to the bar.

We each show our IDs at the door before funneling inside and hurrying up the stairs. We push through the heavy glass doors at the top and walk out onto the perfect night spot. From the street, all we could see were hanging lights and people milling around, bobbing—Ohioans' preferred method of light dancing—to whatever music was playing. But now, up here and part of the crowd, it's so much more. The space that is so much larger than I anticipated is broken up into different sections. A huge bar that extends from indoors to out sits right by the door. Modern and industrial design blend seamlessly with clean lines, wood, metal, and a shock of greenery dispersed across the patio.

One corner has a stage where a band is setting up their instruments. Another space ditches the wide planks and opts for turf. Two games of giant Jenga are playing out while a couple competes in a very intense round of cornhole. High-top tables with umbrellas and barstools are interspersed with giant plush couches and lounge chairs all across the space—a lack of seating never an issue—and flames dance across a long, rectangular fire pit table. It somehow manages to be fun, casual, and romantic all at the same time.

We find an empty table close to the stage, and even though none of us are very hungry, we still order bacon-wrapped dates, truffle fries, and crispy Brussels sprouts when the waitress—Julie, who has an amazing haircut and eyeliner so precise a robot must've applied it—comes by. Oh, and a round of frozen palomas because why the hell not?

"Oh, actually," Ruby stops Julie before she can walk away, "can you put an extra shot of tequila in mine?"

"My kind of woman." Julie winks and scribbles it down on her notepad. "Of course we can. Anybody else?"

"You know what? Why not?" Ashleigh looks like a kid who just stole a piece of candy from the grocery store. I'm pretty sure this is the naughtiest thing she's ever done.

Julie aims a pointed look in my direction. "What about you?"

I feel Ashleigh's and Ruby's stares, and this might be the most peer pressure I've faced in years. Usually, I'd give in. I'm trash for people pleasing and also booze, but for some stupid freaking reason, I can only see Nate's cringing face as he reminded me of my intolerance for tequila. "I'm okay without it, but thank you."

"Did you just deny yourself extra tequila?" Ruby reaches across the table and presses her palm against my forehead. "Are you feeling okay?"

"Ha ha. Real funny. I feel fine." I swat her hand away and contemplate whether or not to tell her what I'm thinking.

If anyone can talk some sense into me right now, it's definitely Ruby. And Ashleigh—forgetting that she has sold both leggings and essential oils since I've known her—has been so supportive and kind since we've met. I know that if I want to keep from locking myself inside my bedroom for another week, I'm going to have to open up to them.

"Okay." I drop my voice to a whisper and lean toward the table. "I need you to both help straighten me out because my mind is all jumbled."

"The entire point of this trip is to straighten you out." Ruby takes a long sip of her water before leaning back in the metal chair and making herself comfortable. "So shoot."

Ashleigh nods emphatically. "I'm not the best at straightening people out, but I am a good listener."

Since she's listened to multiple rants from me and sat quietly during the longest HOA meeting ever, I know this to be a fact.

"Okay." I take a long breath and try to figure out where to start. "So Ruby already knows, but just to make sure we're all on the same page, Nate and I used to be really great friends. Besides Ruby, he was my best friend for quite some time, so he actually knows a lot about me."

"Obviously I've always been her fun friend," Ruby says to Ashleigh.

"Obviously." Ashleigh laughs.

"Anyways!" I pretend to sound annoyed, but I'm sure the smile on my face gives me away. "When I was over at Nate's the other night, even though a lot of time has passed and we've both lived a lot of life, it was really nice talking to him again. There's something so comforting about having a shared history with someone and not having to explain myself. I don't know, it just really made me miss him and our friendship."

"That's kind of sweet." Ruby couldn't sound more annoyed by this. I don't blame her. I feel the exact same way. It's the worst.

"It was. Which is how I got lost in the moment and I forgot what things are really like between the two of us now. I forgot I couldn't trust him to not use what happened with Peter against me."

I keep trying to figure out how I missed his true intentions. But every time I think back on that night, all I remember is sincerity in his hazel eyes and compassion in his deep voice. There was no way I could've known. The saddest part is, even knowing what I know now, if he were to look at me the way he did the other night and open up, I'd make the same mistakes all over again.

"Wait." Ashleigh sits up straight in her seat. "I know you're pissed about the video getting out—as you should be; that was super uncool—but are you saying you think Nate's behind it?"

I can't tell if this is a rhetorical question or not. I look to Ruby for help, but she just widens her eyes and shrugs.

I try to think of something other than *duh* or *are you fucking kidding me* to say, but it's not easy. Becoming a better person is really hard. Maybe I should reward myself with an extra shot of tequila . . .

"Well, yeah," I say after some thought. "I talked to him one night and a few hours later it's plastered all over the HOA website by the woman who is always clinging to him? It doesn't take a detective to piece those clues together."

The part of all this that stings but that I haven't given life to is the woman he told. I might've known that Angela was a bitch the moment I laid my eyes on her, but I can't deny that she's very pretty. Or that she looks an awful lot like Nate's ex-fiancée . . . and the girlfriend he came back to school with after the summer he disappeared on me.

Ashleigh's cornflower-blue eyes dance with mischief, and the smug smile pulling on the corners of her lips looks out of place on her perpetually kind face. "I hate to break it to you, but if you're thinking about a second career as an investigator, you might want to think again."

I tilt my head to the side, narrowing my eyes as I try to comprehend what, exactly, she's trying to say. Ruby, my not-so-mild-mannered friend, slams her hands down on the tabletop and screams, "Come again? What do you mean by that?"

It feels as if the bustling rooftop comes to a screeching halt and all eyes focus on our table. I want to shrink beneath the attention. I want to crawl right back into my bed and throw the covers over my head.

But I can't.

Not now.

Not when it feels like the crux of my entire existence depends on the answer.

Thankfully, Ashleigh must sense my desperation, or—more likely—fear Ruby, because she doesn't hesitate to explain.

"However Angela came across that video, it was not because of Nate," she says. "Rumor has it that even though Angela is married, she has a giant crush on Nate. Which, to be fair, is understandable. Nate is so cute and nice. I met her husband once and he's not terrible to look at, but he corrected almost everything she said and—"

"Ashleigh, I love you so much and you know I love hearing neighborhood gossip, but could we maybe finish about Nate before switching to Angela's husband?" Desperation is dripping out of my pores, or maybe that's all the booze we've been drinking, but either way, I need her to focus.

"Oh yeah, sorry." Her cheeks turn pink, but she gets back to the story at hand. "After you went over to his house, he started posting in the Facebook group, demanding the admins remove the video, and once he did, he went over to her house and in a way only Nate can do, he tore her a new one without ever raising his voice and using words some of the neighbors had to google. He made it clear, in no uncertain terms, that the video was never to be posted and that if she knew the entire story, she'd be ashamed of herself."

"Wow." I pull my lip between my teeth, unsure of what to do with this information. "That was really nice of him."

My stomach starts to feel funny, my sinuses go all wonky, and my stupid memory transports me to the summer before ninth grade when I first realized my feelings for Nate maybe weren't so platonic after all. His dad had flaked out on his baseball tournament—again—and my mom volunteered our cheering services for the day.

Now, it should be stated that I would rather watch profes-

sional wall painting over baseball. I know that it's America's favorite pastime, but I hate it. It's the slowest, longest, most boring
sport ever created and, of course, only played in months where it
feels as if the sun is determined to melt my entire face off. Also, I
physically reject celebrating a sport where math is one of the most
exciting parts of the game. However, because Nate was my best
friend, I tagged along and kept all . . . Fine! I kept *most* of my
negative comments to myself. I'm a really good friend like that.

We were sitting in the car outside his apartment waiting for
him to come out. I was in the front seat, double-checking that my
backpack had at least two books and an adequate amount of
snacks that could last from two to eight hours, when he finally
made his grand appearance.

And grand it was.

The goofy uniform that before that summer always seemed
a little sloppy and ill fitting now fit him like a glove. His tiny arms
weren't so tiny anymore and the fabric clung just right to his legs,
which suddenly didn't seem so chicken-like. Peeking just below
the brim of his baseball hat, his hazel eyes turned up with genuine
happiness to see me. His braces had come off only a few short
weeks earlier, and the power of his straight white teeth hit me in
places that, until that moment, had never been roused.

"Such a nice, handsome boy," my mom had said as he got
closer to the car.

"Ew. Don't be gross, Mom," I lied through my goddamn teeth.

I can still feel the way my skin flamed when I realized my
mom wasn't buying it for a second and the relief I felt when she
patted my leg, wordlessly promising to keep my secret safe.

I sat in the stands that day and paid more attention than I ever had in my entire life. I was completely enthralled, not by the game itself, but by the way Nate was glancing at me from the outfield between hitters, his smile huge when he ran off the field. When he pointed at me before he was up to bat, I rolled my eyes, but on the inside, my stomach was twisting around like our favorite roller coaster at Kings Island.

Just like right now.

I forgot about that day. I guess I forgot about pretty much all the good memories I had with Nate. Which sucks because there were a lot of really great ones.

Thankfully, before I can voice this truly wild walk down memory lane to my friends, Julie strolls back up to the table with a tray full of cocktails.

"Three frozen palomas, two with extra tequila." She places each of our drinks—hopefully—in front of the correct person and her smile widens. "I'll be back with your appetizers as soon as they're up."

We all say our thanks as she leaves and reach for icy glasses overflowing with frozen, citrusy goodness.

"Wait!" Ashleigh stops us before we can take our first sip. "I know we've already cheers'd today, but I think we need one more." She raises her glass to the middle of the table, and Ruby and I follow suit without too much backtalk. "To Collins, Nate, and them finally admitting they want to rip each other's clothes off!"

"I'm not sure I'm that far on team Nate yet"—Ruby taps her glass against Ashleigh's—"but I can get behind Collins hooking up with anybody other than Peter fucking Hanson."

The urge to crawl under the table returns full force as Ashleigh and Ruby start to discuss my imaginary sexual adventures.

"Okay okay okay!" I interrupt their crude debate and clink our cups together. "Cheers!"

We all take giant gulps of the perfect cocktail and groan in unison before the band finally takes to the stage. As the first chords of music rip through the space, I look at my friends and can't believe a day that started with me crying in my room has ended like this.

*T*he rain started with a drizzle and quickly turned into a downpour, forcing us from the rooftop patio to the inside of an Uber.

This driver isn't nearly as awesome as the one who took us downtown, but it's raining and I appreciate his focus. After dropping off Ruby at her hotel not too far from our houses, he takes his time navigating the wet suburban side streets.

"I'll just get out with you," I say to Ashleigh as we pull up to her house. "I'd feel like an idiot having him pull forward a few hundred feet."

While exercise is one of my least favorite pastimes and I'll never pass up an escalator for stairs, this feels ridiculous even to me. Plus, Ashleigh tried to keep up with Ruby tonight and I'm not sure she'll make it to her door without my assistance.

The driver pulls up to Ashleigh's house and slides into her driveway. It's only a few feet, but it makes a huge difference. Ashleigh may be tiny, but she's almost totally deadweight, and if I had to start at the street, there's a good chance we would've gone down.

My finger hasn't even left the doorbell before Grant swings open the door and takes her weight from me. His expression is a mixture of relief, amusement, and love. I don't know what was in those drinks, but watching Grant and Ashleigh makes my heart squeeze a little bit. I'm glad she has that.

He closes the door behind them and I hurry to the sidewalk. Between the empty streets and flashes of lightning in the distance, it feels a little eerie being outside alone. The streetlights are the only thing illuminating this side of the street, and when I chance a look in the other direction, I can't help but notice Nate's porch light is the only one on the entire street that's still on.

I look back to my parents' dark house, my key sitting in my purse ready for me to use, and know that's where I should go. But for some reason, when my feet move, they take me in the opposite direction.

The closer I get to Nate's house, the more of a mistake I know it is. But for some reason, I can't stop myself. Not when I get to his paved walkway. Not as I pass the pruned bushes. Not as I push down on the doorbell and listen to it ring over and over again until I see a hallway light turn on through the window.

Nate swings the door open and stills when he sees me. He's not wearing a shirt. Loose-fitting pajama bottoms hang low on his hips and I struggle to keep my eyes where they belong.

"Collins?" His voice is sleepy, but his eyes are alert. "It's late. Are you okay? Why are you standing in the rain?"

"I heard what you said to Angela. Thank you." My hands fidget by my sides as longing and lust I've hidden away for years claw their way to the surface. "But you know I still hate you, right?"

"Yup." His eyes drop to my chest. My light cotton tee has molded to my breasts and I feel my nipples harden beneath his gaze. "I hate you too."

"Good," I say between heavy breathing.

"Good," Nate repeats.

And that's all we say.

Because it's kind of hard to talk with our lips smashed together and our tongues in each other's mouths.

Chapter 17

*T*he only reason I know the door closed is because my back is pressed against it.

My hands explore his bare back, my nails scraping across the smooth skin. His hands roam my hips and thighs until they make their way to my ass. His fingers press into my ample behind and he lifts me up. I wrap my legs around his hips, clinging on to him. I pull his face to mine, biting his lower lip before our tongues thrash in a battle for dominance. Nothing about it is gentle, but it's hot as fuck and I'm desperate for more.

"Collins." Nate pulls his mouth away for long enough to get the single word out, and I miss it immediately. "What is this?"

This is nothing and it's everything. I can't stand him, but I need him. I've wanted this with him since I knew this existed, and now that I've had a taste of what being with him could be like, I don't know if I'll ever have enough.

"It doesn't have to be anything." I'm trying to focus, to say words that make sense, but all I can feel is his impressive length growing beneath me. I rock my hips against him, trying to sate the need building between my thighs.

"Fuck." He groans and I can feel it vibrating through his body. He drops his head and bites down on my shoulder; the slight sting of his teeth makes my toes curl. He stands like this for a few seconds and I listen as his breathing slows. "I need to know you really want this. I don't want you to regret this in the morning."

I don't think I've ever wanted anything more.

But of course I don't tell him that.

"I came to your house, Nate." I remind him of the facts as I struggle to keep my hips still. "I want this and if I regret it in the morning, then I'll deal with it then. But right now, right here? I would really like it if you took your pants off."

His eyebrows jump in surprise before his eyes darken and his lips curl into the sexiest smile I've ever seen. It's confident and cocky, and if I know one thing about Nate, it's that he doesn't tend to make promises he can't deliver on.

"Well, if that's what you want, far be it from me to deprive you."

He sets me back on the floor and takes a small step backward. My legs feel like Jell-O and I have to use the door behind me to support my body. I watch, enraptured, as he slowly unties the drawstring on his pajamas before they fall to the floor and his massive erection springs to life.

"Holy shit," I whisper in his foyer. "I didn't expect that to be hiding beneath your khakis."

I'll never be able to look at him in his casual business attire the same way ever again.

"Weren't you the one who warned me never to judge a book by the cover?" There's laughter in his voice, but I have no idea if he's smiling or not. All my attention is focused on the way his hand is stroking his impressive length.

My thighs push together, trying—and failing—to find even the smallest amount of relief. "Lesson learned."

I take a moment to fully appreciate the man standing in front of me. I had a glimpse of his body when I saw him out walking, but completely devoid of clothes and distractions, it takes it to a whole new level. It's a thing of beauty, really. The softness of his belly doesn't distract from the strength in his body. His thickly corded quads stand out on his thighs even with his relaxed stance. His biceps flex with every stroke, the bulging muscle evident but not overwhelming. It's a body that's cared for but not obsessed over, and I love every single inch of it.

He takes a step forward and snaps me out of my trance.

"This might be the longest I've ever heard you not talk for." He chuckles and it wraps around me like a physical touch. "Are you okay?"

It takes an immense amount of effort, but I manage to stop admiring the way his chest is covered by the perfect amount of hair and meet his eyes. "I'm not sure I've ever been better."

"Glad to hear it." He leans down, so close that our noses almost touch. "Now how about we take care of this?"

His hands fall to my sides and his fingers trail along the hem of my T-shirt. Goose bumps dance up my arms and down my spine, but not from the chill of my damp clothes. My breathing is shaky as he drags the fabric upward, revealing my midsection and then the lacy bralette I threw on this afternoon, not thinking in a million years Nate would be looking at it later. He pulls it over my head, tossing it to the side somewhere.

Even after all the years I spent with Peter, I always felt uncomfortable being naked in front of him. It was like he was constantly assessing my body, noting what could use improvement and what was acceptable. The gym membership he signed us both up for stung for months.

But beneath Nate's intense gaze, I've never felt more powerful. He doesn't even attempt to hide his desire as his hands explore my bare skin. His cock jumps when his fingers skim across the thin fabric concealing my nipples, and I can't hold back the moan that slips through my lips. His heavy breathing grows deeper, the sound echoing in the empty foyer, before his mouth is back on mine.

The gentle scrape of facial hair I know he'll shave in the morning is a stark contrast to his pillow-soft lips. He nips at my bottom lip, quickly tracing the sting with his tongue. One of his large hands pulls me against him while the other slips into the waistband of the boyfriend jeans Ruby forced me into. I'm hyper-aware of his cock pressing into me and the nuisance of my pants preventing him from giving it to me like I want it.

However, before I can complain, Nate—the wonderful over-achiever he's always been—anticipates my needs. He slips his hand in mine and pulls me behind him up the stairs and down the short hallway to the last open door.

"You're sure about this?" he asks one final time. "I'll be disappointed, but I'll understand if you change your mind."

"If I didn't want this, I wouldn't have rung your doorbell." I admit what I wasn't even sure I was prepared to admit to myself. "I don't just want it now, I need it."

He nods, and a slow, sexy-as-hell grin spreads across his face.

"Good." His lips touch mine and the gentleness of the small touch takes my breath away. "I think I've needed this for years."

Before I can absorb the full weight of his confession, he tugs me into his bedroom. A lamp next to his bed is on, I assume from when I rang the doorbell like a maniac, and casts a dim glow across the space. Unlike the shocking amount of beige in his living room and the kitchen, his bedroom is dark and moody. The walls are painted a dark green that without the burst of light from the lamp I might think was black. His oversized bed is highlighted by a camel leather bed frame, the large headboard taking up most of the wall. His floor's covered by a gigantic sheepskin rug that probably makes climbing out of bed in the morning semi-bearable. But the thing that gets my attention the most is the gallery wall above his dresser. Black-and-white photos of Nate and his friends are framed on the wall, and even though I'm trying not to stare, I can't help but notice how personal this room feels in contrast to the rest of the house.

It feels like a privilege to be invited in.

"I really like your room," I say when I catch him staring at me. "It's nice."

"As opposed to the rest of my house?" He laughs, not offended by my unintentional backhanded compliment. "It's my favorite part of the house, so thank you."

In order to not put my foot in my mouth again, I decide it's time to put something else there instead. We shift positions and now I'm the one pulling him.

"Sit." I give him a gentle shove when we get to the foot of his bed.

"My pleasure." He doesn't hesitate. His naked body hurries up the bed until he's sitting with his back propped up by a generous number of pillows. He tucks his arms behind his head with his elbows splayed wide, watching every move I make from hooded eyes.

I unbutton my jeans, slowly pulling down the zipper and never taking my eyes off him. I shimmy out of my jeans and stand in front of Nate in nothing but my bra and underwear. I obviously wasn't planning on anyone seeing what was beneath my clothes, so I'm not in a cute matching set or anything. But by the way his chest rises and falls faster and faster and his fists curl in the comforter, he doesn't seem to mind the lacy-bra-cotton-undies combo.

My body has always been something I lived with. I never wanted to be a model or anything, but I didn't hate it with the same venom other women I know hated theirs. My modest breasts are the perfect size for me. Big enough to fill in a dress, but small enough that I can wear bralettes with zero support and not think twice. I don't love to work out and I do love pasta, so I gave up a long time ago on caring if my stomach was perfectly flat. And when thick thighs and a generous backside were something to be envious of, the issues I had from my teens began to fade away.

But right now? Standing in front of Nate and witnessing his

undoing just by looking at me? I've never felt sexier. I'm sure that's anti-feminist or something and I should just love myself without the need for validation, which I do.

This is just icing on top of a very sexy cake.

I try to notice everything, from the way my skin is tingling to the feel of his rug beneath my feet, and hope that I never forget a single detail of this moment. A moment where Nathanial Adams no longer looks at me with contempt, but as if I'm the most beautiful person he's ever set eyes on, and I do the same.

I climb on the bed, crawling up the comforter and between his legs. My hands skim the tops of his legs, feeling the way his body tightens beneath my touch. I look up at Nate, holding his gaze as I drop my head and use my tongue to start drawing a line up the inside of his thighs, stopping on occasion to nip at the sensitive skin and then kiss away the hurt.

I watch as his eyes squeeze shut the higher I go. His legs tremble under my touch and his breathing is so frantic, I worry he might pass out. Even though part of me wants to torture him a little longer, my kinder (hornier) side takes over.

Without hesitation, I move my mouth to his cock. My hands work in tandem with my mouth as I lick from the bottom to the top of his impressive manhood, circling the tip. Every hiss of breath, every moan, spurs me on. I start to move faster as I feel him growing in my mouth, but before I can do any more, he scissors off the bed and the room flips upside down.

"Oh my god!" I try to reorient myself. "What did you just do?"

"If this is happening," he whispers in my ear, his raspy

voice sending chills down my spine, "there's no way I'm coming before you."

I can't help the way my legs clench together when his teeth graze across the shell of my ear. His lips move down my throat, stopping to suck and bite the sensitive point above my collarbone that I love so much. It's almost unnerving how well he can read my body. It's like we've been doing this for years instead of mere minutes.

My back arches off the bed as he pulls one nipple into his mouth through the thin lace while his hand yanks down the fabric, exposing my other breast. He alternates sides—sucking, licking, and biting until I'm trembling.

"Oh my god." My hands find their way to the back of his head and I'm not sure if I want to push him away or pull him closer. "You're really good at this."

He doesn't stop as his deep laughter rumbles from his throat. The vibration on top of everything else is almost enough to send me over the edge.

"I'm so glad you approve." He sits back, looking down at me with those hazel eyes of his blazing. "Let's see if I can keep it up."

He watches me closely as his hands move downward, gliding over my rib cage and across my stomach until his fingers loop into my underwear. He tugs and my hips automatically lift off his bed so he can slide them off. Goose bumps trace his movements and the cool air from the air conditioner blowing above the bed causes me to shiver.

And yet, I've never felt hotter.

He throws my underwear off the end of the bed and quickly finds his place between my legs. He spreads my thighs apart, but his eyes never leave mine. I should have known this is what it would be like to share a bed with Nate. All that focus and attention he dedicates to everything he does is directed at the lucky woman he's with. His intensity outside the bedroom transfers flawlessly to his determination in it. He watches me carefully, noting every sound and movement I make. Cataloging everything I like inside that big, beautiful, infuriating mind of his.

By the time his mouth reaches the apex of my thighs, I'm so wound up that just the feel of his breath causes my legs to clench together.

"Oh no, no, no, Colls." Nate slips his arms beneath my legs and wraps his strong hands around them. I try to pull them closed, but in his grip, they don't so much as budge. "You're always hiding, always in control. But tonight? In my bed? That's not how things are going to play out. I'm going to taste you and watch you fall apart over and over again."

I tense for a moment at his words. The idea of being vulnerable in front of—and beneath—Nate scares the crap out of me. But I tried to cling to control of everything in my life for so long and fell in love with a man I thought I could trust. Where did that get me? At least with Nate, I know where he stands. His bed might be the safest place to be. I relax into the mattress and stop resisting his hold.

"Good decision."

He rewards me with the most beautiful smile I've ever seen before his head dips between my legs and his tongue finds its target on the first try. I don't even realize I try to close my legs until his grip tightens, his fingers digging into my thighs. But he doesn't miss a beat. His tongue circles the bundle of nerves, alternating between light and hard pressure. His mouth closes over my clit and every muscle in my body goes taut. My feet push into the mattress and my toes curl. I grip on to the sheets as if I'm in danger of levitating if I let go.

"Fuck. Nate. I . . ." I've lost the ability for speech, my words only going out in fragmented sentences as he pushes me closer and closer to the edge.

Goose bumps and beads of sweat cover my body as tension weaves through my veins. Whimpered moans intermingle with pleas for more. I have no idea what I'm saying. I can't think with the pressure building deep in my belly. I try to shift my legs, to get closer or move away, I don't know. But it doesn't matter because Nate's grip tightens and he pulls my legs farther apart.

I'm not sure what it says about me and I don't think I'm willing to explore it, but that show of dominance sends me soaring. He releases his hold on me as my hips surge upward and my body shakes with an orgasm so intense, it feels as if I'm being ripped apart.

I'm starting to fall back down to earth, my body finally relaxing back into the feather-top mattress, when Nate picks up speed again, this time using his newly freed hand to add fingers into the mix.

"Nate, I can't." My voice isn't recognizable even to my own ears. I try to push him away, but before I can get any leverage, orgasm number two rolls in and stops me in my tracks. "Holy . . . ohmygod."

My hands fly above me like I'm possessed. It's clear I'm not in control here. Not of Nate. Not of my body. Nothing. I pull the pillow from behind my head and use it to smother the screams I can't fight.

As the aftershocks wear off and my body stops convulsing, Nate slowly makes his way to my face. He leaves a trail of kisses in his path, something that feels much too personal and causes my chest to ache.

"That was fun." Nate looks down at me and for the first time maybe ever, I know that smug smile on his face is very well deserved. "Wanna do it again?"

I feel my eyes as they nearly pop out of my head. That was fun . . . one could say too much fun, but I can't do that again. I'm not one of those people who think women can't separate love and sex, but I'm pretty sure that sex with Nate is a drug and his mouth is more addictive than anything else I could possibly try.

I had a lot of sex with Peter, and none of it—okay, well, some of it—was bad. He did what he needed to, and the vast majority of the time, we both left feeling satisfied. But I always felt like him getting me off was more of a chore than something he enjoyed. I mean, he took care of his chore and did it effectively, but there's no comparing him to Nate.

Nate's on another planet . . . in another universe. What he just did wasn't about checking off a box on a checklist to get to the main event. Not at all. Actually, it felt like Nate got as much out of that as I did. And I got a whole lot . . . loads.

Tons.

He showed off and showed the fuck out.

Of course, however, because I am me, the competitive streak I'm a little ashamed of rears its ugly head. No way is tonight ending without Nate knowing how fantastic I am in bed too.

"Now it's my turn to play." I push him to the side and climb over him. "Where are the condoms?"

He points to the table on the side of the bed. "Top drawer, back left corner."

I don't hesitate. I open the drawer and find them just where he said. I pull two out of the box because after the warm-up, I can only imagine that there will be a round two of the main attraction.

After I roll on the condom, with expert precision, might I add, I sit back on my heels to admire my handiwork.

"Like what you see?" Nate asks.

"Don't go fishing for compliments. It's unbecoming." I try to bite back my smile, but it's useless. I'm still basking in the endorphin rush from my two orgasms. "But yes, I'm very much enjoying the view."

"You're pretty fun to look at too." His hands move to my hips and his finger draws a circle on the side of my belly. "I like this little mole. I didn't know you had it, or this one." He points to the tiny mole on the side of my breast. "Now when I see you outside, I'm going to have a lot more to think about."

To tell the truth, I'm not sure I'll ever be able to see Nate the same way again. It was one thing to know what he's packing beneath his khakis. It's another thing completely to know just how well he knows how to use it . . . and his mouth . . . and his hands for that matter.

"You and me both, sir."

I don't wait any longer. My legs are beginning to tremble again like I'm some sort of sex-crazed harlot who can't go minutes without feeling Nate on or inside me.

I grab hold of the base of his cock and climb on top. I lower myself inch by delicious inch, moaning as my body adjusts to his and takes him in. When I've reached the hilt, I sit still for a moment and allow myself to appreciate the feeling of having him inside me. I start rocking my hips back and forth, watching as Nate's eyes slam shut and he bites his bottom lip. His fingers bite into my skin to the point where it's almost painful. A part of me that's never reared its head before hopes he leaves a mark.

I start to move faster, rising up and down to an almost punishing pace. Our groans blend together, our breathing growing heavier by the second.

"Fuck, Nate!" I throw my head back, never losing a beat. "How does this feel so good?"

I thought this round was going to be only for him, that there was no possible way my body could produce another orgasm, but as the familiar pressure builds, I know I was very, very wrong.

"Christ, Colls." He groans, his voice so deep and raspy, it's almost tangible. His grip on my hips tightens and he flips me onto my back. I almost protest, but he grabs both of my hands in one of his and holds them over my head, slamming into me and effectively erasing every thought in my head. "So fucking good."

I pry my eyes open, not wanting to miss a single second of watching Nate finally lose control. Sweat drips from his forehead and the lines on his face deepen. He never slows down, his thrusts are somehow powerful, tender, and relentless, and as much as I want to watch him fall apart, my eyes slam shut as I start to come . . . again.

My vision turns white behind my eyelids and I wrap my legs around him, needing to hold on as wave after wave of pleasure rolls through me. I'm not normally loud in bed, so my screams and groans take me by surprise.

Through my fog, I notice he's released his grip on my wrists. I wrap my arms around his neck and pull his mouth to mine, holding on tight. He begins to shake over me and I swallow his groans as he finds his release and collapses on top of me. His weight is like a warm blanket I never want to climb out of.

"Wow." He breathes into my neck. His lips graze the sensitive skin I love to be kissed and his fingers play with the loose curls that escaped my ponytail. "That was . . ."

His sentence trails off, but I know what he means. There are no words for what just happened between us.

My hands glide up and down his sweat-slicked back. "Yeah, it was."

I've been with enough people in my life to know chemistry like this doesn't just happen. Tonight was special. Even though I know there's a ninety-nine percent chance I'll regret this in the light of day, right here and right now? I've never been happier.

Chapter 18

There's a reason there are no windows in nightclubs and casinos. Everything that looks so sparkly and shiny loses some of its magic beneath the light of day.

It's a mistake I've made multiple times.

You know, the guy who seemed really nice disappears without a trace before you wake up, or the hot guy you swore you were going to marry transforms into his true, douchebag form with the rising sun.

And considering my not-so-wonderful history with Nate, I fully expected the same outcome when I made the decision to lie down for just a minute after round two instead of immediately running home and trying to rid my mind of the terrible, awful, mind-blowing, amazing night with him.

I was hoping for it, honestly.

Because if Nathanial Adams isn't an asshole and his skills in bed are what ruin me for all other men, I will never forgive him.

Nate's quiet breathing is the only noise in his room other than the gentle hum of the air conditioner, and part of me is shocked I'm awake before him. He seems like the type of human who sets his alarm for four a.m. I peel my eyes open and the bright sunlight peeking through the small crack of his curtains immediately sets my nerves on edge. It was going to be hard to sneak back home in the shadows of night, but during the day? I'm going to have to climb fences and hide behind bushes to get home unnoticed.

If a Karen catches even a glimpse of me traipsing out of Nate's house before coffee, the entire neighborhood—including Ashleigh and my parents—will hear all their salacious theories of what went down. And on the list of shit I don't need right now, the neighborhood gossiping about my sex life is at the very top.

I try to climb out of his bed without disturbing him, and my body groans with reminders of all the muscles we put to work last night. I know I came over here thinking this would be a onetime thing, but I quickly begin to think of the countless benefits of doing this until I leave Ohio. If we keep this up, I'm definitely going to have to pull out my old yoga mat or at least start joining my mom on the evening walks she keeps inviting me on.

I scurry around the room trying to find all the pieces of clothing he tossed about last night. Of course, during this search, not only do I not find my underwear, but I also notice that somehow his room seems even more magnificent than it did last night. I need to leave, but I can't pass up the opportunity to inspect the black-and-white prints on his wall without him watching.

Some images I recognize right away. A young Nate smiling up at his grandparents, a cow standing by, with their sprawling farm in the background. An eight-by-ten blueprint of Great American Ball Park, the home of his favorite Cincinnati Reds, is set in a brass frame. The crinkled picture of him with his mom and dad, the only one he ever had, sits behind glass, and my heart constricts for the little boy who yearned for his family more than anything. There are new photos, too, some with people I recognize, like Nate's dad, who looks exactly the same, just a little older, and others with people I don't know. The stark contrast between the before and after, so evident, set out in front of me.

But it's when I get to the end of the wall that the floor falls from beneath my feet.

There in the corner is a four-by-six picture of Nate and me. He's in his old baseball uniform, the one that changed how I looked at him, and I'm wearing jean shorts and a tank top. He has eye black smeared across his cheeks and his gigantic smile takes over his entire face. I'm sticking my tongue out and on my tiptoes holding bunny ears behind his baseball hat. We both look so young.

So happy.

We spent so many days at the baseball field that I can't even remember when this was taken, but here it is. Proof of the love we had for each other. Framed and preserved on Nate's bedroom wall.

I give up my search for my stupid underwear and haul ass out of there. It was already going to be weird talking to him the morning after; seeing this is too much. I didn't realize how many feelings were tied up between us and I know I'm not emotionally stable enough to decipher it so soon.

I tiptoe out of his room and down the stairs, flinching when the old wood creaks beneath my feet. In a stroke of luck I'm not used to having, I see my T-shirt dangling on the back of a chair the second I make it to his foyer. I pull it over my head, ignoring the still-damp fabric, and beeline for his back door. I flip the lock at the same time I hear footsteps hit the ground above me. I pause for a millisecond, wondering if maybe I should stay and talk things out over coffee. But instead of being an adult, I do what I always do.

I run and hide—literally and figuratively—plastering my back against fences and hopping into a bush or two until I make it back to my house without anyone seeing me.

I pause at my front door and attempt to calm my breathing. After a minute, I put my key in the door and push it open, but only once I'm sure I'm not wearing an expression that screams *SKANK*. I walk inside and the outside world falls away as is only possible in my childhood home. The smell of coffee and my parents' soft voices drift from the kitchen. I have a clear shot to my room, where I could shed my clothes and hide all evidence of my night with Nate. It's an easy decision really.

But since when do I ever do the easy thing?

"Hola, parentals." I walk through the kitchen and grab what has become my LIVE, LAUGH, LOVE mug out of the cabinet. "How's your morning going?"

My dad shakes his head for an answer. I'm not sure he'll ever adjust to having a daughter who walks into the kitchen wearing yesterday's wet clothes like it's no big deal. My mom, however, loves it.

"Hey, honey." Her relieved smile is a solemn reminder of the deep worry lines she had yesterday. "Glad to see you're back to your old self. Looks like a night with the girls was exactly what you needed."

"It was a night to remember, that's for sure." I turn to the coffee pot and avoid making eye contact with my mom. Nobody can read me like Kimberly Carter and I need to change the subject before she catches on to where I really was last night. "I still can't believe you got Ruby to come back home."

"Oh, trust me, I didn't have to do anything," Mom says. "After the second day of you ignoring her calls she was already looking at flights."

"What?" My coffee splashes over the rim of my mug as I spin to face her. No way I heard that right. Ruby pledged never to return to Ohio, and she's not one to break a promise.

"I actually had to convince her to take a breath, get organized at work, and then come out. She was prepared to get on a plane four days before she got here."

"Two hotheads," Dad grumbles from behind the paper he insists on having delivered. "It's a miracle you two didn't land in more trouble growing up. Neither one of you knows how to take a breath when you're worked up. Too much alike."

"Anderson Carter. Don't you dare sit at this table and pretend you weren't checking the time on the phone and tracking Ruby's flight until the moment she landed." My mom tsks. "And besides, where do you think these two learned their hothead ways? Could it be from the boxing classes you signed them up for or all those screwball comedies you were constantly driving them to?"

Yes, it's true. My mild-mannered, retired pharmacist, current garden enthusiast of a father is one thousand percent behind my wicked ways. Whenever I told him a story about talking back to a kid at school who tried to mess me with me, he'd give me a high five behind my mom's back. Even when he worked long days, he never turned down watching movies with me. Much to my mom's displeasure, we wore dents into the couch as we bounced from Pryor to Carlin to Steve Martin to Sinbad and back again. We never watched a sitcom without each other, and when I really sit and think about it, my love of storytelling is intrinsically linked to those moments with him.

"Oh, speaking of comedies, Dad." I slide into the seat beside him. "The new script I'm writing is a sitcom. I've never tried this format before, but I think it might be pretty good. Could you look at it for me if you have a chance one day?"

Whatever my mom and dad were doing before I asked is long forgotten. They both snap their attention toward me. Their mouths are hanging open and they're staring like I admitted to robbing a freaking bank.

"Did you just ask your father to read your script?" my mom asks, sounding very suspicious. "Why? What's wrong? Are you sick?"

"Kimmy, quiet," my dad whispers, even though I'm literally sitting right next to him. "You'll scare her off before she lets me see."

"All right, all right. Very funny." I roll my eyes and push away from the table. "I know I can be a little bit secretive, but you're doing too much."

"A little secretive?" my mom repeats after me. "You asked your grandparents for a safe for Christmas so you could lock away all of your writing."

"Whatever," I singsong on my way to the kitchen to put my mug in the sink. "Laugh all you want, but you know that was a good freaking present!"

One of the best presents ever, actually, and it's still in my room.

Except now instead of protecting terrible essays and scripts that I have since burned, it houses three bags of peanut M&M'S, one pack of Sour Punch Straws, and about seven shooters from the liquor store nearby.

Their laughter fades as I take the stairs two at a time. The soreness in my legs and arms has dulled, but there's one more prominent ache between my thighs that I don't think is going any-where anytime soon.

I skip—yes, skip!—into my room and only *just* close the door when the doorbell begins to ring.

Panic stops me in my tracks as I envision countless neigh-borhood lookie-loos standing outside my house, prepped and ready to show my parents video footage of me escaping from Nate's house. A million worst-case scenarios run through my mind, one more awful than the next . . . like Nate coming to return the underwear I left somewhere in his room.

I press my ear against the door to try to gauge what's hap-pening, but instead, all I hear is the sound of footsteps running up the stairs. I hightail it to my bed and grab a book off my night-stand, trying to look as natural and unbothered as possible.

"Oh please." Ruby barges into my room with a breathless Ashleigh on her tail. "You're not tricking anybody with this casual reader bullshit."

"How dare you?" I toss the book beside me and attempt to sound affronted. "I'll have you know that I'm a very serious reader. It's a big part of my craft, thank you very much."

It's true.

A huge part of my time spent as a screenwriter has involved reading scripts and novels. It's not my fault she chose to be a lawyer where she's forced to read boring legal documents all day . . . and also get paid a bazillion dollars more than me.

I have fun. She can afford a mortgage.

Who's to say what's more important?

"You mean the craft you told me you were giving up on forever because your douchebag ex has you blacklisted from the industry you spent your entire adult life trying to break into?" She folds her arms and lifts a single eyebrow. It's her most intimidating stance and I wither beneath her bright blue stare.

"Attack much?" I give up on the good posture and my spine curls into a familiar slouch. "I thought my mom was coming in with gossip and I was trying to play it cool."

"What gossip are you so nervous about?" She's like a goddamn shark.

No wonder she makes so much money. She's told me that on top of keeping a record of her clients' outcomes, she also has a ledger where she records how many of her clients' exes she's made cry.

The number is outrageous.

"I wasn't nervous," I lie through my fucking teeth. "But a person can only hear about who didn't put money in the donation plate and whose teenager was caught vaping for so long."

"She's not wrong." Ashleigh, even in her wild-ass leggings, is a sight for sore eyes. "The gossip around here is terrible. I've been waiting for someone to fill me in on a juicy affair or a white-collar-crime scandal, but the best thing that's happened so far is Collins making a scene at an HOA meeting. But I was there so that tea's cold and stale."

"Affairs and white-collar crime?" I try not to laugh. "I'm going to need you to turn off *Real Housewives* and lower your standards. You live next door to Karen, not Erika Jayne."

Nothing exciting has happened in this neighborhood since Mrs. Richmond walked in on Mr. Richmond with another woman and chased them both out of the house wearing nothing but sheets. And that was when I was in middle school.

"I will never." Now Ashleigh has assumed the power position too. Apparently, *Housewives* is her line in the sand, and honestly? I respect it. "And why wouldn't she just give back the damn earrings? I still don't understand."

"No, I can't go back there." I spent way too much of my life scrolling through Twitter reading everyone's hot takes on Beverly Hills. I refuse to return to that dark part of my history. "But now that we've cleared all that up, do either of you want to tell me why you're at my house so early and not still sleeping off the distillery's worth of booze you both consumed last night?"

"You forgot?" Ashleigh reaches into her purse and pulls out a

T-shirt with my campaign slogan ironed on it. "Today is the Reserve's Freedom Parade and you're in it."

Fuck.

"Never mind, let's talk *Housewives* instead." I try to rewind time, but time travel is still outside my skill set.

"Too late! Time to get our favorite HOA candidate dressed and ready." Ruby is taking way too much joy out of this. Not that I'm surprised. When I told her I joined the race, she laughed for a solid five minutes straight. And then she FaceTimed me so she could laugh in my (virtual) face.

"Have I ever told you that I can't stand you?" I glare, but mine doesn't seem to affect her the same way.

"If by *can't stand* me you mean couldn't live without me, then yes." She takes the shirt from Ashleigh and shoves it in my hands before moving to my drawers to grab a pair of shorts. "And you should be so grateful to have us on your side."

The contrast between her all-American, girl-next-door beauty and her hard-as-nails personality never ceases to amaze me. I've tried to model so many of my characters after her, but I can never do her justice on paper.

"Well, obviously." I grab my outfit from her hands without even looking at the shorts she picked. "But why am I grateful today?"

For forcing me to stay true to my commitments and honor my word? I don't think so.

"Because"—Ashleigh starts to pull out eyeshadow pallet after eyeshadow pallet from her purse, which I'm starting to think is less handbag and more magician's tote—"we're going to get you all glam and perfect so when you're sitting next to Nate all day, people won't even notice him."

Any amusement I was feeling seconds ago shrivels up and dies as dread sinks its sharp claws into my throat until I can't even talk.

"Except for me." Ruby wiggles her eyebrows and shimmies her tiny hips. "You know I thought he was cute in high school, and after hearing you bitch about him these last few weeks, I'm dying to see how he's held up."

I bite my tongue so hard that I nearly draw blood. The urge to tell them both, in extreme detail, what went down last night is almost too much for me to handle. The only thing stopping me is the barrage of questions I know they'll both have and I don't have the answers to. Unless their only question is, How good is he in bed? Not only can I answer that, but I can write poems about it.

"Oh, trust me," Ashleigh says. "He's not only held up but he's gotten better with time. He has this nerdy, uptight thing going on, but it really works for him. Like, I just know that beneath it all, he's a total freak in the bedroom."

Other than a brief stint in middle school of feeling rejected and othered, I've always loved being biracial. I got the best of both worlds. Before I realized I'm not a dancer, I took both Irish step and African dance classes. We ate classic southern dishes my granny taught my dad to make and my mom makes cabbage and corned beef every Saint Patrick's Day. I'm the result of a love that crossed boundaries and continues to show what a world where differences are acknowledged and respected could look like. There are countless things to love, but at this moment, I've never been more grateful for the melanin masking the deep flush burning my cheeks.

All I have to do is roll my eyes and laugh and they'll never catch on.

"Okay! Well, you two enjoy that discussion without me," I shout out instead. "'Cause Nate. Gross. No, thank you."

I may as well have held a giant, neon-lit sign that says SHE FUCKED NATE over my head.

Ashleigh and Ruby both turn to me wearing matching expressions of curiosity and suspicion. When Ruby's posture shifts and her eyes narrow, self-preservation kicks in.

"Gotta get dressed!" I wave my clothes in front of them before speed walking out of my room and into the bathroom.

It's a temporary solution. I've been friends with Ruby for long enough to know I can't dodge her line of questioning for long, and even though my friendship with Ashleigh is on the newer side, she doesn't strike me as somebody who lets things slide. Especially juicy things like her friend sleeping with her noted mortal enemy.

Yup.

I thought I was screwed last night, but my life never fails to humble me by showing me just how fucked I can truly be.

Chapter 19

I revel in being basic.

Pumpkin spice latte? Yes, please. Uggs? I want every color. Top 40 pop songs? I have the lyrics imprinted in my brain. But my most basic quality of all is my love for holidays.

Every single one of them.

Obviously, I have my favorites. Christmas gets top marks from me. I love decorating the tree, listening to music, and I spend a solid weekend every December doing nothing but baking cookies. Plus, gift giving is my love language and I thrive searching for the perfect gifts for my friends and family. Thanksgiving is fantastic because who doesn't appreciate a holiday that's dedicated to eating until you feel like you might explode? And don't get me started on Halloween. Happiness is seeing small children and dogs shoved into costumes. I even like Valentine's Day.

When I was a kid, you couldn't tell me that the Fourth of July wasn't the pinnacle of summer. I mean, barbecue, fireworks, and swimming all in one day? What wasn't to love? But as time has gone on, this holiday has slipped down the list. Don't get me wrong, I still love an excuse to stuff my face with grilled goodness, but I'd be lying if I said the holiday hasn't gotten a little . . . weird over the years. I can't help but notice the coded language that goes into celebrating this holiday for "real Americans" and who they think that includes.

"Wow," Ruby mutters as she takes in the sea of red, white, and blue. "I forgot how patriotic middle America is."

"Isn't it so fun?" Ashleigh jumps up and down and the stars on her pom-pom headband bobble back and forth. Her stars-and-stripes leggings blend in perfectly with the scenery.

"It's . . ." I can tell Ruby is trying not to hurt Ashleigh's feelings and I'm so grateful. Ashleigh spent thirty minutes nailing the blue cat-eye eyeliner look; it would be devastating if Ruby said something that messed that up. "It's really something. You can tell they put a lot of effort into the decorations."

And by *decorations*, she means a plethora of American flags. Some small, some huge, some painted on. There's a flag for everyone. It's quite a sight to behold.

"Ughhhh," I groan. A pang of grief makes my heart ache. "I wish they could've seen Ben before Nate murdered him. He would've been a hit."

The strong showing of patriotism may be a bit alarming, but it's also the proof I need that my instincts for my campaign were right on the money.

"This is all a little too much for me." Ruby stops in her steps. "I think I'm going to go hang with Mr. and Mrs. Carter and save a good seat on the parade route. You two go on without me."

"Are you sure? My husband's around here somewhere."

Ashleigh doesn't hide her disappointment that Ruby doesn't want to hang out with us. "He has a group for his new dental practice and I'm sure there's room for you to join us."

"You're so sweet and I love that you're excited to support your husband by being a part of the parade." Ruby rests a hand on Ashleigh's shoulder before laying down the gauntlet. "But I need you to know that I'd rather die a slow, painful death than be stuck walking up and down these streets in this weather. Or any weather actually."

Welp.

If nothing else, Ruby will always be honest with you.

I pull poor, tenderhearted Ashleigh away from my crass best friend. "Don't take it personally. She's always like this."

I know Ruby won't admit it, but her dad used to take her to all the neighborhood events and she's never recovered. My dad wasn't wrong when he said we're too alike. We're both emotional avoiders, but as bad as I am, Ruby's worse.

Ruby leaves to find a place to sit in the shade and I go with Ashleigh to find Grant.

Our neighbors mill around the clubhouse parking lot, where all the cars and "floats" are lined up. There's a group of kids dressed up as George Washington. They start dancing what I think is supposed to be hip-hop when their adult plays a track from *Hamilton*. Behind them, a group consisting of all ages are rocking their karate uniforms with different color belts tied at their waists. Two of the older members hold a banner advertising the local martial arts studio I tried out the summer before fourth grade.

I wave to the Karens, who are putting the finishing touches on their old Buicks. They started entering the parade when I was in elementary school and still do it up big. A group of moms with strollers decked out in red, white, and blue gather together in matching "All American Mama" shirts. They're passing around a sparkly tumbler in a way that makes me think they aren't sharing water.

Everything is almost exactly the same as I remember, but somehow it's also totally different. New businesses unroll their banners while neighbors I don't recognize wind garland around their antennas and write on their windows. I almost feel sad as I realize how much I've missed. A melancholy settles over me when I think of the memories I missed out on because of a grudge I may have nursed for too long.

"Oh, there's Nate!" Ashleigh points in the direction of a cherry red Mustang convertible and races ahead.

Mr. Wilson is bent over the hood of the car, rubbing it with whatever cloth he always has shoved in his back pocket. He has a look of pure determination on his face, and by the way his car is sparkling, his hard work is paying off.

However, not even a shiny convertible or its shinier-headed owner could distract from the man standing beside it with his arms crossed. I try not to gawk—Kimberly has told me staring is rude enough times—but what can I say? I'm a glutton for punishment . . . and Nate.

He's traded his normal uniform of khakis and a button-up for a more casual pair of chino shorts and a T-shirt. Informal looks really good on him. He's smiling at the older woman next to him and my stomach twists into knots. I haven't had the awkward morning-after thing in years and I don't know what to do.

Spending the night with him was one thing. I went into it not wanting anything more from him, but then he had to mess around and turn out to be some kind of goddamn sex god.

So inconsiderate.

And then, after all that, I had to see that picture on his wall.

It's too much. Feelings from the past are colliding with the present and it's becoming more and more difficult to separate the two.

I manage to pull my eyes away from Nate just in time to dodge a small child in a football jersey. My face almost meets the pavement, but he doesn't even stumble.

"Sorry, ma'am!" he shouts over his shoulder and keeps running.

"Ma'am?" I gasp, never in my life more offended by seemingly good manners. "How dare you! I'm a very young twenty-nine, thank you very much!"

I mean, the nerve of children these days. I have a center part. I wear baggy jeans. I know the lyrics to Olivia Rodrigo's songs! I'm youthful and hip, dammit!

"Wow, Collins." A deep, excruciatingly familiar voice says from much too close. "Yelling at children now? I already knew you weren't going to be competition, but it's like you don't even want to win."

My nerves go haywire. I don't know what's up or what's down. The words he's saying annoy the shit out of me, but the way he says them turns me on. I haven't been this sexually confused since I was fourteen.

But on the upside, at least he's not acting weird.

Or weirder than normal.

"Oh please." I roll my eyes, grateful to know that I'll be able to throw attitude his way no matter how many orgasms he provides.

"You should really give up now. I'm worried your fragile ego will never recover when I crush you on the ballot."

"Besides crafting, what have you done? Have you even studied the bylaws? Do you understand what it really means to be HOA president?"

"Do you know what it really means to be a loser?" I regret it as soon as I say it.

However, to be fair, this is the nerdiest trash talk I've ever witnessed, let alone participated in. No matter what wicked burn I come back with, we're still arguing over the HOA. It's impossible to make this anything other than cringeworthy.

It might be a trick of the light, but I swear I see him smile before he asks, "Seriously?"

I won't dignify that with an answer. Instead, I do the mature thing: I stick out my tongue and do the loser sign.

"Okay then!" Ashleigh steps between us. I guess holding my fingers in the shape of an L is a step too far for neighborhood politics. *Noted. Ten out of ten chance I will do it again.* "Why don't we go get you two set up on the back of Mr. Wilson's convertible? I think he has a list of rules to go over before you can get in."

"That tracks," I say.

"Sounds about right," Nate says at the exact same time.

Mr. Wilson is the man from Shania Twain's "That Don't Impress Me Much." Not only did he shower his car with more love and attention than he ever showed his ex-wife, but he also didn't even seem to really notice when she ran off with another man. If the weather permits, I can always depend on seeing him washing the car in the driveway.

Something the HOA of the past has apparently ticketed him on multiple times, and which will absolutely be how I get his vote.

"Oh wow! Now, look at that." Ashleigh could not sound more delighted by our shared distaste for Mr. Wilson. She loops her arms through ours and drags us along the crowded sidewalk. "You already have so much in common. I think all you two need is some quality time together. This parade might be what you need to come together again."

My mind lives in the gutter now. There's one place and one place only where I'd like to come together with Nate, and it's definitely not riding through the streets of the Reserve at Horizon Creek with Mr. Wilson as our driver.

"Yeah, maybe you're right." I humor her despite knowing this is going to be a total shit show. "It could be fun."

I don't know what it is about Ashleigh that makes me want to go all big sister for her. She's just so sweet and innocent. I'm hardened and bitter, but she's too soft for this hard world. I want to shove her in my pocket and protect her. Oh yeah . . . but also make her participate in all my shenanigans, like excessive drinking in the afternoon and running my campaign for the HOA.

"You get to sit on the back of a car and throw candy to kids." Her excitement is so pure, it's almost contagious. "What's not fun about that?"

Well, the fact that I'm sitting next to the guy I slept with before sprinting out of his house could put a damper on things. But I've been wrong before.

Plus, if nothing else, this will be a perfect scene for my script.

Chapter 20

Life update: I was not wrong.

Trust your instincts, kids.

Not only is participating in the parade not fun, but sitting in the back of Mr. Wilson's car could be considered torture.

His list of rules is exhausting, and I'm certain I'd be better off walking. Not only are we not allowed to keep our shoes on for fear of messing with his leather interior, but we're also not allowed to have any liquids whatsoever. And yes, that includes water. It's July, and although we don't live in the desert, it's still ninety degrees and humid AF. The longer we drive, the more I'm convinced this might be the thing that takes me out for good. We also aren't allowed to make music requests, which means we've been listening to "Born in the U.S.A." for the entirety of the ride.

I get it.

Classics, musicianship, blah blah blah. This is nothing to do with Springsteen—truly, all respect for him—but I think my ears are going to start bleeding if he doesn't play something else soon.

Even Nate can't stop rubbing his temples from what I have to assume is a music-induced migraine.

"Mr. Wilson," I say through gritted teeth. "I know you said no music requests, so please consider this a light suggestion, but there are other songs that talk about the United States. Maybe you want to give one of them a listen?"

Nate's shoulder rattles against me as his body shakes with silent laughter, because he's too chicken—or polite—to speak up.

This leads to the biggest issue of all.

Mr. Wilson was so nervous my denim shorts would scratch his precious car that he laid down a blanket for us to sit on. Now, in theory, this is no big deal, but in reality? It's the fucking worst. The blanket has no grip whatsoever. I nearly toppled off the convertible thanks to the hard right turn he made a couple of blocks back. Now, strictly for safety reasons, Nate and I are so close together on the back of this stupid car that you couldn't slip a piece of paper between us.

"No suggestions either," Mr. Wilson barks, and I want to kick the back of his stupid seat. "That's the problem with you kids these days: no respect for America or music. Listen to this and be proud to be an American."

"Is it safe to assume he has no idea what this song is actually about?" Nate asks under his breath.

"One thousand percent." I grab a handful of candy and toss it to the group of small children waving to us. "I think it's safe to assume he completely lost touch with reality after his wife left him."

It's not a kind observation, but that doesn't make it any less true.

Mr. Wilson flips his turn signal, and Nate's arm automatically shoots in front of me and grabs my thigh. The feel of his fingertips against my bare skin is all the reminder my body needs to transport me back to last night. But in the light of the day, there's another element that wasn't there last night. I'm unable to look away from the way his large hand looks sprawled out against my leg. The contrast of his hand against my sun-bronzed skin. My thighs clench together, and even though it's hot as hell, goose bumps still chase his touch.

I hope Nate doesn't notice; the last thing I need is for him to be aware of how much he affects me. Of course, when I chance a look over at him, he's watching me from under hooded lids. I thought I'd feel embarrassed that he witnessed my reaction to this innocent touch, but it only takes a moment for me to see that I'm not alone. His bottom lip is pulled between his teeth and the flush covering his cheeks is much deeper than it was a few seconds ago.

"I like these shorts." His hand creeps up my thigh, never losing contact as his fingertips toy with the frayed hem of my jean shorts.

"I like yours too. Decided to ditch the khakis, I see?" My breathing becomes labored and my gaze drops to the growing bulge in his pants, which I've been studiously avoiding for the last thirty minutes. It's not easy, but I manage to look up before spectators can follow my line of sight.

"Yeah." He smirks and my stupid heart stutters in my chest. "Someone kept giving me a hard time about my wardrobe. I figured I'd try something new."

"Wow, what a bully." It's a little too breathy to give the effect I was going for, but what can you do? "You should tell them to go fuck themselves."

"Something of the sort happened last night." His fingers flex into my thigh. "I'm hoping I can relay the message again soon though. Maybe tonight even?"

I knew being around Nate wasn't going to be easy after last night, but I vastly underestimated just how hard it would be. For a second I forget the neighborhood is watching and almost launch myself at him.

Thankfully for us, we're riding with the biggest buzzkill in the neighborhood.

"Hey!" Mr. Wilson glares at us in the rearview mirror. "I'm doing my job, you two do yours. Stop the chitchat and throw the dang candy!"

"Sorry, Mr. Wilson." I grab a handful of candy and send a generous amount soaring toward the crowd. "We're on it."

Nate, the hot brownnose, lets go of his grip on my leg and begins to throw candy and wave. "Apologies, sir."

Time ceases to exist as we focus on engaging with the crowd. But by the time we approach my street, Bruce's lyrics are blending together and my cheeks ache from smiling so much.

"You know," Nate says, braving Wilson's wrath when he reaches for a couple of suckers and carefully lobs them to two kids in matching baseball hats. "Who thought it was a good idea to have us throw hard candy with sticks to small children with questionable hand-eye coordination? This seems like a huge liability problem."

"Big facts." I don't want to laugh, he's so freaking corny, but I can't help it. "These parents should have to sign a safety waiver."

Of all the adverse consequences of sleeping with Nate, allowing him to think he's funny could be the most detrimental of all.

When I signed up to run against him, I thought for sure that spending more time around him would remind me why I hated him so much. Instead, it's just bringing back all the good memories we had together. Every minute we're near each other, I find myself softening. Plus, I think because of the number of orgasms I had last night, the happy glow is lingering a little longer than I'm used to.

"Oh, and before I forget, I have something for you." His smile doesn't falter as he waves to the crowds lining the residential streets before reaching into his back pocket and putting his hand in mine. "You forgot these."

I don't know what I was expecting him to hand me, but when I look down and see my underwear in my hand, I almost fall off the car trying to shove them into my back pocket.

"Nate!" I start to yell at him, before quickly remembering where I am.

I don't mean a parade.

That's obvious.

What I mean is on my block. Two houses down from mine, to be exact.

I look in front of me and see my parents both waving like goofy maniacs, but worse than that is the way Ruby is watching.

She narrows her assessing blue stare a moment before total real-ization and understanding cross her face. Her jaw falls open and her eyes go wide.

"Collins Carter!" she shouts from the sidewalk. "Don't you even think you can avoid this!"

Oh crap.

I point to the radio and pretend like I can't hear her, but I know she doesn't buy it. All that time spent in LA and I'm still a terrible actress.

I try to keep my smile so that my parents don't notice any-thing, but as soon as they're out of view, I drop the charade.

I want to punch him, but violence is wrong and people are watching, so I use my words instead.

"You do know that I can't stand you, right?"

"You said that before, but if I'm remembering last night cor-rectly, you changed your tune real fast." He turns to me wearing that stupid smug smile and the worst thing happens.

The urge to slap it off him doesn't come.

Nope.

I want to kiss it away.

Boy oh boy, good to know he's fantastic at mindfucks too.

Even though everyone acts like time is a totally acceptable, logical thing and we use it to do just about everything in our everyday lives, it makes no sense to me.

I don't understand how it moves so fast sometimes but drags on for eternities others or how the past, present, and future are connected but there's no way to change it. Why is daylight saving time a thing? Who decided on the time zones? Why do we act like it's a totally reasonable thing to subscribe to? Same with gluten and money, but I'll save that for a different rant.

The path of the neighborhood parade is only a couple of miles and I couldn't have been sitting next to Nate for more than an hour, so why does it feel like lifetimes have passed when Mr. Wilson parks his convertible back in the parking lot where we started and I'm finally allowed to climb out?

"If I don't have water soon, I think I might literally die." I think the body can only survive three days without it and we have to have surpassed that number already.

"I don't want to call you dramatic, but . . ." Nate lets his sentence trail off and I take his sentence as a personal attack.

"Absolutely not. I reject that." I shake my head and cross my arms. "We just sat on the back of a car for an eternity and a half and weren't allowed to drink water. In no way am I the drama queen here."

Mr. Wilson will forever hold the title in this scenario and anyone who disagrees is a victim of the patriarchy.

"You're not wrong," Nate agrees, albeit reluctantly. "That was a little ridiculous."

"It was a lot ridiculous. I mean, what was the point?" I don't want to be this worked up over Mr. Wilson and a freaking neighborhood parade. I'm blaming dehydration. "Isn't freedom the reason for the season?"

"I don't think Mr. Wilson having rules for his car was a violation of your rights as an American."

"That's what someone who doesn't believe in the Declaration of Independence would say."

I'm not above an easy joke and this one is right there.

"You're such an asshole," he says, but I can tell he's trying not to laugh. "Do you know how many times I've had to tell people that I know Benjamin Franklin really existed? *National Treasure* is my favorite movie!"

Solid movie choice. I worried he became one of those guys who only watches documentaries or movies that make you hate yourself.

"All I'm hearing is you have an unhealthy obsession with Nicolas Cage and believe in conspiracy theories."

"I can't deal with you." He rolls his eyes but makes no move to put distance between us.

If anything, he might come closer. My fingertips twitch to touch him, but the curious eyes of the entire neighborhood keep my hands firmly planted at my sides. He pulls his bottom lip between his teeth and a wave of heat that has nothing to do with the weather crashes over me.

"I'm going to find water if you want to join me." I turn and walk away before he can respond. I'm afraid that if I stay in front of him for any longer, our neighbors are going to get a fireworks display they didn't sign up for.

The parking lot is even more crowded now than before the parade started. Instead of neighbors packing it in for the day and enjoying their nice, air-conditioned homes, they're filing into the clubhouse parking lot carrying a plethora of beach towels and coolers big enough to feed the entire community. Picnic blankets are being spread across the grassy areas as people claim their spots for the fireworks display set for hours from now.

PTA moms are setting up folding tables, covering them with plastic tablecloths and an unrivaled assortment of homemade goodies. I lose count of the different pies sitting atop ceramic stands and almost ditch the pursuit of water in lieu of a sugary treat.

"There's Janice." Nate points across the way to the HOA secretary, who has been rocking the same curly perm since I was in eleventh grade. "She always has a cooler for board members after events like this. I'm sure she'll share even though you're not technically a part of the HOA."

"Yet." I finish his sentence for him. "I'm not a part of the HOA yet. I'm still totally going to kick your ass."

"Sure, keep telling yourself that," he says. "I'm not sure if you're confident, delusional, or both."

"Confident, definitely confi—" I start, but stop when a voice as sugary sweet as the desserts around us calls his name.

"Nate? I thought I might find you here."

Beside me, every line in Nate's tall body goes taut and the color drains from his sun-kissed face.

I follow his eyes and even though I've only seen her face from a small framed photo on his bookshelf, I'd still know that this is the kind of woman Nate was engaged to. She seemed tiny in the picture, but she's even smaller in person. Her cream skin doesn't have a blemish or wrinkle anywhere on her face. With her long blond hair, wide eyes, and delicate features, she looks like a Barbie doll come to life.

Elizabeth's eyes are trained on Nate and she doesn't seem to notice anyone else around us. She shifts back and forth on her heels and nervously bites her bottom lip. It's obvious to anyone watching this scene play out that it took a lot of courage to come and say hello. If I didn't know who she was or what she did to Nate, I might feel bad for her.

But I do know, so all I see in the pint-sized blonde is a whole lot of nerve.

"Nate," she says his name again. "Please, I'm so sorry."

My palm itches to slap her back into whatever hole she climbed out of, but no matter what happened between Nate and me last night, I know this isn't my battle to fight.

The fun-loving, happy-go-lucky guy who was waving to the entire neighborhood is long gone. Frown lines I didn't even know he had deepen around his mouth, which only moments ago was laughing and smiling. He watches her from hardened eyes, and pressure builds in my chest as I watch.

"What do you want, Elizabeth?"

Her features crumble as nosy onlookers watch the scene unfold. I'm sure half of them know exactly who she is and why she's here. I can't decide if she's brave or cocky.

"I made a mistake." Her voice thickens and sympathy I don't want to have builds within me when I realize she's about to cry . . . at a Fourth of July parade. "I wish I could take it back, but I can't."

I try to walk away, but it's like the rubber soles of my shoes have melted and melded me to the spot. I keep thinking of running away this morning and wondering if that was my only opportunity to figure things out with Nate. Did I blow my chance at something I didn't even know I wanted?

It's selfish. This woman could've been the love of his life and I want nothing more than for him to send her on her way.

"You're right." Nate's gentle voice barely carries above the crowd. "You can't take it back."

"But—" Her voice cracks and the tears I suspected begin to fall, leaving trails of smeared mascara in their wake.

As a person who has lived with the ramification of crying in public, the part of my heart that's not completely black hurts for her. Plus, at the end of the day, when I had my scene with Peter, I was leaving a piece of total fucking garbage with no redeeming qualities. I can't imagine having Nate's ring on my finger, a beautiful life laid at my feet, and completely fumbling the bag.

It's tragic.

"Do you know what it was like moving all of my furniture into the house I thought we were going to grow old in together? I thought we had our future planned out. Look at me! I joined the freaking HOA." He lets out a humorless laugh and rakes his fingers through his hair.

The crowd around us gives up on pretending to be discreet and are openly gawking now. It's a sensation I remember all too well, and even though I still have no idea what's going on between us, I can't let Nate go through it alone. I finally become unstuck and move to his side, taking his hand in mine and offering him a small reminder that he's not alone.

Elizabeth's wet gaze drifts to our hands and her mouth falls open in surprise when she finally notices me.

"Oh. I . . . I didn't know." She forces a smile and swipes away the falling tears. "I'm sorry."

I glue myself to Nate's side and his grip tightens like a vise, but I don't even flinch.

"You don't need to be sorry," Nate says to her, and I swear I can hear his heart pounding through his shirt. "It wasn't until very recently that someone made me realize that we weren't right for each other. You weren't wrong to walk away."

The hushed whispers around us come to a sudden halt and the world tips on its axis. I don't know if Elizabeth is still here or if Nate is even talking.

I can only hear one thing playing on a loop in my head. *Someone* made him realize they weren't right for each other. And for some reason I can't explain, I have a sneaking suspicion that that someone is me.

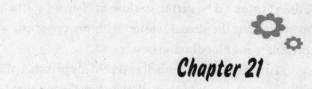

Chapter 21

*I*n case you didn't know, someone's ex-fiancée showing up at the end of a neighborhood parade creates quite the commotion and makes it easy for the person they slept with the night before to make a clean escape.

I know the neighborhood gossip machine is going to be in full force in no time, but I'm hoping Elizabeth's presence outshined the portion where I clung to Nate. The second he let my hand go, I forgot all about my quest for water and took off for Ashleigh's house.

Before the parade, we all agreed her house would be the meet-up point so we could debrief and begin preparations for the final HOA meeting, where Nate and I will state our cases. It's a month away and all I have prepared is a kick-ass motto and a plan to bring doughnuts. We really need to get to work.

Plus, Ashleigh got a panini maker in the mail as a late wedding gift and she promised we could take that bad boy for a spin. As far as incentives go, paninis are high on the list.

Unfortunately for me, when we made these plans this morning, I didn't think I'd be sitting so close to Nate for the neighborhood to see or that the sexual tension with my opponent would be so evident to my bloodhound best friend.

I ring Ashleigh's doorbell and hold my breath. I'm still shaken from seeing Nate and Elizabeth together; I'm not sure I can handle an all-out Ruby assault. Since Ruby watched the parade with my mom, I'm hoping she has held Ruby hostage and is making her tell the Karens all about her illustrious career as a bigwig lawyer in sunny California. If I'm lucky, Mom will keep her occupied until I'm able to have a glass of wine and calm my nerves before she confronts me.

"You had sex with Nate!" Ruby screams before the door's all the way open.

I'm not that lucky.

"Ruby!" I look over my shoulder to make sure none of the nosy neighbors are within hearing distance before I shove her back inside Ashleigh's house. "Can you not? You know how fast gossip spreads around here."

I slam the door behind me just in time to see Ashleigh enter this hellish equation.

"You slept with Nate?" She screams so loud, the windows rattle. "I knew it! I knew you liked him!"

"Whoa whoa whoa. Calm your horses there, cowgirl. Liking him is a stretch, but I'm not hating him as much if that's what you mean."

This is one of the million reasons I didn't want to tell anyone.

I knew they'd read into it when it's no big deal. They're acting like this thing between me and Nate is a full-length novel when it's really just an Instagram caption.

"Seriously, Collins?" Ruby steps in front of me and cuts off access to the kitchen. "The entire reason I'm out here is because you shut me out and you're already doing it again?"

I feel my temper starting to rise and it's an unfamiliar sensation directed at Ruby. We laugh and listen and support each other, but I can't remember the last time we fought.

"I'm not shutting you out, there's just nothing to talk about. You were both saying how I needed to loosen up all night long and I listened." I shoulder past her, needing this conversation to be over, but also wanting my panini. "End of story."

"Not the end of story!" She grabs my wrist and pulls me back. "You're either lying to me or to yourself. This isn't some one-night stand and you know I'm right."

"You know, I got a lot of different cheeses for the paninis. Maybe we should go sit in the kitchen and choose our sandwiches," Ashleigh says in an attempt to defuse the situation.

As far as distractions go, a plethora of cheeses is probably the best technique I've ever come across. But it's still not enough.

"I'm not lying and I don't know why you think I am." My voice begins to rise and I hate it. This is not what I wanted. "You're making this into something way bigger than it needs to be. Nate and I are both adults; we've had flings before."

"Collins." Ruby levels me with a stare that causes my heart to fall to my feet, and I know what she's going to say before she says it. "You know Nathanial Adams isn't some other guy. You don't hate someone the way you've hated him unless you're really hiding some hurt and love deep down. Trust me. I see it every day at work."

"God. You're so fucking annoying." I groan because I know I've lost. "I really wish you would've gone into corporate law and taught me tax evasion or something. That would've been much more useful than this."

"You don't think that as a divorce attorney I don't know all the tricks in the book to avoid taxes and hide money? I could tell you everything, but you don't make enough money for tax evasion." She cuts me to the quick and turns to Ashleigh. "Now, you? Your husband's a dentist. I can help you out."

"Ummm . . ." Ashleigh's eyes shift between me and Ruby, confusion written all over her blemish-free face. "Thanks?"

Poor Ashleigh. I'm sure she's experiencing vertigo-like symptoms dealing with the two of us. This also clears up why Ruby was my only friend until we went to different colleges. I love us, but even I know we're a little obnoxious when we're together.

"Ignore her and show me the panini press." I loop my arm around Ashleigh's and pull her toward the kitchen. "I was watching a cooking show that said the key to a good panini is lots of butter. So once you two literally butter me up, I'll spill all of the details of my night with Nate."

"Are you two not fighting anymore?" Ashleigh asks.

"That little thing?" I wave my hand like I'm swatting her question away. "That wasn't a fight. That was just Ruby knowing me better than I know myself." I lean in closer and whisper, "I'm not sure if you've noticed this about me or not, but I'm a little stubborn."

"She's a pain in the ass," Ruby singsongs beside us. "But don't worry, Ash, I'll give you all my tips to deal with her before I head back to Cali. Usually, food does the trick, so you're already ahead of the curve."

"You two are wild," she says, but it lacks any venom. "I'm into it though."

"Girl, with all these crazy-ass leggings you always have on"—Ruby points at the star-spangled spandex Ashleigh is still wearing—"wild is the only thing you should expect to invite into your life."

I look at Ruby with wide eyes, trying to tell her to shut up with my eyes. I know how proud of this new "business" Ashleigh is and I don't want to hurt her feelings. Plus, this is a massive step up from the oils. The product might be ugly, but at least the leggings people aren't turning their customers into anti-vaxxers . . . or at least I hope they aren't.

Ashleigh looks down at her legs and stares at them in silence for a few seconds.

"Crap." Her shoulders sag and she lets out a deep sigh. "They are ugly, aren't they?"

"Yeah, honey." Ruby nods. "They're atrocious."

It might not be the moment for it, but I can't help it. I laugh and I laugh hard. It's not long before Ashleigh and Ruby join in. We double over, holding on to one another as we wipe away our tears and try to pull it together long enough to stuff our faces with cheese.

. . . .

And then I snuck out of his back door and clung to fence lines and hid in bushes until I made it home." I pop the last bite of my ham, apple, and brie panini in my mouth and take a second to decide if I want another one. "I really think sandwiches are one of the most underrated foods. There's nothing better than a good grilled sandwich."

I expect them to agree with me, but when I look up from my freshly polished plate, they're just staring at me with their mouths hanging open, and their paninis have barely been touched.

"Did you both forget how to eat?" I point toward their plates. "It's not going to be as good if you wait until it's cold."

Neither of them makes a move for their plate and it feels like an insult to the perfect, crispy yet melty masterpieces we spent so much time crafting.

When Ashleigh said she had lots of cheese to choose from, what she really meant is that she bought out the entire cheese section at the grocery store. I've never seen that much cheese in one person's house before. When she told us she had planned on using the leftovers to build cheese boards and host a leggings party, we broke into hysterics all over again.

"Forget about the panini and backtrack for a minute," Ruby says. "He has a framed picture of you in his room?"

"And he . . . you . . ." Ashleigh squeezes her eyes shut and struggles to regain her composure. She's as red as Mr. Wilson's convertible. "How many times did you say again?"

"He has a lot of framed photos in his room." I correct her because the logistics of this story feel very important. "But yeah, there's one tiny picture in the corner that was of the two of us the summer before high school. We were at one of those baseball tournaments we always took him to. It's probably nothing though. I bet it's a placeholder. And for how many times"—I shift my attention to Ashleigh—"do you mean how many times did we have sex or how many orgasms did he give me?"

"I mean . . . I guess both?" Ashleigh reaches for the glass of wine she poured herself when I started talking in detail. Apparently, her group of friends isn't as vivid with their words as I am. "Only if you're comfortable sharing again. I don't want to pressure you into saying something you don't want to."

"Speak for yourself," Ruby cuts in. "I absolutely want to pressure her into saying it all. I'm only here for so long. I can't go home knowing my best friend held out on me. Plus, Collins is a natural-born oversharer. It's bad for her health for her to hold it in."

This is very true.

My dad says my chatty ways come directly from my mom. My mom says it's my dad. He vehemently denies being long-winded, but he has lost entire plots by focusing on details like what vegetable he was grabbing from the produce section when some guy tried to fight him.

I, however, don't credit either one of them for my talkative ways. Being an oversharer is one of the main character flaws of being a writer. I often find the smallest details the most interesting and I love to paint a picture with my words. Even if they make nice, suburban housewives squirm in their seats.

"Okay, so we had sex twice, and for the orgasms . . ." I shut my eyes and start ticking my fingers trying to give an accurate count. "I think five? But that could be wrong."

"So probably only four?" Ruby makes a reasonable assumption.

"I was thinking off in the other direction. It might have been more like six or seven." It feels obscene to say out loud, but I don't even care.

It was glorious to experience.

"And we're still talking about Nathanial Adams, right?" Ashleigh asks. "The man who sold me my house, wears sweater-vests in June, and is on the HOA board? That Nate?"

"The very same," I confirm, my toes curling in my shoes just thinking about him.

"I'm impressed and I'm glad you had that, but . . ." Ruby pushes her sandwich to the side and directs all her focus on me. "I think I'm going to have to be the buzzkill here."

I knew this was coming and not in a bad way. When I'm being shortsighted about anything, I can count on Ruby being there to walk me through things. While I'm focused on the small details, she forces me to zoom out and view the whole picture.

"Okay, I'm ready." I grab my wineglass and hold it close in case I need a sip. "Shoot."

"You know I'm a proponent of having fun and doing what makes you happy. Whether that means a relationship, safe sex with multiple partners, or no sex at all, I think you should do what feels right," she says. I already know this and I'm not sure if this is a reminder for me or her. "But no matter what, I think you need to go into it with your eyes open."

I spin the crystal stem between my fingers but don't drink it yet. "I totally agree."

"I think if you want casual and fun sex, then you need to find someone other than Nate." She rushes out the last words and lands the plane.

I knew it was coming, but it's still a punch in the gut when I hear it out loud. And I haven't even filled them in on Elizabeth yet.

"Okay, I hear you." I take a deep gulp of wine and motion her on. "Now tell me why."

"Because you care about him," she says, simple and easy. Like it's the most obvious thing in the entire world. "And after seeing the way he was watching you on the back of that Mustang, I think he might have some hidden feelings for you too."

"I knew it!" Ashleigh is living her best, know-it-all life right now, and I'm not sure I appreciate it. "I swear, it only took me—I don't know, five minutes to see that beneath all the ridiculous jabs, you two really just wanted to rip each other's clothes off. You're like little kids at the playground."

"Am not." I pout, glaring at the two jerks in front of me.

Then I glare harder when they start to laugh.

"Okay, sure." Ashleigh looks at Ruby with an expression that says *can you believe this girl* written across her face. "Way to prove us wrong."

It's not easy, but I resist the urge to stick my tongue out at them.

"Fine, whatever. So my grudge is a little childish. Who cares?" I stand up and start pacing. The grilled cheese I happily inhaled is starting to feel like a pile of rocks in my gut. "Obviously we're into each other sexually, but I still think you saying he cares about me is a little loaded."

I ignore the way his hand clung to mine when he was talking to Elizabeth and the way she tried to mask her heartbreak when she saw the two of us together. This is just supposed to be fun and wild, a way to fill my time while I'm stuck here. Nothing more.

Not even if it was the best sex of my life . . .

"This is why I don't think it's a good idea." Ruby finally picks up her sandwich and takes another bite. "You're still so stuck in the past that you can't see this clearly. I have my theories about what went down between the two of you in school, but I really think you need answers before you two can have any kind of relationship outside of being HOA weirdos."

"One, you're rude." It's meant as an insult, but she glows like I complimented her. "Two, and I will only tell you both this if you promise not to freak out." I pause and lift my pinkies in the air. They link theirs with mine and we perform the sacred ceremony that is the pinky swear. "Nate invited me over again tonight. I wasn't going to go, but now I don't know. Do you think I should go?"

When I went over to his house it was under the premise that it could be a one-and-done. But that was before I knew about the picture. Before Elizabeth showed up. Before I admitted to myself that there's a possibility I might—deep down—be harboring some not totally negative feelings toward him.

"You're going," Ashleigh says without missing a beat.

"Yeah, duh." Ruby rolls her big blue eyes. "I don't even understand why you'd frame this as a question."

I don't know why I expected them to at least pretend to contemplate their answers. I wasn't even planning on sharing this little tidbit of information. I really only told them because I'm starting to realize that being up front with them saves me a lot of time and energy in the long run. Plus, maybe they're right and I do need answers.

It's terrible, but the hard truth is that I do have a heart and feelings. And since I am nearing thirty, it might finally be time to start acknowledging my hurt instead of pretending it never happened.

Leave it to Ruby and Ashleigh to completely flip my life upside down.

"Fine," I grumble and sit back down. "But if I'm going to go looking for answers, then I'm going to probably need another panini."

Some people go for liquid courage, but I find courage in carbs and cheese.

To each their own.

Ashleigh fires up the panini maker and I pull out all the cheese from the fridge. The conversation moves away from me and we try to come up with ways for Ashleigh to unload her legging inventory. This might not have been how I expected my day to go, but I wouldn't change a minute of it.

Somehow, nestled in this small Ohio suburb, I'm figuring out exactly what it means to be happy and feel loved.

Who would've thought?

Chapter 22

After paninis and an impromptu leggings fashion show—Ruby ended up buying four pairs, by the way—I head home with a full belly and an even fuller brain.

"Collins?" my mom shouts from somewhere in the house as soon as I walk in. "Is that you?"

I kick off my shoes and hang my purse on the hook next to the door. "Nope, it's a burglar."

With the way she refuses to ever lock the front door, I very well could be. I've sent her approximately a hundred true crime articles emphasizing the importance of locking your door and not making yourself an easy target, but she always laughs off my worries instead.

"Oh, don't be ridiculous," she says, and even though I can't see her, I know she's rolling her eyes. It's not a mystery where I get some of my mannerisms from. "Come help me in the kitchen."

I was already heading in that direction, and when I walk in, my heart squeezes at the familiar sight. Almost every cabinet and drawer in the kitchen is wide open. She's standing in front of a counter covered with a plethora of ingredients I doubt she even needs. In a mystery I'll never solve, flour is scattered all over her arms and throughout her hair, yet her apron is spotless. Dad's sitting in his recliner in the living room and *Jeopardy!* is playing on the TV.

"Oh! I know this one!" My mom shouts like if she's loud enough, the contestants can hear her. "What is Manarola, Italy?"

I haven't watched the trivia show since I moved out. It's a jarring sign of time passed to see the new host in Alex Trebek's place. He confirms my mom's random but extensive geography knowledge.

"Impressive!" I lift my hand in the air, forgetting about her flour-covered state until she slaps my hand and a puff of powder explodes around us.

"Thank you very much." She points to the folded apron in the open drawer by the fridge. "But come on and help me out, will ya?"

I don't hesitate to take her up on that offer. She's a chaotic baker, but we always have so much fun in the kitchen. Plus, added bonus, the results aren't always a total disaster.

"What are we making this time?" I look at all the ingredients on the counter, but I can't figure it out.

"Lemon cake." She lifts up a bowl of liquid I'm guessing is lemon juice. "I almost did a strawberry shortcake, but then I got a hankering for cream cheese frosting and had to pivot."

"A hankering?" I laugh. "What a wild word choice."

I wish I had my phone to add it to the list of words I have saved in my notes. Every time I hear a word that I don't think is used enough, I add it to the list and keep it nearby when I'm writing scripts. *Hankering* is definitely list-worthy.

She smirks and hands me a spatula. "I thought you'd like that one."

Beyond all the Bible apps on her phone, once I told her about my list, she downloaded a word-of-the-day app. She tries to weave them into our conversations or texts every day—some with more success than others. Let's just say there's no way to drop *anthropomorphic* into casual conversation.

My mom straightens her glasses and props her phone in front of her as she reads the recipe. We fall into a comfortable rhythm with her measuring the ingredients while I pour and take charge of the mint-green KitchenAid she got last Christmas.

She checks on the cream cheese to make sure it's at an acceptable frosting temperature as I begin to distribute the batter to the pans evenly.

"Four layers?" My hands stay steady as I hold the heavy bowl. When I was a kid, she was strictly a sheet cake and cupcake girlie. "Your cake-making skills are getting better and better."

"Oh no. Definitely not four layers. I tried that once before and it looked like the Leaning Tower of Pisa after I frosted it." She laughs at the memory. "We're making two cakes. One for us and one for Nate. I've been thinking of him since he stopped by that day, and then seeing you two in the parade, I thought this would be nice. Remember how much he liked those lemonade cupcakes I used to make?"

I forget the task at hand and stare at her. This has to be a joke, right?

"Did Ruby call you?" Maybe she snuck off to give my mom a heads-up when I was trying on the hamburger leggings.

"What? No. Why would she call me?" She takes off her reading glasses and focuses her attention on me. "Keep pouring. We need to wash the bowl so I can make the frosting in it."

I resume my cake job, but my mind is still racing. What are the chances that tonight, of all nights, my mom randomly decides to send me marching to Nate's house? I don't know if I want to laugh or break out into a cold sweat. Even though I grew up in a very Christian home, I'm still figuring out what I believe. But right at this moment, I'd be lying if I said it didn't feel like some outside force was pushing me toward the khaki-wearing man down the street.

After we put the cakes in the oven, my mom settles in on her spot on the couch to watch the legal drama my parents have been streaming and I head upstairs. Everything in my mind feels scrambled. Each time I think I have some kind of plan, something else happens that leaves me feeling like I don't know what's up or down. It's almost as if the constant whiplash of the last few months is just now beginning to hit me. I'm always on edge, waiting for the next shoe to drop.

I sit down on my bed and open my computer because if there's one thing that always grounds me, it's writing.

I chose my career because I love storytelling. I love sitting in front of the television and letting the rest of the world fall away as I'm transported into the lives of the characters on my screen for thirty minutes. Having the opportunity to create something that could provide someone else with an escape was all I ever wanted. But, like many people living the constant hustle and trying to find their path in the glitz and glamour of Los Angeles, I became more obsessed with being successful than I was with the work.

I had a vision board next to my bed so it was the first thing I saw when I woke up. It was filled with all the typical "girl boss" quotes. There were pictures of designer bags and houses in the hills, all the crap that would prove to anyone who saw me that I was somebody. I was worth their time and attention. But in chasing the things that, when I really think about it, I don't even want, I lost the reason I started writing in the first place. I stopped writing what called to me and began writing what I thought the market wanted.

Writing became a chore instead of what I loved to do.

I'm not at the point where I can look back at what happened and laugh—that's going to take a while. But as I sit on my childhood bed and open my computer, I can feel grateful that the joy and peace I feel as I tap away on my keyboard has returned.

The stress of what could be and conversations to be had falls away as I lose myself in my script. My main character is arguing with her opponent in front of an elementary school as small children abandon their kickball and games of tag to watch two adults fight. I work *hankering* into Nate's . . . I mean Jack's dialogue and my laughter rings loud inside my quiet bedroom.

"What are you laughing about?" My dad sticks his head into my room.

I look up from my computer and set it to the side to wave him in.

"My new script. It's loosely based on me running against Nate for the HOA crap." It sounds just as ridiculous now as it did when I decided to run.

"I still can't believe you're doing it." His long legs make quick work of my room. He sits down next to me and looks comically large on my tiny bed. "All of my friends are voting for you, you know. I brag about you all the time so they were sold the second they heard your name."

"Thanks, Dad." I bump my shoulder against his. "One more thing to add to all the reasons you're the best."

He looks down at me with that gentle smile of his. The small creases next to his eyes are the only sign of aging on his handsome face, other than the white strands of hair in his beard. Where my mom is loud and over the top showing her love for me, my dad is quieter. It's in every glance, his love always shining in his dark brown eyes. It's in the way he squeezes my shoulder every time he walks past me and how he laughs at all my jokes, even when they're not funny. It's in him mentioning my name in every room he steps in and being proud of me when I'm not proud of myself. It's the way his strength cloaks me in comfort and safety anytime I'm in his presence.

"Well, you make it easy to brag," he says.

"Okay, sure." I scoff because I most definitely do not. The embarrassment that's always lurking beneath the surface rears its ugly head again. "Nothing says brag-worthy like being jobless and living with my parents."

"We love having you here. Obviously, we wish you were able to come home with better circumstances, but your mom and I are ecstatic that you're back." His voice has an edge that wasn't there before and there's a fire burning in his eyes. "My garden would be dead without your help, and Mom's cakes might be edible tonight thanks to you. This retirement thing wasn't as easy as I thought it was going to be; you coming home has made it so much better. I felt like I missed out on so much of your childhood because I was always working. Spending time with you in the garden, even watching those ridiculous shows with the women screaming at one another, has made me feel so much closer to you."

See?

He's the best.

"Have I told you how much I love you?"

He wraps his long arm around me and pulls me into his side, kissing the top of my head. "You have, but I wouldn't mind you saying it again."

"I love you loads."

"Love you loads too. Now"—he pushes off my bed and his knees crack under his weight—"come get this cake from your mom, bring it to that boy, and figure out whatever happened between the two of you."

I start to cough, choking on air. "What?"

"Oh, come on, Colls. Anyone with semi-decent vision who saw the two of you sitting all close on the back of that car could see that there's something between you." He rolls his eyes and shakes his head. "I'm your dad. I knew you two liked each other when you were kids. I kept my mouth shut, but I never liked Peter. Knew it wouldn't last. Nate's a good guy, always has been. I've been waiting years for you two to figure your crap out. Never thought it'd be because of the HOA, but I'll take what I can get, I guess."

I stare at him with my mouth agape. I never knew any of this!

"I didn't know you didn't like Peter!" I start with the easiest part. "You could've told me that, I don't know . . . before he screwed me over."

My parents were my first call after I found out what Peter did. Looking back, I guess they did seem pretty unsurprised when I told them what he had done.

"Collins," he says my name like it explains everything, and I hate it, because it does.

"Fine." I fall back onto my pillow and pout. "I wouldn't have listened, but still. A heads-up next time would be nice."

"Well, if you get out of bed and bring Nate this darn cake, I won't have to, now, will I?" He extends his hand and pulls me up when I grab on.

"Sheesh." I straighten out my clothes and smooth down the curls at the back of my head as I follow him out of my room. "You're feisty."

Because he's used to me and my mom's tendency to lean a bit on the dramatic side, he doesn't so much as grunt to acknowledge that I spoke.

We reach the bottom of the stairs at the same time my mom is walking out of the kitchen holding a beautifully frosted cake atop a yellow ceramic cake stand. She's walking so slow and careful, it looks like she's on a tightrope instead of our oak floors.

"Oh!" She smiles huge when she sees us. "Perfect timing."

I slip on my shoes before taking the cake from her.

"This looks really great." I don't mean to sound so surprised, but not only did I experience her dreadful baking firsthand, there are hundreds of pictures documenting how bad she was at decorating them. "I'm really impressed."

"Well, you know what they say, practice makes perfect." She brushes her hands together after successfully handing the cake off to me. "Now, you be careful walking to Nate's house. I don't want to be dramatic or anything, but if you drop this, I will disown you."

"Real nice, Mom." I know she's joking, but my fingers still tighten around the cool ceramic just in case.

My parents are my last resort—I can't get kicked out of Ohio too.

My dad opens the door for me and they both say-shout their goodbyes to my back. I focus on the step in front of me, my arms starting to burn a little from how tense I am. But even though I'd blame the cake to anyone who asked, I know the real reason I'm so nervous has nothing to do with holding the cake and everything to do with its recipient.

When I reach the bottom of his walkway, I close my eyes and take a deep breath.

I'm coming bearing gifts and he extended an invitation, but for some reason I'm more nervous than I was when I crashed his party and when I turned up in the middle of the night.

Maybe because this time I have expectations and worse— hope.

But even knowing how quickly those things can turn on me,

I don't turn and run—and not just because my mom might kill me if I do.

No, I keep going because everyone is right.

I've tried to hate him for years, but I can't do it anymore.

I might not like the answer, but it's time for me to find out what happened all those years ago.

Chapter 23

*T*he front door opens before I can ring the doorbell.

"You came." His hair is damp and he's wearing gray sweat-pants sitting low on his hips, but nothing can distract me from the nervous smile on his face. "I'm so sorry about Elizabeth. I had no idea she'd be there."

"You don't need to apologize. I could tell she surprised you." My fingers flex around the cake stand and I'm suddenly grateful my mom gave me something to hold on to. My heart pounds in my chest as lost memories of the man in front of me fight their way to the surface. Feelings I've denied for so long become more and more undeniable as the fortress I've been hiding behind crumbles. "Are you okay?"

"I'm better now," he says. "I was worried she scared you away for good."

After the night we spent together, I'm not sure anything could scare me off. It was that good.

"My mom and I made you a cake," I offer instead of blurting

out one of the millions of thoughts bouncing around in my head. "It's lemon."

His eyes go soft and I nearly melt into a puddle in front of him. "I love lemon."

He steps back and gestures for me to come inside. I don't hesitate.

I step into the foyer and welcome the cool breeze of the air conditioning. My stomach flips and my skin buzzes as nerves and anticipation collide. Sweat forms on the back of my neck as I follow him into the kitchen.

"You can set it anywhere." He points to the sparkling granite countertops on his kitchen island. "It looks amazing."

He's the picture of casual, yet I can see how tightly wound he is in the way he moves. For some perverse reason, the thought that he might be feeling as nervous as I am sets me at ease.

"My mom did most of it, but I was an excellent sous chef." My hands feel empty without the weight of the cake in them. My palms itch to reach out and touch Nate, but I don't. I'm loath to admit it, but Ruby's right. I have too many feelings for this to go forward without figuring things out between us first.

"Should we have a piece now or wait until later?" He doesn't wait for my answer before he opens a drawer and pulls out a cake cutter. Because of course he has a cake cutter. "I have ice cream in the freezer. I know you love your sweets as much as you love your cheese."

It's true and it's why cheesecake is the ultimate dessert, but I'd never say no to cake and ice cream. The fact that he remembers that about me makes everything that much sweeter.

"Sugar topped with sugar? How could I refuse?" I settle onto the same stool I sat on after I crashed the HOA meeting. "Although, I'm not sure if you remember or not, but Kimberly's baking is hit-or-miss."

"How could I ever forget? Do you remember those brownies she made us?" His eyes sparkle as he puts giant slices of cake on our plates. "Sometimes I think I can still taste them in my mouth. It's like the unsweetened cocoa powder haunts my taste buds."

I didn't remember those brownies.

Not until now.

It was our freshman year of high school. We'd been studying for a geometry test all week. Nate got an A, I got a C, and I was pissed. But in my defense, shapes aren't math and I will die on that hill. I was on the verge of tears all day. To this day, I hate the feeling of not quite getting something—feeling like I'm missing what others understand so easily.

Because Nate knew how much I loved sweets, he called my mom and asked her if she could surprise me after school. When we got home, a tray of brownies was sitting on the kitchen counter. He and my mom high-fived like total dorks before we cheers'd our brownies together. We held eye contact as we took matching, giant bites—and watched each other's faces change from excitement to disgust as we raced to the trash can.

Dad ended up bringing home Dairy Queen.

When I went to sleep that night, my stomach ached not from the fail brownies and ice cream, but from laughing so hard with my best friend.

It's bittersweet, remembering the good times but knowing how abruptly they came to an end. Pain intertwines with happiness and something breaks free inside me. The fear of what I might hear dissipates and an overwhelming need to understand what happened between us comes over me. I have to know how we went from best friends to enemies.

"What happened?" I ask.

"What do you mean?" Nate looks up from the carton of ice cream he fished out from the bottom of his freezer. His confused expression flickers from me to the plates to his counter. "Did I drop something?"

A kinder person might be more delicate in their approach to this sensitive and long-overdue conversation, but I can't. I know that if I wait or dance around the question, I'll never ask. I might not be some shrinking violet afraid of making others upset, but I am a person who constantly felt on the outside of everything.

As writers, we're taught that all our characters have a story they're telling themselves. Something that they believe with all their heart, even if it's not true. Some characters may feel like they are unlovable while others believe that love makes you weak. It's up to us as writers to figure out this story and show how it's affecting their life. But even though I would consider myself pretty damn good at doing this for my characters, I'm only just now seeing that I've been ignoring mine for years. This belief that I'm not good enough, that I don't belong, and that nobody will ever choose me has been haunting me all along.

Nate abandoning me, and choosing the popular kids over me,

reinforced everything that I already knew to be true. It triggered every ounce of self-loathing I had percolating through my hormonal, awkward teenage body, and I hated him for it.

And in my hurt, as the main character in my own story, I never once thought about what he could've been going through. It was so much easier to be angry than it was to be sad that I never once thought to ask him why he walked away.

Until now.

"You dropped me." Blood rushes through my ears like Niagara Falls. "You left for the summer and then we never talked again. What happened? What did I do to make you leave me like that?"

I'm not sure I've ever felt so vulnerable. I've spent my entire adult life masking my anxiety and fears with humor to try to avoid looking weak. Allowing Nate to see me like this, knowing he's hurt me before, is terrifying.

"Fuck." He drops the ice cream scooper and runs his fingers through his hair. "I knew we were going to have to talk about this one day."

My instincts to walk it back, tell him we don't have to talk about it, light up like the fireworks that have been setting the sky ablaze all night.

I hold firm.

"If we're going to move forward, then yes. I need to know." My voice holds steady, but beneath the counter, I'm pinching my leg so hard it may leave a bruise. "If we don't talk about it, I'll always think you're going to walk away again."

I had prepared myself for his immediate response to be defensive. That's what mine would be. But when he nods and his hazel eyes look at me with nothing but understanding shining through, I'm reminded once more of why losing him hurt so damn much.

"I know." He slides the plate in front of me and walks around the island to take a seat beside me. "I need you to remember that I was a kid. I know we thought we knew everything back then, but I was so young and stupid. I had no idea how to express what I was going through."

I'm afraid to look at him. I keep my eyes trained on the plate and nod, hoping he'll keep talking.

"I don't know how much you remember about that summer," he says, and I keep quiet, not wanting to tell him that I remember every single thing. The plans before he left, the unanswered calls while he was gone, feeling as if he'd plunged a knife through my heart when I saw him back at school holding Rachel Shroder's hand. "I told you I was going to see my grandparents but I lied. That was the summer I stayed with my mom."

All the air in my body leaves me in a sudden whoosh.

"What?" I gasp.

"Yeah." He nods. "I can't remember if I ever told you that she still called sometimes. A few times a year I'd get a present in the mail with a letter telling me how much she missed me or that she wanted me to come visit."

"You never told me that." I'm nervous to speak, afraid I'll say the wrong thing and cause him to shut down. "I'm sorry I wasn't there for you more or if I ever made you feel like you couldn't talk to me."

"There's nothing to be sorry for. Seriously, you and your family did more for me than anyone else in my life." He reaches beneath the counter and takes my hand in his. "If I'm honest, I loved your mom so much that sometimes I felt ashamed of myself. Like I was betraying my mom for wishing she could be someone else.

"With her, it was always empty promises. I think I stopped believing she'd ever follow through when I was nine or ten. But that summer . . . that summer was different." He takes a deep breath and part of me wonders if he's ever told anyone this before. "Before the end of the school year, she called and told me my grandparents had given her money to buy a plane ticket for me to see her in New York and I'd be staying with her instead. I wanted to tell you, but to be honest, until I saw her waiting for me at the airport, I didn't think she'd follow through."

Millions of questions race through my mind, but I can tell he needs to say this without any interruptions. I tighten my hand in his, hoping it relays at least a small bit of how much I care.

"When I got there, she was so excited to see me. She couldn't stop hugging me or telling everyone we passed on the street that I was her son. She had all these huge plans for us too. We were going to go see a Yankees game, check out Times Square, take a boat to see the Statue of Liberty. She told me about this little Italian restaurant down the street from her apartment that had the best chicken Parmesan in the entire city." He takes a deep breath and all my muscles go taut. "But most of all, she couldn't wait for me to come to some little theater off-Broadway to see the show she was starring in. She was so proud, she kept telling me it was finally going to be her big break."

The air turns static as pieces to a puzzle I didn't know existed begin to fall into place.

"The first week was so great that I almost called you and told you everything. Her place was small and a little junky, but in a New York City way I thought was cool. She walked me around her neighborhood and introduced me to all of her neighbors. I ate so many hot dogs that I almost threw up my second or third night there." He smiles a bit at the memory. "I hated Times Square, but she insisted that I'd like it one day. She'd keep telling me I'd been in Ohio for too long, that I needed to expand my horizons if I wanted a real future.

"The second week was when things started going downhill." He leans forward on the stool, and all I want to do is wrap my arms around him. "I was tired of tagging along with her to rehearsals. I was a teenage boy who liked baseball and math; musicals weren't my thing. I tried to seem enthusiastic because I could tell that's what she wanted, but she saw through it until she gave in and let me stay at her place alone.

"The first night she came home with pizza. I remember that. I was worried she was mad at me, but when she got home she seemed fine. She taught me how to eat New York–style pizza and we watched some movies from the eighties that she loved. But the next night, she didn't come home."

"Nate—" I don't know what to say. My heart breaks thinking of him all alone in that junky New York apartment.

"She came back the next morning with bagels and coffee," he

says. "She told me I'd love the coffee. It was black, too strong, and it burned my tongue. But I drank it all. I didn't want to hurt her feelings and make her disappear again."

I, an almost-thirty-year-old woman, can't stomach black coffee. I can't believe an adult would push a fifteen-year-old kid to drink it. But I guess considering this was the same woman who left her son all alone in a strange apartment, nothing should surprise me.

"For the next few days, it was a crapshoot if she'd come home or not. The groceries she had stocked up were starting to run out and I was lying to my grandparents more and more about how things were going. It wasn't great, but it was only for a month and I thought I could tough it out."

The story already has me so angry that I can't imagine it could get worse, but somehow I know he's barely scratched the surface. I want to tell him that he doesn't have to tell me the rest, that I understand and we can move on, but something is telling me he needs to get this out as much as I need to hear it.

"One night, I can't remember how long I'd been there, she got home really late. I was sleeping, but I guess she lost her key or something so she just started banging on the door, yelling at me to let her in. As soon as the door opened, it was like someone hit me over the head with a bottle of whiskey." His voice is flat as he stares unseeing straight ahead. "She stumbled inside and the smell of alcohol filled the entire apartment. When I tried to get her to lie down, she started screaming at me. Telling me that getting pregnant ruined her life. She said my dad was the worst mistake of her life. How he tried to trap her in Ohio to keep her small like him and I was just like him, pulling her down, and it was a mistake to have me visit her. She said she should be a star and it was everyone else's fault that she wasn't."

It's hard to breathe.

My first year in LA, I bruised two ribs.

I became friends with this girl in my dorms whose cousin was a stunt double. Her cousin had just landed a role as a stunt double in a major action film and invited us to train with her one day. I was eighteen and an idiot who didn't think anything bad would ever happen to me. So when her cousin asked if we wanted to learn how to look as if we were getting hit with a baseball bat, my dumb ass didn't think twice. Of course she accidentally hit me. Because I never did the whole team sports thing, I'd never gotten a serious injury before. I'll never forget how painful it was to do something as simple and necessary as breathing. I vowed I'd never do something stupid like that again.

Yet, here I am, sitting in Nate's kitchen, feeling as if shards of glass are tearing me apart every time I inhale.

"I waited until after she passed out to call my grandparents. They bought me a train ticket back to Ohio the next day," he says quietly. "The train ride was almost twenty hours and I don't remember much of it, but the one thing I remember vividly is how fast the sadness morphed into anger. I spent the next two weeks at my grandparents' farm and my mom didn't call me. Not once."

The urge to track the woman down and beat the living daylights out of her is almost too much to handle. I can't imagine anyone treating anyone that way, but your own son? It's unfathomable.

"I'm so sorry." It's not enough, but it's all I have. There aren't any words to make what he went through any less terrible. "But I'm still not sure I understand why you didn't tell me any of this."

"I know it's not fair, but I was mad at you." His grip tightens and he prevents me from pulling my hand away. "I spent all that time alone on the train and then two weeks with my grandparents just stewing on everything. I was pissed, but my grandma kept telling me how I only get one mom and although she may not be perfect, I had to love her anyways."

"You know that's not true, right?" I'm still not sure how this is going to end, but I won't be able to leave here unless I know he's created healthy boundaries in his life. "You don't have to accept anyone hurting you. Even your mom."

It might not be a popular opinion, but I'm of the firm belief that nobody is deserving of space in your life if they only cause harm.

"I know that now, but I didn't then and I needed my anger to go somewhere. And you know what they say." He pauses and takes a deep breath before looking at me. "You hurt the people closest to you. For me, that was you."

He's getting closer to the answers I wanted, but now I don't know if I want to hear them anymore.

"Nate—" I try to stop him, but he keeps talking.

"You were still texting and calling every day. You'd record those ridiculous three-minute voicemails you used to leave all the time." He rolls his eyes and I decide this isn't the time to inform him that I still leave those voicemails. Ruby's voicemail box is always full because of them. "You'd tell me about what shows you were watching and about the book you were reading. Those were fine, but then you'd complain about how your parents were driving you crazy. Or you'd talk about how you ran into someone from school that you hated and how you couldn't wait to move to LA."

"Oh fuck." Realization finally dawns on me. Guilt that I didn't expect to feel hits me like a freaking dump truck, which is fitting because boy oh boy do I feel like trash. "I'm so sorry. I didn't know. I—"

He cuts me off again.

"Don't apologize. You didn't know, and even if you did, you were allowed to complain about your parents. I'm pretty sure that's your job as a teenager," he says. "And looking back, I don't think you could've done anything right. I was so embarrassed, my ego wouldn't have let me tell you anyways. But also, everything my mom said penetrated deep. I knew you wanted to move to LA and I figured it was only a matter of time before you left me just like she did."

And I did.

I close my eyes and fight back tears on the verge of falling. Not only did we lose out on so many years together, but in trying to protect ourselves, we confirmed everything we already feared. That we weren't good enough or deserving . . . when in actuality, we were both.

I understand why he stopped talking to me, but I still have a couple of questions that I need answered.

"Why were you all of a sudden best friends with the football jocks? And why, out of all the people in our school, did you have to date Rachel?" The football guys I kind of understood. They were assholes, but they were funny. Plus, the quarterback's parents were loaded and they were always taking him and his friends on vacations. But Rachel? She was a bitch and Nate hated her. She made my life a living hell in middle school and even as an adult, I can't think of one redeeming quality about her.

When I saw them holding hands in school together for the first time, I almost threw up.

"Because I knew you hated them. I knew if you saw me with them, you wouldn't ask questions I didn't want to answer. You'd think I changed and you'd be pissed, but you'd stop trying to figure out what happened." He says it like it's the most obvious thing in the world. "Plus, they were safe. They were too into themselves to notice if something was wrong with me, and I knew they weren't going to up and leave me. They were happy living in Ohio and you resented it. If it makes you feel better, though, Rachel never stopped being awful and I was miserable when we dated."

"That does make me feel a little better." I try to smile, but I don't do a great job.

Neither one of us says anything and a heavy silence settles around us.

Years of questions, years of anger, and after one conversation, it's all gone. I've walked with this lingering fear not only that I could lose anyone at any time, but that it was only a matter of time before I pushed them away. Until this moment, I didn't realize how heavily this has weighed on me. I see him with a new set of eyes and appreciate the man he's become more than I could've ever imagined. All the feelings I've been suppressing for so long flood to the surface. I want to pull him into my arms and make up for all the years we lost . . . all night long.

After what feels like an eternity but is probably only a minute or two, I slice my fork through the piece of cake sitting next to a melted puddle of ice cream, and take a bite.

"It's pretty good." The tart lemon and cream cheese frosting is the perfect combination. "Try it."

Instead of cutting his piece, he reaches across and cuts into mine. His eyes light up when he chews.

"I was afraid you were messing with me," he says. "This is great. I'll have to swing by and thank your mom. I mean, if that's okay with you."

I put the fork down and twist my body so I'm facing him on the stool. I rest one hand on top of his leg and the other on his shoulder, unable to hold back from touching him any longer.

"That's more than okay with me," I say with total sincerity. "Maybe you could come over for dinner tomorrow? I think they'd really like it. I know I would."

His shoulders fall, and when he smiles, I can feel it between my thighs. "You would?"

This time, I decide not to answer.

Not with words at least. I wrap my arms around his neck and pull his mouth to mine. And with his lips pressed against mine, I realize that I don't hate Ohio at all.

In fact, I think I like it here . . .

Maybe even love it.

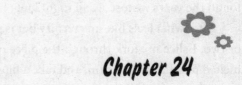

Chapter 24

*T*o say my mom was happy to have Nate sitting at her dining room table again is perhaps the understatement of the century.

For her, it was like the president (a good one), the pope, and Oprah came to dinner.

Except better.

Because the president is married, the pope can't marry, and Oprah won't marry. With Nate, however? There's a chance. And that small sliver of hope is all my mom needed to go from one dinner to whispering in my ear every chance she got about what a nice boy Nate is and how cute we look together. Something, it's important to note, she did not do once when I was dating Peter.

But while I might give her a hard time about her constant meddling and her overboard love of Nate, I'd be lying if I said I wasn't loving being around him too. After we laid everything out in the open, it was like we were right back to being young again. Except this time Nate has his own house and we kiss.

Oh yeah . . .

And there's also the sex. So. Much. Sex.

Let's just say the first night was not a fluke. In fact, I'd venture to say it keeps getting better. If that's even possible. I feel like I've been walking on sunshine for the last two weeks. Which is much better than what I'm doing right now, which feels like I'm literally walking on the surface of the sun.

"I don't understand why you're still running," Ruby complains beneath the brim of the giant hat protecting her skin from the sun as we canvass the neighborhood. "Weren't you only doing it to spite Nate? What's the point now that you don't hate each other?"

I can't lie. After Nate and I made up, I did consider dropping out of the HOA race for a second. But then I started thinking about how fun it would be to force him to call me president and it reinvigorated me all over again. Plus—and I will deny this if asked—I've really enjoyed getting to know my neighbors and feeling like an important part of the community.

Ohio is doing weird things to me.

"You know how competitive I am. You don't think I'm going to tap out because I let Nate tap in, do you? I'm not quitting this thing no matter what happens." I take one of the flyers we made from Ashleigh. "Also, how are you still here? Don't you have to go back to LA soon?"

I know she said she'd stay, but I didn't think she meant it. I figured she'd be on the first flight out of here as soon as she knew I was okay, but it turns out I'm not the only one who secretly missed being home. She checked out of her hotel and has been splitting her time between my house and Ashleigh's. She still hasn't seen her dad, but that's a topic for another day. Or maybe another century.

"I told you I have a lot of time off and I can do work on my computer." She slaps one of the "Vote for Collins" magnets we made the other night on the side of the mailbox we pass. "Plus, now that I've invested so much of my time and energy into this campaign, it would be a waste if I missed the final debate."

"Well, I for one am glad you're still running and that Ruby's still in town," Ashleigh chimes in. She's wearing her favorite pair of wedges and is the only one of us who hasn't complained about her feet hurting. "I've been having fun preparing for the debate. Plus, do you remember that makeup party I went to the other night?"

"We remember." Ruby and I have been talking her down from becoming a lipstick rep all week. I've never seen anyone so into MLMs in my entire life. I think Ruby and I might have to stage an intervention.

"Anyways"—Ashleigh rolls her eyes and Ruby laughs—"I forgot to tell you that I met this woman named Vanessa who lives over on Wabash. I guess one of her neighbors is friends with Angela and the other one is an older woman who goes on walks with Nate. Apparently news of you and Nate is the topic of the neighborhood. She said she's never been to an HOA meeting before, but she's coming this week just to see you and Nate."

I wish this was news to me, but it isn't. There's been so much interest in the upcoming meeting that we had to move it from inside the clubhouse to outside so we could accommodate more people.

"I know." I try to sound irritated but don't succeed. "My mom told the Karens about me and Nate when she saw them at church. I can't confirm this, but I'm pretty sure they have a phone tree in place for good gossip."

It wasn't even an hour after they left Bible study that Nate's phone started lighting up with texts and Facebook messages asking if we were together. I can't help but be impressed with the efficiency of their wicked ways.

Also, if I'm being honest, a part of me is thrilled to have the news out. Sneaking around was fun for a second and I'm glad we had time to figure things out without the nosy gaze of the neighborhood bearing down on us, but getting to parade him around outside is even better.

There was a reason Nate was my best friend for so long, and he has slid seamlessly back into my life. We have so much fun together, and I haven't smiled or laughed this much in forever. I don't want to hide or limit that. I want to go on morning walks with him and go on dates. Plus, there is also the fun added bonus of rubbing it in Angela's bitchy face.

"Yeah." Ruby nods. "My mom called me to ask about you and Nate and she moved out of the Reserve five years ago. She's very happy for you, by the way. Said she always thought you two would've made a cute couple."

"I love your mom. Tell her I said thanks." Dr. Amanda Dunlap, formerly Peterson, is smart, funny, and even though she raised Ruby, still very sweet. After news broke about Mr. Peterson's affair, she checked out for a little while, but I think that's to be expected. She moved to Denver a few years ago for a new job, and from what Ruby's told me, she's thriving. "Maybe we could all take a trip to Denver and visit her one day. Does your one cousin still live there?"

Ruby's family isn't very big, but her mom's cousin and his daughter came to visit a few times when we were younger and I always really liked her.

"Brynn?" Ruby asks. "Yeah, I think she owns a bar or something? I'm not sure. I'll have to ask my mom."

We stay on the sidewalk, stuffing mailboxes with flyers and magnets. We pass houses for sale and I try to bite back my giddy smile seeing Nate's face on the signs that still have wiggle eyes plastered onto them. We greet our neighbors and make small talk as we pass by. Like a good candidate, I tell everyone why I'm running—well, I leave out the part about spite and pettiness—and how I hope as HOA president to make it less about rules and fines and more about living in a community where we care and treat one another with respect.

"Okay, I have to tap out now," Ruby says when we reach the end of the block. "I have a video conference in an hour and I need to take a shower. Plus my feet hurt and I don't want to do this anymore."

We've been out here for almost two hours. She's lasted about an hour and a half longer than I thought she would. Of course, while I'm all sweaty and the size of my bun has doubled from humidity since we've been out here, she looks like a dewy supermodel ready to step on set for a photo shoot.

It's rude.

"I think I'm going to go with her." Ashleigh hands me the

small stack of flyers we still have left. "I found a new recipe I want to make for dinner and have to run to the store. You and Nate are welcome to join us if you want."

When I dated Peter, we never had any couple friends . . . or single friends for that matter. Ruby lived on the other side of town, and with LA traffic, she might as well have been living in Texas. When we did manage to get together, Peter never tagged along. I see now that it wasn't so much that he knew Ruby hated him—which she did—but that he didn't care to put in the effort to do anything that didn't directly benefit him.

Becoming friends with Ashleigh, and by proxy Grant, has made me realize how empty my life really was in LA. I worked, came home, and worked some more. I squeezed in time for people when I could, but it wasn't often. I was too busy struggling to write the next big hit to do anything else. Now I have friends, family, I'm writing a script that I love, and I get to kiss a really cute man while I'm at it. I think this is what people are talking about when they say they want balance.

"Let me ask him, but that sounds fun," I say. "Even if he can't go, I'll be there."

It's too hot for hugs, so we wave as we go our separate ways. I flip through the remaining flyers to gauge how much longer I'm going to have to be out in these streets. Canvassing with friends is much more fun than doing it alone.

I turn the corner to the next street and immediately run into another FOR SALE sign with Nate's face—with googly eyes still intact—on it. This time, though, there's an OPEN HOUSE sign right next to it that causes me to hesitate.

He's working. It'd probably be best to keep walking and send him a quick text wishing him luck. Or I could go inside and watch his butt as he gives me a tour of the house I don't have the desire or funds to buy.

Obviously, I choose option two.

It's later in the afternoon. Other than Nate's Buick—which I still give him a hard time over—there aren't any cars parked outside and I hope I'm catching him alone. I assume I can walk in so I push the front door open without knocking. I'm immediately greeted by the smell of freshly baked cookies and spotless wood floors gleaming beneath the sunlight pouring in from every opened window.

"Hello," Nate calls from somewhere inside the house when the door closes behind me.

"Hello!" I call after him, following the sound of his voice.

I'm walking through the living room when he rounds the corner and causes my steps to falter.

"Hey. I thought that was your voice." His eyes are soft and his smile is gentle as he closes the space separating us, touching his lips to mine when he reaches me. "What are you doing here?"

His sleeves are rolled up to his elbows, exposing his forearms, and his hair is mussed as if he's been running his hand through it all day. I think it's my first time seeing him wear a tie and I'm surprised at how into it I am. He looks so freaking hot it takes me a minute to focus long enough to answer.

"I was handing out flyers and saw your open house sign." I wrap my arms around his neck and pull his mouth to mine once more. "Thought I'd come in and see you in action."

"That's nice of you, but I think you might've overestimated the action part of real estate."

"Maybe," I say. "But I still want to see the house. Pretend that I'm a potential buyer and show me around."

He looks hesitant for a second, but he gives in immediately when I stick out my bottom lip.

Sucker.

"Fine, I'll give you a tour." He shakes his head and smiles down at me. "But this means you're going to have to let me read the script you've been working on one day."

After what happened with Peter, not only did I think I'd never write again, but I knew there was no way I'd ever feel comfortable sharing my work with anyone. But for some reason, when Nate asks, I don't think twice.

"Deal." I extend my hand and he envelops it with his large one. "Now, let's start upstairs and work our way down."

Because if he's going to tell me about this twenty-five-hundred-square-foot craftsman, I want to begin the tour by watching his butt climb the stairs.

And that's the house," he says when we step back into the kitchen with custom-made cabinets, soft-close drawers, and quartz counters. "As you can see, it's a steal of a deal and will be the perfect choice for you and your family. I'm sure little Suzie and Sally will love it here."

Halfway through the tour, I stopped being me and turned

into Debra, wife and mom of two looking for the perfect home for me and my family. Nate showcased the Jack and Jill bathrooms and the bedroom closets, which have enough space for all the toys now, but will transition flawlessly to their teen years. He highlighted all the storage in the master bedroom and the custom window coverings that not only look wonderful but will save on my energy bill. By the time he finished, I caught myself trying to figure out how I could afford this house.

"I know you're going to think I'm being sarcastic." I grab one of the chocolate chip cookies off the tray on the counter. "But you're really freaking good at your job and I think it turned me on a little bit."

"Okay." He rolls his eyes and laughs even though I'm being dead serious.

Obviously I think Nate is very attractive, but now it's crystal clear why all the women in the neighborhood are so obsessed with him. While he walked them through their houses and sold them on a dream, he became tangled in the fantasies of their perfect suburban lives.

"I don't know why you're laughing." I push the tray to the side and hop on top of the counters he described as indestructible. "I just watched your ass for twenty minutes as you waxed poetic about storage, counter space, and energy-saving appliances. That tour was practically X-rated. If you started an OnlyFans page giving house tours, I bet you'd make a fortune."

I grab his tie and twist it around my fist, pulling him closer to me. He pushes into the counter and I wrap my legs around his hips, pinning him close to me.

"Oh really. You liked that?" His eyes darken as they watch my lips.

"Yes," I whisper as I scoot forward, feeling the bulge in his pants as it begins to strain against the zipper. "But there is one thing you didn't tell me about this kitchen."

My voice is breathy and my hands are trembling. I've never been more aware of an unlocked door and opened windows before, while at the same time, I couldn't care less.

He's so close that I can feel the whisper of his breath against my lips. "What didn't I tell you?"

I struggle to keep my eyes open as my back arches and my breasts brush against his chest. "You didn't tell me what it would be like if someone were to bend me over this counter."

"That's because that's not something I can tell you." He sucks in air through his teeth, his hazel eyes never once looking away from me as he presses his groin into my center. "That's something I have to show you."

Before I even know what's happening, I've lost the little bit of control I thought I had.

His mouth is on mine, his kiss hard and demanding as his tongue tangles with mine. He moves his hands up my back until they're cradling the back of my head, and he lays me down ever so gently against the hard stone.

I let go of my hold on his tie as he straightens above me and looks down at me spread out across the countertop for him.

"Fuck, Collins," his gruff voice whispers in the silence of the house. "You're so fucking beautiful. I can't believe you're in front of me right now."

One of my more problematic traits is that I always have something to say. Some people might argue that I say too much. But right now, staring at Nate as the cool tile seeps through my thin cotton tee, I couldn't string a sentence together if my life depended on it. All I want in this moment is to feel his hands on me.

To feel him inside me.

And luckily for me, Nate knows what I want without my having to say it.

His hands graze across my torso and hook into the waistband of my shorts and underwear. His eyes never leave mine as he pulls them off in one quick downward motion. The cold quartz against my bare skin shoots chills up my spine before Nate's warm hands are splayed across my hips. I clench on the edge of the counter as he tosses my legs over his shoulders and bends down so his face is level with the counter.

My breath lodges in my throat as anticipation makes my toes curl.

In the recesses of my mind, I know there's a very real possibility of someone walking in on us. It should be enough to tell him to stop, and that we can pick this up at his house in a few hours.

But when his mouth latches on to my center I lose all ability for rational thought. And when he pushes a finger inside me, moving it in perfect rhythm with his tongue, I do nothing but feel. He begins to move faster, his mouth more urgent as his finger finds the spot deep inside me.

"Yes." My hands find his head and I hold him to me as I rock my pelvis forward. "Please don't stop."

He says something in response, but I don't hear it. I feel it, the vibration of his voice pushing me over the edge as the sudden orgasm crashes over me. Wave after wave of pleasure rushes through me. Nate's mouth never leaves me. I try to catch my breath as I ride it out and I can feel him in every inch of my body.

Once I've come down, he kisses his way up my stomach until he looks down at me with a small smile pulling on the corner of his mouth. "That was fun."

"It was," I agree. "But it's not over yet, is it?"

"Greedy." He laughs and touches his mouth to mine. "But I don't bring condoms to work, so we might have to wait until later to finish this party."

As good as Nate is with his mouth, he's the anomaly who's just as wonderful without it. And while I love a good appetizer as much as the next person, I want the main course. I could wait until later. I wouldn't like it, but I don't think it would kill me. I just really, really don't want to wait.

With anyone else, I wouldn't even consider taking this step so soon after sleeping together, but add it to the list of reasons why this thing between Nate and me is so weird. We might have changed the status of our relationship a couple of weeks ago, but time feels irrelevant with him. Besides Ruby, he probably knows more about me than anyone. I trust him to keep me safe, physically and emotionally.

"After I realized Peter wasn't shit and couldn't be trusted, I went and got tested," I blurt out. There's really no tactful way to have this conversation . . . especially with my pants off in a stranger's house. "I got a clean bill of health and I have an IUD. If you're comfortable without a condom, so am I."

"I'm comfortable," he says, fire lighting his hazel eyes. "I've always used condoms and my last screening was all clear."

Wow.

Look at us being all spontaneous and responsible at the same time. Safe, fantastic sex at its finest.

"Then what are you waiting for, Adams?" I wrap my legs around him and pull him close. "I don't know much about open houses, but I'm guessing it's safe to assume we don't have all day."

Nate is a perfectionist in everything he does, and this extends into the bedroom. He takes his time and he does it right. Very, very right.

So when he looks down at me with a glint in his eyes and says, "Hold on," I'm not sure what to expect.

I tighten my grip on the poor counters that we've defiled as he positions my legs around his back.

Then I see stars.

He slams into me, rough and fast but with the same control and finesse he has when we're in his bedroom with all the time in the world. I moan as I struggle to hold on to the quartz growing slippery beneath my palms.

"Oh. My. God," I breathe out between powerful thrusts as embers in my belly start to spark.

"Yes, Colls. That's it," he groans, moving his hand between my legs, his thumb rolling over me without slowing down or missing a beat. "Give it to me."

My coiled muscles spring to life and explode, the sheer force of it knocking my breath out of me. I scream out, but no sound comes out as time ceases to exist and the world turns white. Somewhere in the distance, I hear Nate's moan as buries himself deep inside me and finds his release. He falls on top of me, his damp forehead resting on my shoulder. I wrap my arms around him, trying my hardest to cling to this moment as we both float back down to earth.

I lie there, appreciating the feel of his weight on top of me as my breathing begins to slow. The world around me drifts back into view and everything seems a little brighter, more sparkly. The man I thought I couldn't stand is actually the man who brought me back to life. It might not be fate, but even I have to admit how truly serendipitous this is.

"That was . . ." He pauses and searches to find the right word. "That was indescribable. You are indescribable."

"You're not so bad yourself." I keep my thoughts on serendipity to myself. Even though I could lie beneath him for the rest of the day, I remember that time is of the essence. "I should probably get dressed though. I can only imagine what your Yelp review would look like if the owners walked in on us like this."

His deep chuckle causes my thighs to clench all over again, and I have to push him off me before I demand round two.

I run to the bathroom, and when I come back, he's finishing up cleaning the counters.

"So I'm thinking," he says as he tucks the cleaning supplies underneath the sink. "How do you feel about going on a date this weekend?"

Butterflies wreak havoc in my stomach and a smile I don't even attempt to fight causes my cheeks to hurt. A real date with Nate Adams?

"Yes, please." I don't even attempt to play it cool. I mean, we just had sex in a stranger's kitchen. Playing it cool at this point doesn't exist.

"Good." He walks around the counter and pulls me into him for a kiss just in time for us to hear the front door open.

My eyes go wide. We got lucky in more ways than one.

"Okay, so . . . yeah." I stumble over my words as a young couple and their toddler walk into the kitchen. "Bye!"

Well, one thing's clear: Nate may know more about real estate than I do, but I didn't overestimate the action.

Not even a little bit.

Chapter 25

*N*athanial Thomas Adams!" I slap his shoulder when I finally realize where he's taking me. "Are you freaking kidding me?"

The Ohio State Fair spreads out in front of us and childlike giddiness bubbles inside me like a shaken pop. I start bouncing in the passenger seat of his—very nice—Buick as I'm inundated with memories of summer days spent wandering these fairgrounds.

"You're excited?" He looks at me out of the corner of his eyes as he navigates the crowded parking lot.

"Again I ask, are you freaking kidding me?" I look at him with my best *duh* expression before I start slapping his shoulder all over again. "Fried food, a petting zoo, rides that may or may not be up to code? What's not to be excited about? I fucking love the fair!"

I went to Disneyland a few times when I lived in LA, but it's just not comparable. Don't get me wrong, Disneyland is wonderful. There's a castle and the parade is dope, but it's too shiny for me. Everything is overpriced and the lines are a hundred hours long. I like my rides with a little bit of dust and rust, like stepping onto the ride is daredevil enough.

A lot of my tastes turned LA while I lived there—yes, I will fight you for a good coffee and I paid an exorbitant amount for avocado toast—but my love for sketchy-ass fairs will never fade. I can't wait to tell Ruby—she's going to be so jealous.

"Good." He lets out a sigh of relief. "I remembered the summer I went to visit my mom, we were supposed to go to Kings Island when I got back. This was as close as I could get for the time being."

I was already excited, but my heart melts into a tiny little love puddle when I hear him say that.

"You can't take me to the fair and be sweet," I say. "It's too much. I can only handle a certain level of awesomeness before my head explodes."

Which is probably why I stayed with Peter for as long as I did. He never even came close to approaching that line.

"Okay." He laughs. "I'll try my hardest, but I can't make any promises. I have been told that I'm pretty awesome before."

"I both doubt that completely and believe it wholeheartedly." I unbuckle my seat belt after he pulls into a parking spot not too far from the main entrance. "You, sir, are a walking contradiction. But as luck would have it, I'm super into it."

"Says the person running for HOA president even though she claims to hate the neighborhood and is afraid of heights but loves roller coasters."

"I don't know what you're talking about." I shrug, tucking my hand in his as we walk up to the front gate. "All of those things make perfect sense."

He rolls his eyes but doesn't argue. He either sees the logic in my statement or—more likely—knows I will argue about this for the rest of my life and he's better off dropping it.

I walk in the direction of the long line leading into the fair when Nate tightens his grip on mine and pulls me to the side.

"I bought tickets online." He shows me the tickets on his phone. "We don't have to wait in line."

Holy crap.

Is this what it's like to date an organized, responsible adult? Someone is always prepared and you're not rushing around, trying to do things last minute?

The date has barely begun and it's already my best date ever.

I look down my nose at all the couples waiting in line, judging the Joe Schmoes who didn't think ahead like Nate did as we walk past them and the fair opens up in front of us. Who needs the pearly gates of heaven when this is accessible on earth?

We walk past the giant cardinal statue at the entrance and into the crowds milling around. Game booths and food trucks line each side of the pathway leading deeper into the fair. Picnic tables are scattered about and filled with adults and children eating giant corn dogs and trying to lick their ice cream cones before they melt all over them.

We make it to the end of the path and reach our first fork in the road. Rides sit to the left of us while more food trucks are straight ahead and the arenas are on the right.

"What do you want to do first?" Nate lets me take the lead. "If I remember correctly, you had some kind of schedule you used to make us stick to."

It sounds a little unhinged when he says it like that, but it's true. There's an art to getting optimal enjoyment out of a fair. If you start with food, you end up with your head in the toilet when you move to rides. If you start with the arena shows, your legs get all tired, and then you need to inhale sugar, which will also disrupt the rides.

It's science.

"Thank you for remembering. I do take my fair agenda very seriously," I say with total sincerity. "We need to see what the show schedule is, but the general outline is rides first, then food, then a show, back to rides, and grab a final treat on the way out."

If I had this level of focus and discipline in any other area of my life, I could run the world. But as it stands, I run the fair and that's good enough for me.

After we settle on the lumberjack show and petting zoo, we head to the rides. Nate pulls me to the ticket booth and we each get a wristband so we can ride as many rides as we want to.

Peter took me to the Creative Arts Emmys one year. I bought a new fancy dress and had my hair and makeup professionally done. It was a fantastic date night.

It doesn't hold a candle to this.

I don't know what day of the fair it is, but the lines to the rides aren't too long. Nate follows me from ride to ride as I zigzag my way through the most dangerous-looking ones first.

"Oh my god! Do you remember that ride?" I grab Nate's hand and point to the Gravitron. "It's the one where you stand in front of the board and as it spins around, you're suctioned to the wall and it moves up and down."

It was my favorite ride as a kid. It felt like magic as I climbed upside down while my cheeks were being pushed to my ears. I'm not sure my adult body will handle it as well, but I'm willing to give it a try.

"Is that the one we went on with your dad and he ended up sitting on a bench with a warm pop for the rest of the day?"

I laugh remembering the way my poor dad came off the ride looking so pale, he was almost the same shade as me. He couldn't even speak; it was like he'd witnessed war and not just gone on a ride with his daughter and her friend.

"Yup, that's the one." After that day, the only ride he'd ever get on with me was the Ferris wheel and the very occasional go on the Tilt-A-Whirl. My mom, on the other hand, loves a ride as much as I do. I might have to come back again with her. "Do you think you can handle it or are you going to pull an Anderson Carter?"

"My goal is to live as closely as possible to Anderson Carter in just about every aspect of life," he says, looking down at me with a knowing smirk. "But I think I'm going to stray a little on this one."

Even though we've moved past most of our issues, when he

says that, I can't help the wave of annoyance that rushes over me. If he admires my dad so much, how was he so quick to issue the HOA fine that launched a thousand wars? I don't want to be the one who causes this truly perfect date to go sideways, but as we stand in line and wait for our turn, I can't stop thinking about it.

"Can I ask you something?"

Worry creases his forehead, but he still nods. "Of course. You can ask me anything."

"The HOA fine." I take a breath and think about how to ask my question. I don't want him to become defensive. "If you love my dad so much, why did you issue the fine?"

Since Ashleigh tends to lean a little—a lot—more on the gentle side of things, Ruby has taken full control of debate prep. She's a goddamn monster and has forced me to read the bylaws more times than anyone should ever have to read HOA bylaws in their entire life. It's cruel and unusual punishment, but the masochist can't get enough of it.

But in repeating the bylaws to Ruby word for word and answering mock questions, I know that there was nothing wrong with my dad's landscaping. Since the tree that was already there was knocked down by an act of God, he didn't need to submit plans for approval from the HOA to replace it.

"I forgot about that." His shoulders relax and a mischievous smile tugs on the corners of his mouth. "There was never a fine."

The screams coming from the surrounding rides fade away as my focus narrows on the man in front of me. "What do you mean there was never a fine?"

"I typed up the letter at home," he says. "I was soaking wet and pissed because you sprayed me with the hose. I had things nice and organized and then you waltz back in, turning my life upside down all over again. As soon as I saw you outside of Cool Beans, I knew I wasn't over you. It was like no time had passed and all of the growth I'd done since high school flew out the window. I tried to think of something I could do to you that would convince you to leave, but I knew you'd brush it off. But your parents? *That* you'd take seriously. The joke was on me though. I thought you'd leave. I never expected you to show up at that damn meeting. I almost threw up when you stood up and announced you were running."

I try to glare.

I want to be pissed that I might end up being the president of the HOA because Nate printed a letter in his home office.

But instead, I laugh. "You're an evil genius."

"And, Collins Carter"—he bows and draws the attention of everyone standing in line with us—"you're the most worthy opponent."

This I know, but I still like hearing it.

"Thank you, sir." I curtsy. "And now knowing this entire election was built on a bed of lies, I can't wait to destroy you at the polls."

"It's a punch ballot that they drop in a glorified shoebox, but yes. Same energy."

In front of us, the riders start to filter out of the exit. Every single one of them is a disheveled mess, but other than two people who look like they might throw up at any minute, they all run straight to the back of the line for round two.

And standing next to Nate, I totally understand the need to keep going back for more.

*B*y the end of the day, Nate definitely agrees that my schedule is the only way to do a fair.

Not only did we outlast almost every person we spent our early afternoon with, we also rode every ride multiple times, demolished lunch, learned about chain saw safety, fed baby goats, and now we're back for dessert before we hit the road.

"I'm getting the corn bread funnel cake." I make my final decision, looking at the deep-fried cookie dough once more . . . just to be sure. "Yeah, definitely going with the funnel cake."

Classic with a twist. Perfect fair food.

"Would you judge me if my dessert was another donut burger?" Nate asks.

"There's no judgment at the fair," I tell him. "Unless you're that one person who brought their own salad. I mean, leave the virtue signaling at home, lady. Nobody wants to see that nonsense."

Fresh vegetables? How dare she.

The only produce I want to see at the fair is freakishly large and earns someone a blue ribbon.

"That salad really pissed you off, didn't it?" He laughs before he leans down and touches his lips to mine.

I used to be anti–public displays of affection, but with Nate, I find myself wanting to touch him anywhere and everywhere. I feel like a teenager again . . . except not, because I didn't have a boy-friend until I went to college.

I drop the salad talk and start to walk in the direction of the funnel cake booth. When they hand me a funnel cake bigger than my head topped with whipped cream, caramel, and a heart-stopping amount of powdered sugar, I know I made the right decision.

"I don't care what anyone says, this is art." I stare at my picture-perfect dessert trying to decide the best way to attack it. "Somebody should make one of those ice cream museums, but with fair food."

There'd be a funnel cake maze, a corn dog carousel, and an exhibit where it looks like you're walking on giant clouds of cotton candy. The only locations would be scattered across the Midwest and it'd be a freaking hit.

"I want to know what it's like inside your brain." Nate stares at me with a mix of wonder and amusement.

"I think it's probably like a kaleidoscope or something." I try to put words to the chaos running through my mind at any given moment. "Tons of bright colors and half-formed sentences inter-spersed with flashing pictures of food, your butt, and Little Mix songs playing all the time."

"My butt?"

"You have a fantastic ass." I pop a piece of funnel cake in my mouth. "It lives rent-free in my mind."

"Glad you like it." He smiles at me and I add that to the list of things always in my brain.

"I like *you*."

I don't mean to get so sincere in the middle of the fair, but I can't help it. Not only has this been one of the best days I can remember having in . . . maybe forever, but all my time with him is turning into the best day ever.

"I like you too." He turns to me and takes my free hand in his. "I more than like you."

Suddenly, the kaleidoscope in my brain turns black and I can't think of anything to say. I'm frozen to the spot, staring at Nate beneath the neon lights of the food booths and carnival rides. It's hardly a fairy-tale setting, yet nothing has ever seemed more romantic or perfect.

Because somehow, against all odds, in the aftermath of going through our pain, we found happiness and comfort . . . in each other.

Serendipitous indeed.

Chapter 26

"R emember." Ruby grabs me by the shoulders and bores into my eyes. "On this stage, Nate is not your boyfriend. He's not even your competition. For the next hour, he's your enemy and you will not stop until you destroy him!"

I told my mom not to let Ruby have that third cup of coffee, but does anyone listen to me?

"Rubes?" I take a small step back. She gets a little scary when she's this intense. "I love you, but I'm going to need you to take it down by, like, seventy percent. This is for the homeowners' association, not the Senate."

I love that she stayed to support me through this, but my girl is jonesing for litigation. I need her to get back in the courtroom ASAP because these video meetings just aren't doing it for her. Last week she made me pull an all-nighter and laminated my note cards.

I didn't even study this hard in college.

"You're going to do great." Ashleigh tucks a stray curl behind my ear and paints my lips with the makeup we weren't able to talk her out of signing up to sell. "People don't care about the rules; they want to connect with you. They want to know how you're going to help them. You know why you're here, so speak from the heart and it will be perfect."

I never thought the loud woman who lived next door and only wore wedge sandals would be the calming force in my life, yet here we are.

If anyone would've told me a year ago that I'd be living with my parents, dating Nate Adams, and running for the HOA board, I would've laughed in their face. I mean, I lived it and I still can't quite believe that I'm here or that what started as a petty attempt to piss Nate off has turned into something I actually care about . . . against someone I care about even more.

If by some crazy chance I win this thing, I really want to make my parents and my community proud. I think I could be really good at this.

"Yeah, sure. Speak from the heart or whatever." Ruby rolls her eyes. "Then you fucking bring Nate to his knees. You can kiss and make up afterward. Which, by the way—"

Before she can finish, someone knocks on the door to the conference room in the back of the clubhouse we've claimed as our headquarters for the day.

"I'll get it!" I jump at the opportunity to avoid whatever lecture Ruby was about to inflict on me.

Ashleigh's soft giggle follows me as I feel Ruby's glare burning a hole in my back. I pull open the door, expecting to see my mom or one of the other board members telling me it's time to get started, but instead I'm greeted by Nate's smiling face.

He looks nothing short of wonderful.

He traded out his trademark khakis for a pair of slim-cut navy slacks and paired them with a brown leather belt and a striped button-up folded at the sleeves. I may not have proof, but I'm pretty sure no other HOA hopeful has ever looked so hot.

"No fair!" I look him up and down, unable to help where my eyes happen to linger. "You look like a damn thirst trap. You're rigging the vote."

"And what's this?" He gestures to the form-fitting V-neck button-up dress Ashleigh forced me into this morning. "You're telling me *this* is fair?"

"We get it. You're both hot and you want to make out and have fantastic sex." Ruby groans. "Give it a rest."

"Hey, Ruby," Nate says, unbothered. "Ashleigh."

"Nate the Snake." Ruby refuses to update the nickname she gave him in high school. "Hope you're ready for my girl to kick your ass."

"I apologize for my angry friend. She's not used to being around people who like each other," I explain. "It's too calm around here and she thrives in chaos. Something I'm sure a therapist would have a lot to say about." I shout the last sentence because she's canceled three sessions with her therapist since she's been here.

"Oh my god. Fine! I'll call Monique," Ruby shouts across the room. "But I want you to know you're a real pain in my ass."

"Being your pain in the ass is my greatest honor," I throw over my shoulder as I follow Nate into the hallway.

As soon as the door shuts behind us, his hands and mouth are on me. It's not over the top, nothing like our open-house rendezvous, but it's enough to get my heart pumping and for the blood to go directly between my legs.

Have I said what a good kisser he is?

Because he's a really good kisser.

"What was that for?" I ask when he pulls away. "Not that I'm complaining."

Every minute we spend together, I'm forced to remember how crazy life can be. When we kiss, it's as if some greater force is whispering *You're welcome* into my ear. Nate brought out the worst in me, but through that, I really think I discovered the best in me.

"I started your script this morning."

My stomach plummets and I get a little light-headed. "You did?"

I've been sharing my scripts for years and it never gets easier. Every time I send a script to someone, it's as if I jumped out of a plane butt naked, with a faulty parachute. The moment I press send there's no turning back and I don't know if I'm going to crash or soar. It's exhilarating, terrifying, and the most exposed I ever feel.

"You'd always write those little short stories when we were kids and I remember thinking you were talented." He leans in, his big body shielding me from the outside world. "But this? I don't feel worthy enough to read it. It's so good that I don't even know how to put it into words."

As a writer, you learn rather quickly that you can't rely on praise for validation of your work. You have to learn to find that within yourself, because no matter what you create, someone out there will not like it. If you hang your worth on the opinions of others, you won't survive this career.

But that doesn't mean I still don't love it when someone enjoys my work.

"Really? You liked it?" Or that I don't fish for additional compliments every now and again.

"It's amazing," he says. "I laughed out loud the entire time I was reading. The characters felt so real, the idea is so clever. All of it. You're a genius."

"Stop it." *Tell me more, tell me more!* "You're just saying that."

"Oh please, you know it's amazing. I know you well enough to know you wouldn't have sent it to me if you didn't think it was." He catches on to the game I'm playing rather quickly, but he still plays along. "Plus, how could you go wrong with that smart, charming character who looks great in khakis? You should really thank whoever inspired him."

"You caught that, did you?" I thought about changing the character so he wasn't so on the nose, but why fix what's not broken?

"I did." He touches his lips to mine, but it's much too fast. "But really, it's fantastic and I'm not just saying that. You're brilliant and it's only one of the many things I love and admire about you."

I'm not sure I heard him correctly.

Did he say *love*?

I can't tell if he meant to say it, and as we stare at each other, neither of us says anything. The distant chatter in the clubhouse is the only thing filling the space between us.

He opens his mouth to say something, but before he gets the chance, Ashleigh and Ruby swing open the door and march into the hallway.

"Showtime! Let's go show the Reserve what Collins Carter is all about." Ashleigh's wearing her "Collins for President" T-shirt and has a matching tote bag stuffed with magnets, ChapStick, and fans to hand out. I'm not above bribery and neither is she. "And, Nate, good luck, but my money is all on this woman right here."

"Can't say I blame you," Nate says to Ashleigh, but his eyes never leave mine. "She's pretty hard not to cheer for."

Warmth swirls through me like hot cocoa on the first day of winter. I lean toward him, hoping for one more kiss before I go.

"No!" Ruby grabs my face in her hands and pulls me nose to nose with her. "Don't let him make you go all soft, not before you go onstage."

"There's no stage," I correct her. "I think it's just a long table."

"Life is a stage, Collins! Come on!" she shouts in my face. "Get your head in the game."

I wonder if this is how she treats her clients before she gets them on the stand. No wonder she has such a high success rate and has made so many people cry. *Intense* is an understatement.

But weirdly, her screaming in my face kind of works.

"Sorry, Adams," I say once Ruby loosens her grip on my cheeks. "But you're going down."

And then maybe later, he can go down again . . .

. . .

I knew more people were planning on coming to this meeting than the last one I came to, but I vastly underestimated the community's interest in me and Nate.

My hands fidget beneath the table as I look out into the crowd of at least a hundred people. There's nary a cloud in the sky and the sun is shining bright, its brutal rays beating down on me as beads of sweat drip down my back. My palms are wet and even though I made fun of her earlier, I've never been so grateful for Ruby and her love of a laminator.

"Welcome to the Reserve at Horizon Creek's Homeowners' Association meeting," Janice greets the crowd from in front of the table. She's trying her best to sound warm and welcoming, but nothing can mask the disdain always lurking in her voice. "Today is a special meeting. As you all know, our former president, Harvey Bridgewerth, moved to Florida and resigned from his position as president of the HOA. Today we will hear from our two candidates and have a chance to ask them a few questions before we place our votes. First up is Collins Carter, followed by Nathanial Adams, then we will conclude with questions."

She gestures for me to stand up and I go blank. I hate public speaking. Why did I decide to do this to myself? I'm unable to move. It's like my butt has been superglued to the seat. I look around, trying to find Ruby and Ashleigh in the crowd. They'll know how to get me out of this.

Before I can spot them, Nate's hand latches on to mine.

"Hey." He leans in close to my ear. "You got this. If you were able to stand up in the middle of that meeting and win the crowd over with no preparation whatsoever, they don't stand a chance against you now. Plus, Ruby might murder both of us if this meeting gets canceled."

He's not wrong.

About any of it.

"Thank you." I close my eyes and take a deep breath, and when I open them, I remember who the fuck I am.

I stand up on steady legs and round the table, staring back at curious eyes more interested in my relationship status with Nate than my stance on neighborhood policies. But I don't care what they came for; all I know is what I'm going to give.

Ugh.

Moving home made me so corny.

"Hello, everyone, thank you so much for coming out today." I finally spot my friends and family in the audience. Ashleigh and my mom both give me a thumbs-up while Dad and Ruby nod in approval. "I'm sure for some of you, this may be your first home-owners' association meeting and you don't know what to expect. To that I say, I know how you feel.

"When I went to my first homeowners' association meeting, I was prepared to take a nap and raise hell." The crowd, minus a few exceptions like Karen Two in the first row, laugh like I hoped they would. I positioned a small joke early on, hoping their re-action would provide me with a little encouragement, which it does. "Never in a million years did I think I would volunteer to run for president that night. I can't stand here and lie to you by saying I knew what I was getting myself into. In fact, I had no idea whatsoever. I had just moved back from Los Angeles and I hadn't been a member of this community for a long time. If I'm honest, half of the reason I went that night was to get under the skin of my opponent." When I look at Nate over my shoulder, the way he's watching me gives me butterflies and I can't help but go off script a bit. "And I guess you could say that was a massive success."

He winks, and his massive smile, which outshines even the afternoon sun, makes it almost impossible for me to look away. The collective sigh coming from the audience is the only thing that pulls me back. I can hear Ruby in the back of my mind screaming at me to stay on topic, but at least I know I gave a solid fifty percent of the people here exactly what they came for.

"But seriously, when I stood up in the middle of the meeting, I had no idea what this community needed." I find my way back on track, the nerves slowly drifting away as I find my groove. I don't even need the note cards I was clinging on to so tightly. "And I'm here today to tell you I still don't know."

I can tell this isn't what they were expecting me to say.

I have them right where I want them.

"No single person can know what our community needs, and as president, I promise not to speak for you. I promise to make room for you to speak and be heard. I promise to care less about the bylaws than I do my neighbors." My voice is strong and steady. I hope they can all hear the sincerity in my words. "I grew up in this community. I watched as neighbors looked out for one another and lifted each other up when they were in need. That's what I believe the homeowners' association should be: a place where we can come together and express ourselves and our needs. It shouldn't be about riding around on golf carts and issuing fines, but instead about building this community into a place where we all feel safe and welcome. You bought your homes. You pay your dues. The HOA is for you, not the other way around. If that is the vision you see, then I hope I'll have your vote. If not, I still know that Nate will do an amazing job as a leader. Thank you for listening."

Before anyone has the time to respond, Ruby is out of her seat and on her feet.

"Yes, Collins!" she shouts. "That was amazing!"

It doesn't take long for the rest of the crowd to join in. Other than my family and Ashleigh, nobody is as enthusiastic as Ruby, but the applause mends something I didn't know was broken inside me. For so long, I felt like an outsider, like I didn't belong.

Not anymore.

I finally feel at home . . . and it only took me running for the HOA to make it happen.

I hate that Nate's speech was good. I really thought he was going to bomb," Ruby grumbles as she grabs a piece of cheese off the charcuterie board Ashleigh brought over to celebrate me not falling on my face.

"I don't know why." I slump down into the chair next to her. My entire body aches. I didn't realize how tense and stressed I was until the meeting ended. "He's been on the HOA already and he's always been good at public speaking."

He spoke at our graduation and I may have hated him at the time, but I still had to admit it was a really good speech. There's something about the way he carries himself, confidence in the way he moves, the thoughtful inflections of his voice, that make him damn near transcendent when he talks.

"Well, I think you both did a phenomenal job." Mom drops a bowl of pita chips and hummus next to the board. "I didn't know if you were going to stick this out, but you did. No matter what happens next, I'm so proud of you."

At almost thirty, I thought I wouldn't need my parents' approval anymore. But as I sit at the table, hearing my mom say she's proud of me, warmth flows through my veins and my vision begins to blur. These last few months have been so tumultuous; I went from low to high to low again. I had no idea how much of my self-worth was tied to my career and finding success in Los Angeles until I lost them both. Moving back home, I didn't know if I would ever feel proud of myself, let alone make my parents proud.

"Thanks, Mom." My voice is thick with unshed emotion. "That means a lot to me."

Instead of saying anything, because she knows I will cry and I don't want to cry at a table with my friends, she takes my hand and gives it a gentle squeeze.

It says everything words could never.

Before things get too emotional, the doorbell rings.

"Finally!" Ruby shouts. "That better be Nate with the wine. You can't do charcuterie without wine."

"You're ridiculous." I push out of the chair to go open the door.

I may or may not have told Nate that if there's a way to win Ruby's heart over, it was through quality wine. It's a long shot, but he jumped on it. Plus, even if it doesn't work, at least we'll be properly boozed.

He's earlier than he said he'd be. It's only been a couple of hours since I saw him last, but the anticipation of seeing him again spurs me to walk to the door a little faster. I swing open the door, fully prepared to launch at him, when I come to a sudden halt.

Because it's not Nate.

"Hey, Colly. You're looking good."

It's Peter.

Chapter 27

*T*he wheels in my mind spin as I try to process what is happening. The last time I saw Peter, he was watching me destroy his car through our apartment window. As far as I know, there are still charges pending against me and I thought we weren't supposed to be within one hundred yards of each other. Yet here he is, standing on my parents' sidewalk in all his California god perfection.

Even though he's a trash human whom I truly wish nothing but the worst for, I'd be lying if I said he wasn't gorgeous. He was handed cards from modeling scouts more than once when we were together. From his permanently tanned skin to his square jaw, whiskey-brown eyes, and long, lean surfer's body, he is what dreams are made of . . . and he knows it.

He was quick to turn on the charm and use it to impress the young, impressionable girl in the classroom he was in. To manipulate, lie, and steal from those around him. From those who trusted him most.

So even though he's standing in front of me, aiming his megawatt smile that could grace magazine covers? I'm not impressed.

No.

I'm pissed.

My fingernails bite into my palms. The urge to wrap my hands around his throat hasn't lessened over the months.

"What are you doing here?" I whisper so that I don't scream. If I'm lucky, I'll get him to leave without anyone being the wiser.

"Really, Colly?" The nickname I used to love makes my skin crawl coming out of his mouth. "Don't be like that."

My throat burns as I swallow the poison I want to throw at him.

"Don't be like what? Like a person still pissed that you stole my fucking work, sold it as your own, and instead of admitting what you did, doubled down to get me blacklisted from the only career I ever wanted?" Any hold I had on my temper slips away as the memories and feelings I've been suppressing since I stepped onto that Delta flight months ago resurface. "And then you show up at my parents' house and expect me to be what? Happy to see you? Are you fucking insane?!"

Just like I knew would happen, footsteps echo through the house as everyone inside rushes to see what's wrong.

"Well now, this is quite the development," my mom says over my shoulder. Her calm and steady presence takes some of the edge off . . .

Until Ruby rounds the corner and sees what's happening.

"You've got to be shitting me!" She comes barreling out of the front door and I barely manage to grab her by the arm and pull her backward. It doesn't do much. Her long reach stretches in front of her as she jabs her finger into his chest. "You have some goddamn nerve to show your face here."

"Ruby." Peter quickly masks the surprise of seeing her behind his condescending smile. "You're as pleasant as ever. Can't say I'm thrilled to see you again."

"Can't say any of us are thrilled to see you." I throw his words back at him as my hold on Ruby loosens. "Hurry up and tell me what you're doing here so you can leave."

During all the years we were together, I can count on one hand the times he let his guard down and was really vulnerable. I was so used to the persona he was playing, I had no clue it was all an act. But standing in front of me with Ruby about two seconds away from inflicting physical harm, I watch as he deflates.

"Can we talk . . ." He looks at the small crowd that has gathered around me. "Alone?"

The ever-present ego melts away along with his always superb posture. I notice the dark circles beneath his eyes and the lines on his face that weren't there a few months ago. Gray streaks his thick brown hair, which is longer than I've ever seen it. He's a mess.

A better person would feel bad for him.

"Why? They all know how you stole my script and then lied to make me seem like some unhinged ex-girlfriend." I let go of Ruby when I'm sure she won't attack and fold my arms in front of my chest. "Anything you have to say to me, you can say in front of them."

I stand firm, refusing to budge no matter how uncomfortable he is. He shifts from foot to foot as his gaze flickers to the faces I know are all shooting daggers at him. People are always so enamored with him, he doesn't know how to handle open hostility. I know he's going to turn and walk away.

But he doesn't.

"I need you."

He's so quiet, I'm sure I misheard him.

"What?" I ask.

"I need you to come back to LA," he says, louder this time, and my breath catches in my throat. "I need your help."

"And why should she help you after what you did to her?" my mom asks with more venom in her voice than I've ever heard before.

"Because," he says to my mom, but his light brown eyes peer into mine. "If she does this, she'll not only get her script back, but she'll have the career she always dreamt of."

Ashleigh took Ruby back to her house and my parents are pretending not to listen from the other room. Peter is in front of me, my mom's favorite Corinthians verse above his head as he sits awkwardly on my parents' couch.

It's his first time in our house. Almost a decade of dating, and the first time he came to my parents' house is to ask for something.

Typical.

"Tell me what happened."

I wish I was strong enough not to ask. I wish his words meant nothing to me and I was able to send him away without hearing him out. But I'm not. I can't help the way the possibility of moving back to LA, spending my days writing in my favorite coffee shop, and resuming the career that was snatched away so carelessly sparks the flame that I thought was long extinguished.

"It's your show." He shrugs, resignation in every line of his strong body.

"Well, duh, Peter." I slip my hands beneath my thighs to try to keep still. "It was always my show and that didn't stop you from acting like it wasn't. I want to know what changed. Why are you here? Why now?"

Even though I've grown to really enjoy being home, I can't lie and pretend everything's perfect here. I have my family, Ashleigh, and, of course, Nate, but I don't have any job prospects, and even without rent, I'm running out of money. Writing is a huge part of who I am, and while I can write from anywhere in the world, my career is in Los Angeles.

"I know what you think, but I really did plan on having you in the writers' room," he says, and I feel my temper rise all over again.

"You said you would look at my résumé." I remember it clear as day. "To work on the show . . . that I wrote."

It sounds so insane hearing it out loud that it almost makes me question my memory. How could anyone think that's okay?

"I couldn't just staff you without interviewing you first. You didn't have many credits behind your name and it would look like favoritism if I hired you without going about it the proper way. I didn't think you'd want people to assume you got the job because you were my girlfriend."

He says it with such sincerity that for a moment I wonder if he's being reasonable and I'm the one overreacting. Then I remember that he *stole my fucking script and sold it as his own.*

"Do you hear the words that are coming out of your mouth?" If it was medically possible for my head to explode, I would yell for my parents to call an ambulance. "It was my show! You weren't worried about favoritism. You were worried that someone would figure out that you were a thief."

"I messed up. I get it." His demeanor shifts as he becomes more defensive. "Is that what you wanted to hear?"

I mean, it doesn't hurt.

I stay silent.

"I thought I could get us what we both wanted and it would be fine. You'd have a job you liked. I could finally be a showrunner." He falls back into the couch and scrubs his hands across his face. "But every decision I've made has been wrong and the studio's pissed. It's a mess. I need you to come back. You can be supervising producer, lead the writers the way you want, anything."

"Why should I help you?"

The truth of the matter is, I don't care if he fails. Plus, the thought of sitting next to him in a writers' room for hours at a time makes my skin crawl. I don't know if I could manage to be civil long enough to create an entire television show.

"Because it's not about me," he says. "It's about your show."

My stomach dips as I remember the countless hours I poured into that script. The time I spent carefully crafting my characters, endlessly workshopping the dialogue until it was perfect. Years of my life were put into that project. Am I willing to throw it all away because of my hatred for Peter?

I'm not sure.

"I have to think about it." I'm not comfortable giving him an answer tonight. "How long until you have to report back?"

"The studio gave me three weeks to come back with something new," he says. "I got on the plane to you as soon as I left the meeting."

I don't know if that's supposed to make me warm to him or what.

"Okay, well . . . I guess I'll call you?" I stand up and he follows suit. "When do you fly back?"

If he would've talked to me about everything before he did what he did, we could've figured it out. I knew I wasn't prepared to be a showrunner by myself. I still have so much to learn and I would've been happy to share this with him had he just asked.

This entire mess of a situation is all his doing and nothing he could ever say can change that.

"I leave tomorrow morning." He shoves his hands in his pockets. "You know, you really do look good . . . happy. I don't know who you were expecting when you answered the door, but I remember when you used to look at me like that. Whoever it is, they're really lucky."

"Yeah," I agree, my shoulders falling at the thought of Nate. "We both are."

I might be imagining it, but I swear, for a split second, I see sadness and maybe even regret cross his handsome features.

But I can't be sure.

Because as if conjured by thought, the sound of the front door opening pulls our attention just in time to see Nate walk into the room.

"I brought the wine!" he shouts before he takes in the scene in front of him and comes to a sudden stop. He eyes Peter up and down before turning his attention to me. "What'd I miss?"

"So, so much." The exhaustion of the day weighs in my voice. "Peter, this is Nate. Nate, this is Peter."

Nate's wide eyes fly back to Peter.

"The same Peter who stole your script?" Nate asks, and Peter's cheeks turn red. It's nice to see he's at least a little embarrassed by what he did. "What's he doing here?"

"What do you think?" I ask. "Begging for me to come back, of course."

The air leaves the room as Nate turns his attention back to me.

Because as much as I want to pretend I'm going to say no, I think we both know that's not how this is going to end.

Chapter 28

*P*eter scurried away quicker than the cockroaches in my first LA apartment soon after Nate arrived. He might work out every day, but it's clear to anyone who sees them next to each other that even in his ironed slacks, Nate could kick Peter's ass. And considering the angry vibes radiating off Nate in droves, I wasn't so sure he wouldn't do it.

Not soon after Peter left, Nate and I followed suit.

I knew my parents would give me the respect and privacy to have a conversation with Nate alone, but we both felt it would be better in Nate's house.

The cool evening breeze blows the stray hairs off the back of my neck. Awkward tension that hasn't been present in weeks lingers between us; only the sounds of far-off squeals of laughter from the neighborhood kids enjoying their summer cut through the silence.

I try to keep my mind focused on the now, but I can't help the way it drifts off to the what-ifs and maybes that come with the opportunity that's been presented to me. By the time we walk into his house, I have a full list of pros and cons running through my head.

I follow him into his kitchen. Without saying a word, I watch as he pulls out two wineglasses from his cabinet and opens one of the bottles he brought to my parents' house to celebrate. I can't help but realize he's opening it for a much different reason now.

"I don't know if I'm going to go," I tell him. "I told him I'd think about it. I could say no."

He rounds the kitchen island and slides a glass in front of me. His heavy pour causes the deep-red wine to dance dangerously close to the rim.

"Collins." He says my name as if he's just given an hour-long speech.

"Don't 'Collins' me." I hate when he does that.

He used to do it all the time when we were younger. Saying my name like it explained everything in the world. The frustrating part is that he's usually right.

I guess the bad thing about being with someone who knows you so well is that they know you so well, they won't even let you lie to yourself.

He lifts the wine to his mouth, his full lips settling on the glass, but never takes his eyes off me.

"Stop it." I want to shield myself from his knowing gaze, but there's nowhere to hide. He recognizes pieces in me that I have yet to discover about myself. "I'm serious. If I go, I'm still going to have to work with him and I don't know if I can do that. How do I let myself be vulnerable enough to create with someone I can't trust?"

My stomach twists as the reality I'm facing sets in.

Peter is dangling my dream in front of me. Everything I worked so hard for is at my fingertips but firmly held in Peter's grip. If I walk away, he has no incentive to admit any wrongdoing or clear my name. I'll still be blacklisted from writers' rooms, agencies, and production companies. If I don't go now, I might miss the window to ever return.

I thought I was going to hate my time at home, but it was the break I didn't know I needed. I'm just not sure if it's plausible for me to stay forever. *HOA**holes* is the strongest thing I've ever written, and if I don't figure things out now, it will live in my computer instead of out in the world where it belongs.

"You told me how much that script meant to you, how many years you spent working on it," he says. "If you care about something that much, you do what you can to see it succeed. Even if it hurts."

He's not talking about the script anymore.

"Nate—" Emotions clog my throat. I can't speak.

"No." He sets his glass on the counter and turns to me. He holds my face in his hands, wiping away tears I didn't even know were falling. "If I didn't love you so much, I'd ask you to stay. I'd beg you to forget about everything and stay here with me, forever. But I can't do that."

I was sixteen when I experienced my first big loss. My grandpa had a stroke and died. It was unexpected and we were all in shock.

My dad didn't talk for an entire day after he found out. I was devastated. Nobody I knew had ever died before. The thought that he'd never call me on Sunday night to hear about my week and what I had planned for the next was almost incomprehensible. How could someone be there one minute and not the next? The finality of it, knowing I would go back in time and do whatever I had to do to hear his voice one more time, to have another week of it, broke me in a way that even after I healed, I was never the same.

And here with Nate, I feel a new crack breaking me apart.

"Maybe you could come too?" The tears are falling faster. I can't get ahold of them. "Or we could do long-distance. It won't be like the last time I left. I'll come home more."

He looks at me with a sad smile and I know what he's thinking before he says it.

"Me with my love of khakis and sweater-vests in California? You know that wouldn't work." His laugh is hollow, but I can't find it in myself to even try. "I know you'll come back and I'll be waiting at your parents' house, but then you'll leave again. Your dreams are in Los Angeles. I've seen firsthand what happens when someone tries to stand in the way. I refuse to do that to you."

His mom.

I cry harder. My chest aches. The sobs feel as if they're being pulled from the bottom of my soul.

"You knew I'd hurt you." White-hot memories flash bright in my mind. This is why he stopped talking to me all those years ago. He was afraid I'd hurt him just like his mom did, running away from home to chase far-off goals. I clawed my way back into his life only to do the exact thing he was afraid I'd do.

I struggle to breathe as guilt like I've never known before ensnares me in its grip. I feel dizzy with regret as I process the mess I've made. The damage I've done.

I bury my face in my hands. I can't look at him.

I can't let him see me.

"Collins." His voice is muffled like I'm underwater. Before I know what's happening, his arms are wrapped around me and he pulls me off the stool. The same stool where things began . . . where they're ending.

He carries me up the stairs and I wrap my arms around his neck, clinging to him as I cry into his shoulder.

"I'm so sorry. I'm so sorry."

I don't know what else to say. I want to tell him I love him, that I might have always loved him, but it feels cruel. Too much hope lives in those words and this feels hopeless.

"Please look at me," he whispers, his voice soft but his tone firm.

It takes a moment for me to garner enough control to stop crying long enough to give him at least that.

I focus all my attention on the man in front of me, the man I loved even when I hated him. The intensity staring back at me from hazel eyes steals my breath away.

"There's nothing to be sorry about. You are going to go back to California and you're going to do what you always said you would do. You're going to write shows and win awards and I'm going to be right here watching, telling everyone I know that I beat you in the race for the HOA."

I don't want to laugh, but I can't help it.

"You don't know if you won yet." My hoarse voice is almost unrecognizable.

"Trust me," he says. "I won."

"I don't think you're talking about the HOA anymore."

"I'm not." He brings his mouth closer to mine, so close that I swear I can feel it. "Yes, you're going to California. But we never know what tomorrow is going to bring and we don't need to."

My breathing deepens, my chest rising and falling a little faster as I struggle to keep my eyes open. I try to imprint every second into my mind. I don't want to forget any of this.

"We don't?"

"We don't." He shakes his head and I watch as his hazel eyes turn black. "We have right now and it's up to us to make sure every moment counts. If we do it right, tonight can last forever."

I fight back a fresh wave of tears.

When his mouth touches mine this time, it's different. Our full lips press together, no longer exploring, just feeling. There's no rush, no frantic energy as our tongues tangle together while his hands hold me tight. We take our time.

It's a slow burn gradually building with every graze of his fingertips, every brush of his lips.

When he lays me down on his bed, he doesn't make a move. He stares down at me, his eyes lighting a fire as they drift down my body.

"Perfect," he whispers, finally letting his hands follow the path his gaze forged into my skin.

By the time he puts his mouth on me, I nearly combust.

I can't watch anymore. The sight of his head between my

thighs is too much. I'm not ready for it. I close my eyes and push him away. I try to fight it as my stomach tightens and my back arches off the bed, but it's no use.

Because even with my eyes closed, he's all I can see.

Pleasure has never hurt so good. It rips through me, tearing me apart from the inside out and taking my heart along with it.

Nobody's ever touched me the way Nathanial Adams touches me. Nobody's ever looked at me the way he looks at me. As the final waves rock through me, I'm worried nobody else ever will.

And then, just when I thought it was impossible, the tears begin to fall again.

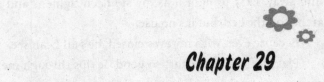

Chapter 29

*W*hoever said it's always sunny in Southern California clearly didn't account for the smog.

The dry heat feels oppressive and I yearn for the humidity I thought I hated. Everything I missed about Los Angeles has been less sparkly since I've been back. It's been the longest month ever.

I miss my parents, I miss my friends, and I really fucking miss Nate.

Not one night has gone by without me dreaming of the last night we spent together. I wake up thinking of his eyes and fall asleep trying to conjure the feel of his touch. I've dialed his number so many times that I've lost count, yet I still haven't called.

Peter let me move back into our apartment and is staying with a friend until I figure things out. It's smaller than I remember and I miss the comfort of my room back home. The king mattress is too big after sleeping in my twin bed. The coffee shop around the corner I used to go to every day isn't as good either. The plants on the patio are a sad excuse for a garden next to my dad's and the neighbor who made me go viral is a downright disgrace compared to my MLM queen, Ashleigh.

But I've been trying to tell myself that's not why I moved back here.

When I came to LA as a bright-eyed, slightly-less-jaded eighteen-year-old, I didn't come to make friends or sit around drinking lattes all day. I came because I'm a writer, and as cheesy as it sounds, I want to share my stories with the world. I'm finally getting the opportunity to do it and I can't let some boy from my hometown be the reason I lose focus.

My phone buzzes and just like it has since I stepped foot in the airport, my traitorous heart leaps at the chance that I might see Nate's name on the screen and then breaks all over again when I don't.

"Hey," I greet my best friend, who's still in freaking Ohio.

"You thought I was Nate again, didn't you?" Ruby asks.

"No," I lie. "Have you bought your ticket back to California yet or are you just moving into my bedroom?"

"I always told you to get bunk beds. If you would've listened when we were younger, you wouldn't have to worry about being out of a place to sleep when you come to visit us."

"When they discover time travel, bunk beds will be my first plan of action." I grab the keys to the rental car Peter is also funding off the table and lock the front door behind me as I leave. "But seriously, when are you coming back?"

Heavy silence lingers over the line and I think I've lost her.

"Ruby?" I look at the screen to see if we're still connected. "Are you there?"

"Yeah, I'm still here. Sorry." There's a hesitation that sounds foreign in her perpetually overconfident voice.

I know what it means before she tells me.

"You aren't coming back, are you?"

I unlock the car and climb in, blasting the air conditioning as Ruby's voice transfers over to the car speakers.

"I applied for a job at a law firm in C-bus." She confirms what I figured was true days ago. "I can't go back there, Colls. I hated the person I was turning into there. All I did was work and yell. I forgot what it was like to have a life outside of the office."

"I'm proud of you." I am. She's been needing a break for years, but selfishly, I'm also really disappointed. I miss my friend. I thought I was coming back to my life, but more and more, I'm starting to feel like I left it. "What did Monique say?"

"She said it's good as long as I continue to make changes and don't expect moving to magically change my life." I can almost hear her eyes rolling. "I think she was probably wondering why I picked Ohio, but she didn't ask."

"I hope she at least told you to never say C-bus again." No matter how much I'm missing home, I'll never get behind C-bus. Ever.

"Hater," she says. "But enough about me, let's talk about you. How's the show going? What's it like working with Peter?"

I knew this question was coming from the moment I saw her name on my phone.

"It's amazing! I can't believe I'm finally a supervising producer. It's a dream come true."

As soon as the last sentence leaves my mouth, I know I've taken it a step too far.

"That bad, huh?"

Worse.

"It's not great." I put the car in reverse and start my traffic-filled trek to the studio. "I don't know what I thought it'd be, but it's not this."

I miss my parents' minivan as silence fills the small sedan with surprisingly terrible gas mileage. I wait for Ruby to say something—anything!—but she stays quiet. It's one of her favorite techniques to get me to spill my guts. I hate how effective it is.

"I don't think this will surprise you, but I'm the only Black person in the room and there are only two other women. I'm the supervising producer, but it's clear that the older white men in the room don't value or trust my position. And they've destroyed my show."

It's the last part that's been the hardest to come to terms with.

My gorgeous script with so much humor and nuance is now totally flat, overrun with easy jokes and missing the spark that made it so special to begin with. If I was working with assholes, but they were constantly coming up with fantastic ideas that made the show stronger, that'd be one thing. But it's clear that Peter staffed people going off how well he knew them instead of how well they worked.

Pretty ironic considering his reasoning for not hiring me in the first place was to avoid rumors of nepotism.

"What are you going to do about it?" She asks the million-dollar question.

I've been up at night, asking myself the same question over and over again. I've been rereading my original script, trying to figure out how to get back to the heart of what I was trying to say. The only problem with that is I'm not the same person I was when I wrote it. I still love the script and the characters, but I can't connect to it like I once did. And I'm not sure if it's because of everything Peter put me through or because I can't stop thinking about *HOA**holes*.

"I'm not totally sure," I say. "But I'm on my way to a meeting with Reggie Fulton and I guess I'll just have to see what he has to say."

Reggie was the first showrunner I worked for and he always touches base with me if he needs a new writer. He was one of the few people who didn't completely blow me off when the Peter fiasco first went down. He never loved Peter and I have a feeling he knew something about what happened was amiss. He told me to keep in touch and reach out if I was ever in town.

I emailed him after my first day in the writers' room. He told me to send him anything I've written lately, so I sent over *HOA**holes* and I've been praying every day since that he didn't hate it.

"I hope he says something you want to hear," she says. "Now you focus on driving and call me after. I'm going to Ashleigh's house to help her set up for some makeup party this evening and she won't stop texting me."

I laugh picturing Ruby as Ashleigh's wingwoman. Those party

guests don't know what they're in for. I hope their credit cards have a high spending limit.

"Sounds good. Tell everyone I said hi."

I don't have to say his name for her to know I'm talking about Nate.

"If I see Nate, I'll be sure to tell him."

See.

She knows me so well.

"Thank you." I blink away the tears because LA traffic is *not* the place to have a breakdown. "Laters."

"Laters, babe."

Then the line goes dead and I'm left alone with my thoughts.

Again.

I thought Reggie and I were only going to have a quick meeting in his office, but he surprised me and took us to Sotta instead. It's a little Mediterranean restaurant in Burbank, and it's—chef's kiss— so delicious. And because Reggie is an A-plus human, he makes sure we order extra hummus, stuffed grape leaves, and sweet potato fries.

It's the first meal I haven't wanted to weep through.

"So." He leans back in his seat once he's polished off his chicken kebab. "Tell me about everything. How's it going working with Peter?"

The question of the day, apparently.

"It could be better, could be worse." I try to keep my answer vague and casual. I like Reggie, but as I've seen before, LA is small and people talk. I need to be careful with my words. "I'm grateful to have a job and be back."

He narrows his eyes but stays quiet . . . watching. Assessing.

Sheesh!

Did he and Ruby coordinate this?

"Why do you look like you're about to laugh?" he asks.

"I had almost this exact conversation with my best friend on the way to meet you." I pop a piece of hummus-covered pita bread in my mouth and finish chewing before I speak. Basic manners that Kimberly would be proud of. "She's a lawyer and you two have very similar techniques in yanking the truth out of me."

He sits up a little straighter.

"So does that mean you're going to tell me how you really feel?" A glimmer of excitement twinkles in his eyes.

I guess nobody is above the thrill of being on the receiving end of hot gossip.

"Fine, but the only reason I'm telling you is because you're the only person who reached out to me after my brush with viral fame." I look around the restaurant to make sure we're shielded from prying ears before I lean in. "I'm fucking miserable. I hate it so much. I have no idea how Peter has tricked so many people into thinking he's a genius, and I'm ashamed I fell for it for so long."

His smile grows with every syllable I utter. When I'm finished, he's grinning like a lunatic across the table.

"I knew it!" he booms, gaining the attention of the entire restaurant. "He's a goddamn asshole and I knew you saw it!"

"Reggie!" I whisper-shout across the table, a frozen smile plastered across my face. "Could you say that a little louder? I'm pretty sure there are a few people in the Valley who didn't hear you."

"Oh, fuck 'em." He tosses his napkin on the table. "A schmuck can only be a schmuck for so long before people start to catch on, and people are starting to catch on to Peter's crap."

My ears perk up at this news.

I'm working on what is still Peter's show and he did apologize—though it didn't seem like the most sincere thing in the world. I'm not sure it says great things about me that I'm so excited to hear some not-so-great things about him, but I can't help it.

My grudges are long-lasting for minor offenses. For what he did to me? It could last lifetimes.

"Well, don't get quiet now," I say. "Tell me the goss!"

It's all the encouragement he needs.

The rest of the diners fade away as all my attention narrows in on the wonderful storyteller in front of me.

"I'm good friends with one of the big executives involved with your project," he says, and it's a very promising start to the story. "I remember him reaching out to me about the script when he had it in his hands, and I thought it sounded similar to the script you told me you'd been working on. When I asked him who the writer was and he said Peter, I called bullshit immediately. But Peter had a good reputation and some other guys vouched for him, made it an easy sell."

My blood starts to boil all over again as I think of how hard I've had to work to prove I'm deserving of being in a room, when shitbags like Peter and his friends do nothing but shake hands and somehow land the best jobs.

"I told my guy not to trust it and when I saw that video of you on his car, I knew I was right. But this industry, for as many steps as we've taken in the right direction, is still a boys' club run by white men." His arms are gesturing all over the place and I'm worried he's going to knock his glass over. "It's a load of crap and that's coming from a straight white man!"

"I can't say I don't agree with you there." I reach for his water and pull it closer to me for safety. "The writers' room Peter stuck me in is basically the advertisement for the boys' club. I'm the supervising producer and they spend the majority of the day talking over or just flat-out ignoring me."

"Well, let 'em," he says. "Let them talk over you and take all the credit. I know you just got brought on staff, but if you can manage it, I think you should step all the way down."

"Are you serious?" I feel my brows furrow in confusion. This is the opposite of the advice I thought he was going to give me. I was preparing to stage a coup to regain power, not throw my hands in the air and walk away.

He pulls his water back across the table and takes a deep gulp. "As a heart attack."

Brilliant writer, still makes dad jokes.

"All right then." I sit back in my chair, ready to listen. "I'm going to need you to explain this one to me first."

He nods, obviously expecting a little pushback.

"Listen," he says. "I'm not sure of the exact details, but I know whatever is happening over in Peter's part of the woods is not good. He's worked with students for too long; I don't think your script is the first one he's passed off as his own. The whispers that have always been in the background are getting louder, and I get the sense that a reckoning is coming. You are not going to want to be associated with him when it happens. Your script, as wonderful as it was, is going to go down with him."

I'm not sure if it's because I grieved the loss of this project months ago, but the sadness I would've expected at hearing his news is nowhere to be found. Rather, in its place is relief so deep I almost shed a tear. The weight of building this project back up while knowing that Peter would receive the praise has been too much to bear. I dread going to work and I've started to resent the project. I never want to feel that way about writing.

"You don't look too broken up over it," Reggie says, watching me closely. "That's the reaction I was hoping for."

He piques my interest yet again.

"And why, may I ask, is that?"

"I want to start by telling you what a fantastic television writer you are. It's why I call you whenever I've had staff openings and it's why, if after you hear me out you still want in a room, I'll do whatever I can do to help get you there," he says, and my hackles rise. "But I read the project you sent me and I have to tell you, that's not a television show."

I regret the last bite of pita bread I ate as the Mediterranean food I downed turns in my stomach. I've been in this business for long enough to know it's highly subjective and not everyone will love what I write, but that doesn't make hearing it any easier. Rejection, no matter how thick your skin, still stings.

This rejection, however, feels more like a bullet wound than a quick jab of a needle. I didn't only send him the pilot episode; I sent him an entire season.

Without the restraints of Hollywood breathing down my neck, I was able to create without boundaries. I wrote the entire season not thinking I was wasting my time, but that I was investing in my craft. It was an amazing way to look at it and I thought it unlocked something I'd been afraid of letting out.

But maybe I was wrong, too wrapped up in the characters to be objective.

"And I sent you so much." I force out a laugh that I hope disguises my disappointment. "I hope you didn't force yourself to read the entire thing."

"What? No." The lines on his forehead deepen and he shakes his head. "You're not hearing what I'm saying. I loved it. I read every word you sent to me."

I attempt to follow what he's trying to say, but he's all over the place and I feel like I'm getting whiplash.

"You're right, I'm not hearing you." I throw my hands in the air like a petulant teenager. "Tell me again, but slower this time."

"It's not a television show, it's a movie." He spells it out for me. "One of the best rom-com scripts I've come across in years. Your voice is great on TV, but it shines as a movie, and I think you've finally found your lane."

I sit back in my seat, trying to digest what he's saying to me. I think back to my script, trying to see what he sees, and it only takes a moment to recognize how on point he is. I had tunnel vision before; I couldn't see outside writers' rooms. But now? It's like the entire world is opening up before me.

I can write a film script from anywhere in the world.

Italy. France. Ohio.

"By the way," he adds, as if he hasn't blown my mind enough already. "The main characters? Talk about chemistry. I couldn't get enough. And the hero who loves khakis? Brilliant."

Oh.

He has no idea.

I don't even wait until we leave the table to email Peter my resignation . . . or book my red-eye flight back home. Where my life is waiting for me.

Chapter 30

As soon as the wheels touch down at John Glenn Columbus Airport, I feel like I can breathe again . . . and not just because my mom's phobia of flying has rubbed off on me over the years. Yes, I know it's the safest mode of transportation, blah blah blah, but a metal tube hurtling through the sky will never not terrify me.

The moment I step into baggage claim, I'm immediately swarmed by my people. Ruby and Ashleigh bull-rush me like freaking linebackers. We jump up and down like three elementary school girls, but I don't care how ridiculous we look. If the last month taught me anything, it's to live in the moment and follow my heart. And right now, my heart has never been happier to see these two women.

Ruby's devoid of the normal designer gear and perfect makeup she's always wearing. She's in jean shorts and a T-shirt, her hair is in a bun on top of her head, and she's never looked more stunning.

"You're glowing." I take a step back and check my friend out. Happy looks good on her.

"Thank you." She curtsies. "It's what happens when you stop working eighty-hour weeks, start sleeping eight hours a night, and swap wine and caffeine for water."

"Who would've thought?" Heavy sarcasm falls from my tone. "Certainly not your best friend, therapist, or any person with basic health knowledge."

"Smartass."

"Oh!" Ashleigh pipes in. She's wearing her trademark wedge sandals and makeup that must've taken at least thirty minutes even though it's not even five in the morning. "And she's been going on walks with me. You should start coming too!"

A few months ago I would've played it cool with a swift and firm "hell no," but now I'm singing a different tune. I was so lonely in Los Angeles. I'll do whatever it takes to make sure my friendship with these women never fades. Plus, a little cardio never hurt anyone.

"Tell me when and where and I'll be there with bells on."

"Damn," Ruby says to Ashleigh. "She must have missed us more than we thought if she's agreeing to exercise without a fight."

Considering how much I complained about having to canvass the neighborhood, it's a fair observation.

We stand arm in arm in front of the conveyer belt waiting for my suitcase to come through. Not surprisingly, the airport isn't packed at this time of day. But of course, my suitcase is taking forever to come through.

"Nobody told Kimberly I'm back, right?" I ask the two women sandwiching me between them.

"Not even a clue." Ruby could not be more pleased with

herself and I can't blame her. Pulling the wool over my mom's eyes is a feat to be admired. "And your dad asked her to go with him to the garden center, so I think that should buy us a few hours."

After all it took for me and Nate to come together in the first place, it didn't feel right to barge back into his life by knocking on his door. He's done so much for me, it's my turn to do something for him.

I just really hope that he likes it . . . and that he hasn't moved on yet.

I might've gone a little overboard.

"This. Is. Amazing!" Ashleigh can't contain her excitement as she takes in the makeshift carnival once we're all finished setting up.

Carnival games intermix with the giant inflatable slide and bounce house behind the clubhouse. I wanted to get a Ferris wheel to really re-create our date, but it was like five thousand dollars, so inflatables are going to have to cut it. The sun is beginning to set and the fairy lights we spent much too long hanging up sparkle overhead. I connected my playlist to the built-in speakers and the random playlist of all Nate's favorite songs from when we were kids is playing in the background.

When I first came up with the idea, it seemed perfect. At the clubhouse where I first challenged him for HOA president, but with elements from our date to the fair. But as I look at it sprawled out in front of me, I worry I've done just a tad bit too much.

"You don't think it's too much?" I gnaw on my bottom lip. "I think maybe I took this rom-com-movie-writer thing too far."

Maybe I only need two games instead of all six. People don't do things like this in real life. He's going to think I'm proposing and run for the hills.

"It's a lot," Ruby says and I feel my blood pressure spike. "But it's not too much."

"Are you sure?"

Ruby is my honest friend, so I know she's not lying. But my nerves are beginning to ramp up and I don't know how to calm myself down. Because even though Nate and I ended things on really good terms, there's still the fact that I haven't talked to him in a month.

Soon after I left, we sent each other a few text messages, but that was it.

He went back to his life. My mom always filled me in on who he went on his morning walks with, while Ashleigh kept me up-to-date on what he was planning as the HOA's newly instated president. Ruby, despite her feelings for men in general, reached out to him to help her look for a condo. It was like he didn't miss a beat settling back into his old life.

I, on the other hand, was a complete mess and I'm freaking out that instead of reading this grand gesture as romantic, it's going to come off more as a crazy stalker he needs to escape from. Who's to say he hasn't met someone else and realized, just like he did with Elizabeth, that I wasn't the person for him?

If I thought having my writing rejected hurt, I could be in for a world of pain.

"Stop it right now." Ashleigh, not Ruby, grabs me by the shoulders. "You're getting in your head and I don't know what you're telling yourself in order to get out of this, but you need to stop. Nate was head over heels for you and trust me when I say that doesn't just go away in a month. Go pour yourself a glass of champagne and relax. Ruby and I will take care of the rest."

I'm not used to Ashleigh being the truth teller, but I appreciate it.

I give them both a quick hug, then I do as they say.

I pour a glass of champagne for me and Nate, only taking small sips of mine because bubbly tends to go straight to my head, and just like the last time we were together, I want to remember every moment.

I'm fighting the urge to pull out my phone and check the time when I see Ruby and Ashleigh escorting a blindfolded Nate down the staircase leading to our carnival.

"You two better not be planning on throwing me in the pool," he says. "I know how to swim. You won't be able to take me out that easy."

"I don't know why you don't trust us." Ruby winks at me over his shoulder. "If this surprise kills you, you'll come back from the afterlife to thank us."

"I don't know if that's a good or bad thing." He's starting to fidget beneath the blindfold. I silently motion for Ruby and Ashleigh to speed it up.

"Why don't you see for yourself then?" Ashleigh asks, and knowing what's about to happen, the butterflies in my stomach start a riot. "Take it off in three . . . two . . . one."

Ruby and Ashleigh let go of his arms and take a step back. Even though I know they want to stay and watch, they turn and hurry away instead.

Have I mentioned before that I have the best friends?

The second prior to him pulling off the blindfold feels like an eternity. Every worst-case scenario runs through my head, but the second his hazel eyes meet mine, all my worries drift away.

It's only been a month, but somehow, he's even more handsome than he was before. His haircut is different—shorter, and I wonder what it will feel like to run my fingers through it. He's a little bit tanner, probably from all the walks he's taking without me, but mainly, it's the way he's looking at me, like I'm the most incredible sight in the entire world, that turns me upside down.

"You're here," he whispers, his eyes never leaving mine. "What are you doing here?"

"I was thinking I could really go for a carnival." I gesture to the games and inflatables surrounding us. "But there was only one problem."

"Oh yeah? What was that?"

We're both moving closer to each other, like there's some invisible force pushing us together, but we're both too afraid to make a sudden movement. As if this moment could be taken away from us just as quickly.

"There's only one person I wanted to go with." My mouth goes dry and my hands won't stop shaking. "He lives all the way in Ohio and is super busy with his default victory as HOA president, so I have to bring the carnival to him."

"But what about your script?" he asks, and the love I thought

I had for him multiplies. "You can't just leave your career. You know you won't—"

"I didn't leave my career," I cut him off. "But even if I did, you made one major miscalculation last time."

He's right in front of me, close enough to touch, and my body lights up in recognition. Every part of me calls to this man. From the way he touches me to the way he believes in me to the way he drives me absolutely insane, I'm a better person with him by my side.

"I did?" he asks. There's a cocky tilt to his smile and I want to kiss it away. "I doubt that."

"You did." I can't wait to touch him any longer. I wrap my arms around his neck and pull his face down to mine. "You said my dreams are in Los Angeles, but you were wrong. My dreams are right here. With you."

And when his mouth finds mine, I know I'm right.

When I moved back home, I had no idea what I was looking for, but somehow I managed to find my forever.

Epilogue

When the old gavel hits the table, I have to resist the urge to run to the front of the room, push Nate on the table, and rip the striped button-up shirt I bought him straight off his body.

What can I say? I'm a sucker for powerful men.

I had a video conference with the producers of *HOA**holes* and didn't think I'd be able to make it to the meeting today, so he's not expecting me. I linger at the back of the conference room, watching with a fascination that hasn't lessened even a little bit as he throws his head back and laughs at something Mr. Griffin told him.

After I moved back, part of me feared it was another reckless decision I was making without thinking it through all the way. What if I only felt chemistry and excitement with Nate because part of me knew it wouldn't last? Would it be the same without all the obstacles between us? I mean really, how long could he put up with my antics, and how long could sweater-vests hold my attention? As it turns out, well over a year, and I don't see it fading anytime soon.

Karen D. taps him on the shoulder and as he turns to talk to her, his eyes catch mine, and I watch as they go soft.

Add the way he looks at me to the list of things that will never get old.

He holds up a finger and I nod my head. I, more than anyone, know not to ignore a Karen. Plus, now that Karen D. took over for Janice as HOA secretary and volunteered to use her gossiping super-powers for good, I take great pains to stay out of her way. She's thriving as the official notetaker and never before have a home-owners' association's minutes been so detailed or organized.

It only takes a few minutes—a record for dealing with a Karen—before he's weaving through the crowd and making his way to me. I bite back my smile as he's stopped every few steps to answer a question he didn't get to during the meeting. This is an-other one of those moments when I feel very grateful I conceded my presidential run for a short-lived move back to Los Angeles.

"Hey, Mr. President," I greet him when he finally makes it to me. The butterflies I always feel whenever he's near start to go crazy in my stomach. "You looked very official and very hot with that gavel."

"Oh yeah?" His eyes crease at the corners and he bends down to touch his mouth to mine. "I'll see what I can do about getting one for home."

I'm certain I'm the only person in the entire world who might be developing an HOA kink, but I won't be shamed for it.

I link my fingers through his and pull him out of the con-ference room before any other well-intentioned neighbor can steal him away from me. "Promise?"

"Would I ever lie about something so serious?" He holds open the clubhouse door for me and we step outside into the most perfect night. His eyes twinkle beneath the setting sun, mischief lingering behind the hazel eyes I could stare into forever.

"Speaking of something serious . . ." I let my sentence trail off. I've been wanting to have this conversation for the last month, but every time I start to bring it up, I chicken out and change the subject. Now I'm running out of time and it's now or never.

"Please tell me this is about your lease," he says and my mouth falls open, because it absolutely is.

"How'd you know? Did Ruby tell you?" Or it could've been Ashleigh; she has been stopping by more often lately to drop off leftovers from the food she's been making to demo the cooking products from the latest MLM she joined. Or maybe it was my mom . . . or my dad.

Dammit!

See, this is what happens when you live someplace and have a real community around you: you can't pinpoint which person is making sure you don't self-sabotage . . . again.

"What? No." He laughs and puts his arm around me, tucking me into his side as we walk down the sidewalk toward his house. "I was there when you signed for your apartment. I've been wanting to ask you about it for a while now, but I didn't want to be pushy or pressure you into making a decision you weren't ready to make."

I've been living in the apartments Nate lived in when we first met. And while it may not be Ruby's luxury apartment with a pool and more amenities than I can count, it's nothing to sneeze at. It also costs a fraction of the rent I was paying in LA and doesn't have a neighbor who posts videos of me online. And I'd call that a win.

It's been nice to live on my own and prove that I can take care of myself without my parents' help or relying on a boyfriend to split the rent with. It's just that, after a year of living there alone, I don't want to be alone anymore. I want to make dinner with Nate and sit on the couch watching old comedies together without having to make the drive back home. I want to add my books to his shelves and replace the pictures on his walls with pictures of us. But mostly, I want to fall asleep and wake up beside him. Every single day.

"What if I've already made a decision and you're not ready for it?" I'm aware of what a big step this is. It needs to be right for both of us.

"When it comes to you, I'm always ready." He stops walking and turns to me, sincerity replacing the mischief from earlier. "Whatever you need, whatever you want. I'm ready for it. You want to stay in your place another year? Okay. If you want to move into my place and turn it into a home for both of us? I'm ready. I cleared out half of the closet last week. Whatever you want, I'm on board."

My heart speeds up as the world slows down.

"You . . . you cleaned out your closet?" I was there last night and I had no idea. "You'd be okay with me moving in?"

"Yes, I'd be okay with you moving in." He says it like it's the most obvious thing in the world. "I've loved you since I was fourteen, Collins. I've been waiting for you to come home my entire life."

"Okay then." My voice is thick with the emotion of a woman who was just handed the entire world. "Let's go home."

Acknowledgments

I can honestly say that writing the acknowledgments for my seventh book is a dream so big, I didn't dare dream it. So first and foremost, thank you, reader, for picking up this book and for coming along on this journey with me. It truly wouldn't be possible without you and I am so grateful.

I first thought of a ridiculous idea to write a romance set around a homeowners' association in 2018 and I never thought anyone would let me write it. I couldn't be happier that I was wrong! Thank you, as always, to my wonderful agent, Jessica, for not only not laughing in my face when I told her this idea, but for encouraging me to write it.

Kristine Swartz, thank you so much for everything you do. You are an editor extraordinaire and I love working with you. Your encouragement has gotten me through many writing slumps, and no compliment means more than when you say something I've written has made you laugh.

Acknowledgments

Jessica Mangicaro, Chelsea Pascoe, Mary Baker, and everyone at Berkley, thank you for everything that you do and the love you put into these books.

Amber Burns and Phoebe Wright, your friendship means the world to me. Thank you for letting me crash your Friday meetings and never kicking me out. Your creativity, kindness, and determination is an inspiration and I couldn't have finished this book without you. Melissa Gill and Artavia Jarvis, I will always feel like the luckiest person on the earth that you both read my books and still chose to be my friends. My life is so much richer with you in it.

Lindsay and Maxym, this year has been pretty wild, but thank you for sticking by my side. Suzanne, I don't think either of us knew what we were getting into as mentors, but your friendship has been a touchstone in this wild world of publishing. Rosie Danan, Andie J. Christopher, Harper Glenn, Falon Ballard, and Jen DeLuca, I don't know how I tricked so many talented people into being my friends, but I'm glad I did!

Lin, my writing partner since day one, I don't know if I'd have been brave enough to go on this journey without you by my side. *Revelle* is amazing, you're amazing, and I can't wait to see what you come up with next.

Abby, Taylor, Brittany, Natalie, Shay. I love writing about friendships in part because I've experienced the most wonderful friendships firsthand. My life wouldn't be the same without you.

Mom, I've been feeling your presence a lot lately and I miss you terribly. I feel like you've found the peace you craved so desperately when you were here and I pray I'm right. I hope you're with Dad, Grandma, and Grandpa. It gets a little lonely without you all here, but I'll be forever grateful for the time I had with you.

To my family: Derrick, DJ, Harlow, Dash, and Ellis. Thank you for being my home. You are my touchstone and my reason. I love you with all my heart and I would go to the ends of the earth for you . . . even to Ohio.

NEXT-DOOR NEMESIS

ALEXA MARTIN

READERS GUIDE

Questions for Discussion

1. When *Next-Door Nemesis* begins, we find out that Collins has recently moved back into her parents' home after a video of her misbehaving goes viral. Have you ever gone viral? How do you think you would react to becoming "internet famous"?

2. Collins and Nate have two very different views of the HOA and what it does. Does your neighborhood have an HOA? How do you feel about homeowners' associations?

3. Collins's neighbor, Ashleigh, joins multiple multilevel marketing groups. Have you or would you ever join one? If you started your own MLM, what would you sell?

4. You are officially running for your neighborhood homeowners' association. What is your campaign slogan?

5. In order to get back at Nate, Collins decides to run against Nate for the HOA board. What's the most ridiculous thing you've done in the name of petty revenge?

6. Collins often speaks about her experience of feeling "othered" growing up and how it has affected her into adulthood. How do her past experiences impact her ability to open up to Nate and trust her community?

7. Throughout the course of the book, Collins's idea of where and what home is transforms. What does home mean to you?

8. Collins uses her writing to express her feelings. What hobby or passion helps you when you're feeling overwhelmed?

9. If you were elected to your HOA board and could create any bylaw for everyone to follow, what would it be?

10. Nate and Collins have a bumpy history together that colors the way they see each other years later. Are you a grudge holder? What's the longest grudge you've held?

Keep reading for a special look at
another romance from Alexa Martin

BETTER THAN FICTION

I KNOW IT'S NOT THE POLITICALLY CORRECT THING TO SAY, BUT school is most definitely for fools.

Listen, I get it. I won't tell the kids, but I already fell victim to the great con. I was a good student—not full-scholarship good, but solid—went to a decent college, majored in something other than art. And where did it get me?

A high-paying job on Wall Street where I laugh at the peons around me complaining about school debt?

Not even close.

It landed me as the owner of a bookstore I most definitely didn't want to own, pretending to care while this woman drones on and on about the difference between women's fiction and romance. But, you know, good thing I aced that AP Chemistry exam.

"I'm so glad you're able to find something you love here." I pull out one of my many well-rehearsed responses. I hope it will send her on her way so I can do inventory—or pull out my hair—but then she cuts me off and hits me with something no amount of rehearsal could prepare me for.

"And I want you to know . . ." She reaches over and grabs my hand. I fight the urge to yank it back. Physical touch is def not my love language. "I'm just so sorry about Alice, she was always so kind to me."

My fingers curl into hers, my aversion to touch temporarily forgotten as I seek the comfort I have yet to find since my grandma passed away a year ago.

"Thank you." I can't get the two small words out without my voice breaking. Sympathy swims in the woman's eyes the same way I'm sure unshed tears are swimming in mine.

The woman, whose name I don't remember, gives my hand one more gentle squeeze before walking away, off to bury her problems in a book with a happily ever after that's so elusive to actual humans.

Alice Young was the best person I've ever known. The best person anyone has known. Every stranger who walked into her little bookstore walked out with more books than they probably wanted—and a new friend. The Book Nook sells books, obviously, but the real draw was getting to come and chat with Gran. She was wise beyond her seventy-two years and had a way of listening that made you feel like your biggest problem was actually just a pebble in your shoe. She made you feel as if you could accomplish anything. In the age of e-book conglomerates and chain bookstores dominating the market, the Book Nook never struggled.

Until she left it to me.

It's not that I have self-esteem issues as much as I know my strengths and weaknesses. And my strength is definitely not sitting with a sympathetic ear and listening to other people's problems. I've never been good at it, but I'm especially terrible at it when my own problems seem so big.

Huge.

Gigantic.

Insurmountable.

Because yeah, this isn't my dream job or anything, but Gran left the bookstore to me. And sure, sales were through the roof the first couple of months after she passed away, with well-wishers coming to show their support. But now that the months have crawled by, people are going back to their lives. Unfortunately for me, that doesn't include spending money at a store where Alice no longer greets them with her cheerful smile and welcoming ear.

If I don't figure it out soon, I will lose the only tangible link I have left to my grandma.

On that thought, the bell above the front door rings and I look just in time to see Collette, Vivian, Mona, Ethel, and Beth file through the front door.

Oh shit.

I really need to check my calendar more often.

"Drew!" Mona's voice bounces off the overstuffed bookshelves. Even at seventy, she strides through the store in her trademark three-inch stilettos, which make my feet wince. Her gray hair has not a strand out of place and her pink-painted lips stand out on her pale, gently wrinkled face, which has aged gracefully over the years. "What are you doing standing over here looking all sad? Is it because you're wearing those sandals again?"

"The way you come for me every time you see me is still completely unnecessary, Mona." We live in Colorado: Birkenstocks are not only a completely reasonable footwear choice; it's practically mandatory for all Denverites to own a pair.

Also, it's still strange for me to call her Mona instead of Mrs. Fuller, but as I transitioned into adulthood, she insisted that I call her by her first name only. It's weird, but I acquiesced. Respect your elders and all that jazz.

It is kind of nice to feel like I'm on an even field with them now. Even though they're a lot older than me, they're still the coolest people I know.

"Coming for you? I just want you to join us and sit with some old ladies for a little while."

"Well, if you insist." I play it cool, but there's actually not a chance in hell I'd ever pass on the opportunity to listen to them very self-righteously talk shit about every person they know.

I aspire to be just like them when I grow up.

Minus the book club, obvi. Maybe I'll start a podcast club or something.

She links her arm through mine. Her nearly translucent skin is a stark contrast against my golden-brown skin.

"How's Mr. Fuller?" I always ask about her husband of almost fifty years when I see her.

"Old and cranky. Happy golfing weather has returned, though not as happy as I am to get him out of the house." The snide words don't match the dreamy look that crosses her face whenever his name is mentioned.

I love seeing how happy she still is. My best friend, Elsie, married her high school sweetheart before she could even legally drink—I still tease her relentlessly for her sparkling grape juice toasts—and is blissfully happy with four kids. As for me, however, I'm very much *not* into the idea of marriage.

I don't even like myself half the time and you're telling me it's a good idea to latch myself on to one other person until death do we freaking part? Or more likely, until they cheat, get bored, or whatever other reason fifty percent of marriages end in divorce.

Yeah. No thank you.

It's probably a good thing I have no interest in marriage. I'm not fighting off a swarm of potential suitors. Apparently my winning personality isn't doing it for them.

Their loss.

When we reach the back corner of the bookstore where the Dirty Birds—the name they chose for their book club—meet on the second Wednesday of every month, they're cackling just like their name would suggest. Copies of whatever romance novel they decided to read this month are sitting on the coffee table and each woman is in her unofficial-official chair. None of the chairs are the same. Gran and I would take weekly trips to the flea market, and she'd treat me to a fancy coffee and pastry before we'd spend hours wandering around, hoping to find the next treasure to grace her store. It took us months before we found all seven chairs that now occupy the nook portion of the Book Nook. I sanded and painted them all a creamy shade of mint while Gran sewed cushions to top them.

Now when I look at the chairs filled with all her friends, laughing and chatting like she imagined, I struggle to remember the joy we had creating them. All I see is the empty seventh seat.

Her seat.

"Did you finally read this month's book?" Collette, the most crass of the Dirty Birds, narrows her eyes when I sit. Her hair is dyed a bright red that turns a little orange and always clashes with her red lipstick.

"You know I didn't." I've never participated in a book club and I never will. Once I watched the movie instead but was shamed so intensely for it, I avoided them for a week. The Dirty Birds are vicious.

"You do know you own a bookstore now," she reminds me, as if I've thought of anything else since the lawyers read Gran's will all those months ago. "You have to read books. You can't keep this place running if you don't know the products."

"Geez, Collette, give the girl a break. She just inherited the place!" Sweet Beth sticks up for me. "Not even you could read all the time when you were working. Just because you're retired now doesn't mean she can do whatever you think she should be doing."

I want to high-five Beth, but I resist when Collette's knowing glare cuts my way.

"Fine," she mumbles, leaning back into her seat. "But you're going to need to start reading something. You can't own a bookstore and hate books!"

She's not wrong. This is why I thought Gran was only leaving me her necklace I loved so much.

My fingers drift to the pendant always resting on my chest.

She still left me the necklace; it's just that now it feels more like an apology than a gift. Especially since she left me to fight off her son too.

"I'll figure it out." I wave off her concern, sounding much less worried than I actually am. "What book are you reading this time?"

Vivian leans forward, the creak of her chair cutting through the quiet chatter. "*Last Hope*, by Jasper Williams." Color fills her cheeks as she summarizes the book for me, and I can't help but wonder exactly how dirty these Dirty Birds are getting. Maybe I should start reading along, given how single I am. "Oh, and it was just so lovely. The way he writes. I'll never get over it."

"You've read him before, haven't you?" I recognize the name right away. It's a popular one in the store; soccer moms and pierced pixies alike request his work weekly. Jasper Williams stands out among the shelves of female romance authors despite the understated covers that grace all his books.

"You'd know that if you'd read the damn books with us." Collette's raspy smoker's voice rises and I bite back my smirk. I didn't mean to, but getting her worked up is one of my favorite pastimes.

"Maybe next month," I lie. And by the exaggerated roll of her eyes, she knows I'm full of it.

It's not that I don't like stories. Of course I do. I'm human, after all. I just like my stories told to me in a different way. I like visuals. The countless stories photographs can tell. The real-life images where the curve of a mouth can tell more than any book can. The perfectly framed shot of a mountain that allows your imagination to drift to the countless lives that have graced the landscape. Those are the stories I'm drawn to. I love conjuring hope myself, not being force-fed broken promises or lies telling me love is for everyone and I'm right around the corner from a happy ending of my very own.

"Oooorrrr . . ." Ethel drags out the word. My spine snaps straight. I recognize that tone and the meddling that always follows it. "You could read it before this weekend because Jasper Williams has agreed to come to the store. He's going to join our book club and do a reading."

I shake my head, trying to understand. "What do you mean? Shouldn't I know about in-store events?"

"Well, now you know, dear." Mona reaches for her copy on the table . . . the one with about eight hundred sticky notes popping out from the pages. "It's Saturday evening. The reading begins at five, followed by a discussion lasting until six or so, but he said he's flexible. I put it on your calendar. I thought you would've seen it by now."

I grab my phone out of my back pocket and open up my calendar, but nothing is there. I swipe around a little more, trying to see if she entered it somewhere else by mistake.

"It's not on my calendar."

"Oh no, not on your phone." Mona laughs and shakes her head like I'm being silly. "I said your calendar. The one on your desk."

I barely manage to fight back my groan.

This is just one of the problems that come with inheriting a business from your grandma. Mona and Ethel helped me get organized when I officially took over about nine months ago. And by that, I mean they nagged me about how I did everything and tried to force a day planner on me. For some ridiculous reason, I assumed that once the adjustment phase was over, they would step away completely. I should've known better.

"Mona, you know that was Gran's planner, not mine." And I avoid it like the freaking plague. I made the mistake of opening it once, and seeing her heavily slanted penmanship covering the pages with plans she would no longer be here for broke me.

"Well, she left you the store and that includes everything in it. Besides"—Mona lifts her chin in the air, looking down her nose at me—"if I don't put it in there, how am I supposed to schedule things for the Book Nook?"

"Ummm . . . I'm not sure?" Sarcasm is heavy in my voice. "Maybe don't? Or ask me?"

"Nonsense. It's going to be amazing. You'll thank us." She waves me off like I'm the little girl I was when she met me and not a grown woman trying—and fine, whatever, maybe failing—to run a business. "Now, where should we start? I think that little bit by the lake in chapter two was interesting."

On that note . . .

I stand up, ignoring the way my chair groans beneath my weight, and make my way to my office in the back to cancel the booty call—I mean the date—I had scheduled for Saturday and add Jasper Williams to my calendar.

A Saturday night spent listening to some old guy mansplain what women want?

Can't freaking wait.

Love isn't always by the book, but
if you're lucky, it can be . . .

Don't miss this perfectly bookish, opposites-attract rom-com to curl up with!

Available now

HEADLINE
ETERNAL

FIND YOUR HEART'S DESIRE...

VISIT OUR WEBSITE: www.headlineeternal.com
FIND US ON FACEBOOK: facebook.com/eternalromance
CONNECT WITH US ON TWITTER: @eternal_books
FOLLOW US ON INSTAGRAM: @headlineeternal
EMAIL US: eternalromance@headline.co.uk